116

Treve

ALBERT PAYSON TERHUNE

Treve

Grosset & Dunlap

PUBLISHERS

NEW YORK

My book
is dedicated to
ELLEN COMLY
Treve's friend and mine

CONTENTS

CONTENTS

Treve

CHAPTER I: THE COMING OF TREVE

THE rickety and rackety train was droning along over the desert miles—miles split and sprinkled by cheerless semi-arid foothills. At dusk it had shrieked and groaned its way over a divide and slid clatteringly down the far side amid a screech of brakes.

Out into the desert-like plain with the scatter of less dead foothills it had emerged in early evening. Now, as midnight drew on, the desert ground—with its strewing of exquisite wild flowers here and there among the sick sage brush and crippled Joshua trees—took a less desolate aspect; though it was too dark a night for the few waking passengers to note this.

The Dos Hermanos River lay a few miles ahead—many more miles on the hither side of the Dos Hermanos mountain range. The half-fertile land of the river valley was merging with the enroach of the desert.

Fraser Colt got to his feet in the rank-atmosphered smoking section of the way-train's one Pullman; hooked a fat finger at the porter to find if his berth had been made up; then loafed through to the baggage car for a last inspection of his collie pup, before turning in.

Now it is a creditable thing for a man to assure himself of his dog's comfort for the night. Often it bespeaks more or less heart. But, in the case of Fraser Colt it did nothing of the sort; nor was it creditable to anything but his interest in his dog's money value.

As to heart, Fraser Colt had one;—a serviceable and well-appointed heart. It pumped blood through his plump body. Apart from that function, it did no work at all. Or if it beat tenderly toward any living thing, that living thing was Fraser Colt alone.

Into the ill-lit baggage car he made his way. There were not less than ten occupants of the car. Two of them were normal humans. The third was Fraser Colt. The remaining seven were dogs.

This was by no means the only westbound train, of long or short run, to carry dogs, that night. For at eleven o'clock on the morrow the annual show of the Dos Hermanos Kennel Club was to open. Exhibitors, for two hundred miles, were bringing the best in their kennels to it.

Seven crates were lined up, along the walls of the baggage car, when Colt slouched in. The baggageman was drowsing in his tiptilted greasy chair. In a far corner sat an oldish kennelman who had just taken from a crate a police dog, which he was grooming. Because the night was stiflingly hot, the car's side door was rolled half-way open to let in a sluice of dust-filled cooler air.

Fraser Colt went over to a crate, unlocked and opened its slatted door and snapped his fingers. At the summons—indeed, as soon as the door was opened wide enough for him to wriggle through—a dog danced out onto the dirty floor.

Then, for an instant, the newly released prisoner halted and glanced up at the man who had let him out. The wavery light revealed him as a well-grown collie pup, about eight months old. Golden-tawny was his heavy coat and snowy were his ruff and frill and paws. He had about him the indefinable air that distinguishes a great dog from a merely good dog—even as a beautiful woman is distinguished from a merely pretty woman.

His deepset dark eyes had the true "look of eagles," young as he was. His head and foreface were chiseled in strong classic lines. His small ears had the perfect tulip dip to them, without which no show-collie can hope to excel. But, though three show-collies out of five need to have their ears weighted or otherwise treated, to attain this correct bend of the tips, here was a pup whose ear-carriage was as natural as it was perfect.

You will visit many a fairly good dogshow, before you find an eight-month pup—or grown collie, for that matter—with the points and classic beauty and indefinable air of greatness possessed by the youngster that was now returning Fraser Colt's appraising gaze.

There was no love in the pup's upturned glance, as he viewed his owner;—although, normally, a pup of that age regards the whole world as his friend, and lavishes enthusiastic affection on the man who owns him.

This pup was eyeing Colt with no fear, but with no favor. His look was doubting, uncertain, almost hostile. But Colt did not heed this. His expert eye was interested in scanning only the young collie's perfection, from a show-point. And he was well satisfied.

He had paid a low price for this collie; buying him at his breeder's ill-attended forced sale, three weeks earlier. Colt was a dog-man; but that does not mean he was a dog fancier. To him, a dog was a mere source of revenue. He had foreseen grand possibilities in the pup.

He had entered him in three classes, for the Dos Hermanos show; whither now he was taking him. This he had not done through any shred of sportsmanship; but because he knew the type of folk who visit such western shows.

He was certain of carrying the pup triumphantly through his various classes and of annexing several goodly cash specials. For there were, and are, few high class show-collies in the Dos Hermanos region; though there are scores of wide-headed and splay-footed sheep-tending collies scattered among the ranches there.

Fraser Colt knew that rich ranchmen and others of their sort would be glad to pay a fancy price for such a pup; especially after he should have won a few blue ribbons under their very eyes. There were certain to be fat offers for the puppy, at the show; and the fattest of these Colt was planning to take.

Thus it was that he had come for a last look at the youngster before going to bed. He wanted to make sure the pup was comfortable enough, to-night, not to look jaded or dull in the ring, to-morrow.

He stooped and ran a rough hand over the golden-tawny coat; not in affection, but in appraisal. The puppy drew back from his touch; in distaste rather than in fear. Then the deep-set dark eyes caught sight of the police dog in the far corner.

Perhaps in play, perhaps in lonely craving for friendliness, the collie scampered gayly across to the larger dog.

The latter was submitting in dumb surliness to his handler's grooming. The big police dog had not relished being yanked from his crate, late at night, for brushing and rubbing. Indeed, he had not relished any part of the joltingly noisy ride. He was not in the sunniest of tempers.

Over to him scampered the friendly collie pup. As he came within a foot or so of his destination, the car gave a drunken lurch, in rounding a bend of the track. The capering puppy was thrown off his unaccustomed car-balance. He collided sharply with the police dog.

The impact set the larger dog's ruffled temper ablaze. With a roar, he hurled himself bodily upon the unsuspecting collie stripling.

Now a collie comes of a breed that is never taken wholly by surprise. Even as the big dog lunged, the pup recoiled from the onslaught, at the same time bracing himself on the swaying floor of the car. He recoiled; but not far enough.

The larger dog's ravening teeth missed their mark at the base of the spine; but they seized the puppy's left ear; biting it through. At the same time the police dog shook the dumbfounded pup savagely from side to side.

Before the puppy could make any effort to defend himself, the handler and Fraser Colt had rushed into the fray. The police dog was hauled back, snapping and snarling. Colt's rough hand restrained the collie from doing anything in the way of reprisal. The very brief fight was ended.

Colt glanced over his pup, once more; this time with more worry than mere appraisal. Battle-scarred canine visages do not impress dogshow judges favorably.

Then, from Fraser Colt's thick throat avalanched a torrent of lurid blasphemy. For he saw something which affected him as might the loss of his garish diamond scarfpin.

One of the puppy's tulip ears still tipped gracefully forward from the point. But the other ear hung down from the side of his head as limply as a sodden handkerchief. In brief, if one ear was tulip, the other was wilted cabbage leaf.

From the down-hanging lacerated ear, blood was trickling; in token of the police dog's bite. The shaking of the mighty jaws had wrenched and broken the cartilage and muscular system of the stricken ear into raglike loppiness.

Ear-carriage is an all-important detail in the judging of show-collies. Lack of perfect ear-carriage may perhaps be condoned to some extent, if the dog's other points be good enough to counteract it. But no collie-judge on earth would give a ribbon to a dog with one semi-erect ear and one ear that hangs flappily down the side of his head.

No, the pup's show possibilities were gone,—absolutely gone. Two minutes earlier he had been worth perhaps $400 of any fancier's cash. As he stood, he was worth as much, for all show-purposes, as a one-eyed woman in a beauty contest.

That savage wrench of the police dog's jaws had harmed no vital spot. But it had ripped hundreds of dollars out of Fraser Colt's bank account. Why, nobody, now, would be willing to pay as much as $50 for the collie, as a pet! Who would want a lopsided, clowish-looking dog, when a handsome mutt could be bought for half the price?

To Colt, a dog was as much an insensate chattel as was a bank note. This particular dog had just deprived him of a rare chance to annex many bank notes. In illogical fury, he brought his open hand down over the puppy's bleeding head, with a resounding and stingingly painful slap. In Colt's present frame of mind, he must needs take out his furious disappointment on something.

The blow knocked the puppy half way across the car. Striding after him, Fraser Colt swung his hand—fist clenched, this time—for a second and heavier blow.

In righteous indignation at the injustice, and in unbearable pain, the collie met the second attack, halfway. As Colt's big fist smote at him, the pup shifted deftly aside from the descending arm. Slashing as he jumped, he scored a deep red furrow in his owner's wrist.

With a howl of rage, Colt flung himself, mouthing and foaming, upon the luckless puppy. He snatched up the young collie by the nape of the neck, and hurled the vainly protesting furry body out through the open side doorway of the car.

Now, by all laws of averages, a puppy thrown off a train going thirty miles or more an hour, should have landed on the hard track ballast or the right of way, with enough force to break several bones or even his skull.

But the law of averages was kind to this particular puppy. Perhaps out of pity for his wrecked show-career; perhaps because the pup was born for great deeds.

For several seconds the rumble of the train over the ballast had given place to a hollower sound. Also, the thirty-mile speed had slowed down perceptibly. All this by reason of the fact that the engine and front cars had begun to cross the cantilever railroad bridge which spans the Dos Hermanos River in the very heart of the Dos Hermanos Valley.

The pup catapulted out into windy space, in the arc of a wide circle. But he did not smash sickeningly against the hard ground beside the track. There was no ground alongside the track. There was nothing alongside the track but night air.

Through this air, head over heels, spun the flying tawny-gold body. Down and down he fell, past the level of the bridge span; missing an outthrust concrete-and-stone buttress by a fraction of an inch.

With a loud splash that knocked the breath out of him, he struck the sluggish water of the Dos Hermanos River. The rush of his fall was broken, in part, by this breath-expelling impact. But enough momentum remained to carry him several feet below the surface.

The train chugged drearily on. The stillness of midnight crept down again over the lonely valley. The ripples had not died on the disturbed water when a classically wedge-shaped head re-appeared above the surface; and four sturdy feet began to strike out in confused but energetic fashion toward the nearer bank. Still in sharp pain and fighting for his lost breath, the puppy swam on; letting the easy current carry him downstream in a slant, rather than to waste extra strength in fighting it.

Lionel Arthur Montagu Brean was far too

accustomed to the roar of passing trains to let
such sounds awaken him from slumber. As the
engine and cars rolled hollowly over the bridge,
a hundred yards upstream, they did not so much
as penetrate his sleep-mists in the form of a
dream. But presently a far less noticeable sound
stirred him to wakefulness. This because the
lesser sound was also less familiar to the wanderer's subconscious self.

Through his sleep he heard a despairful panting and an accompanying churn of the quiet
stream on whose bank he had pitched camp for
the night. Brean sat up, stupidly, rubbing his
eyes. In front of him, not twenty feet from
shore, something was plowing a difficult way
through the yellow water, toward the spot
where he sat.

Brean got to his feet, wondering. The advancing shape took on size and form. The swimmer
was emerging from the water. Through the
dim starlight, the man was able to make out that
the oncomer was a very wet and bedraggled
collie.

At sight of the man, the pup hesitated, half
in and half out of the water. Brean bent toward
him and called:

"Come on, son! Nobody's going to hurt you."

The voice and the gesture that went with it
were reassuringly friendly. The dog read them

aright. He was still little more than a baby. He had been cruelly and unjustly manhandled. His heart ached for the human kindness he had known before he fell into Fraser Colt's posses- sion. Hesitant no longer, he came straight up to the man.

Brean petted him, speaking friendlily. Then, as the light was elusive, he went over to his smoldering camp fire and stirred it into life. The flare showed him every detail of the pup; even to the bleeding and lopped ear. At sight of the injury a long-dormant professional instinct flared up in the wanderer, as suddenly and as brightly as the fire had just flared from its embers.

Lionel Arthur Montagu Brean had once pos- sessed the right to tack the courtesy title of "Honorable" in front of his name. For he was the fifth son of Lord Airstoken, an impecunious Irish peer. There had been four older brothers; and Lionel had been allowed to follow his own yearnings to become a physician. He was a natural-born surgeon; and, from the start, he won for himself an enviable name at Guy's Hos- pital.

But he was a natural-born crook, as well. Thus, within three months after his graduation with honors, he was a fugitive from justice;

through the clumsy forging of a check, wherewith to meet certain pressing gambling debts.

He smuggled himself to America by steerage.

Penniless, hopeless, afflicted with a love for
wandering, he had sunk presently to the philo-
sophical leisure of tramphood. Life was easy
for him. He followed the climate, north and
south, through a belt of the Far West; picking
up food and rudimentary clothes as best he
could. Half forgotten was his British home.
Wholly forgotten had been his almost uncanny
skill at surgery;—until the sight of the collie
pup's broken ear revived it.

Partly in self-derision, partly in amusement,
he set to work, before the crackling campfire,
treating the ear. In his final year at Guy's, he
had won a wager from a collie-breeding friend.
The latter had claimed that a collie's broken ear
is incurable. Brean had made such an ear as
good as new. True, then he had had all manner
of appliances for the task; while now he was
forced to rely on ingenuity and on such meager
makeshifts as his battered kit contained. Yet
the old skill was throbbing in his fingertips.

The pup did not wince under the deftly light
handling. He seemed to know the tramp was
trying to help him. If the operation hurt, the
accompanying words soothed.

"Puppy," apostrophized Brean, "you're a most honored dog. Do you realize that the hand operating on you might now be operating on the King of England, if the luck had broken differently for me? They all said nothing could stop me from going straight to the top. And then a little oblong of scribbled paper sent me straight to the bottom, puppy. But it's lucky for you that it did. For if I were back in Harley Street, with a 'Sir' stuck in front of my name for my surgical preëminence,—why, don't you see I couldn't be working over you, now?

"That'd mean you'd have to go through life with one-half of your grand head looking like a lop-eared rabbit's. Yes, you're an honored dog; and a lucky dog, too. . . . Now don't shake your head or rub it against anything, before that dressing gets set!

"This is known as the 'Treve Operation.' Because I tried it, first, on Noel Treve's dog, you see. I think I'll name you 'Treve' in honor of your own operation. Like the name?

"How about something to eat? I ask the question merely as a bit of rhetoric. For there isn't a crumb of food in the larder. We're on our way to the Dos Hermanos ranch, Treve. Last year, when I dropped in there, they gave me a sumptuous breakfast and told me if I was caught on their land again, they'd shoot me,

Let's hope their memory for faces is short, puppy. I'm taking you along as my welcome. It's only a matter of twelve miles to the ranch house. Now, let's go back to sleep, shan't we?"

Neither Royce Mack nor his sour old partner, Joel Fenno, had or ever would have the right to prefix their names with "Honorable";—either by dint of being the sons of British lords or by election to legislature or Congress. But, unlike the Honorable Lionel Arthur Montagu Brean, they never had had to worry as to where the next meal was coming from.

Their big sheep ranch covered eighteen hundred acres of grazing land. And, in the dry season, their flocks went northward, at an absurdly small price per head, into the richer government grazing lands, on the upper slopes of the twin Dos Hermanos peaks.

They were working hard and they were making fair money. Their chief cause for woe in life was that their neighbors, the cattle ranchers, looked upon them and on all sheepmen as something lower than skunks.

This contemptuous hostility on the part of the cattlemen did not annoy Joel Fenno in the very least; so long as it was confined to mere words and looks. Fenno was ancient and hardbitten and surly and with the mental epidermis of a rhinoceros. Mack, being younger and more sensitive, girded at the thought that any man or collection of men on earth could look on him as an inferior.

The partners had ridden out from the ranch house before daylight this morning to their Number Three camp, where the spring "marking" was going on. Having seen that the marking gang was satisfactorily at work, they walked over to the Number Three foreman's shack, for breakfast.

The shack was like a thousand of its sort, from Arizona to Oregon; the single room's walls decked with fading and yellowed and frayed pictures cut from long-ago Sunday Supplements; its untidy furniture sparse and in dire need of repair. Its one distinguishing feature was a fast-graying lump of sugar which adorned a broken corner bracket, in a place of honor among a litter of fossil bits and snake rattles and the like.

This lump of sugar was the sole and treasured memento of the foreman's sole and treasured spree at Sacramento, three years agone. There he had eaten at a restaurant. In a bowl at the restaurant were many such cubes of white sugar. Never having seen sugar in such shape before, the reveler had stolen one of the lumps and brought it home to show to admiring friends.

The foreman had finished his breakfast and,

had hurried back to his gang; as is the way of foremen when the boss or the bosses chance to be on hand. But Mack and Fenno were lingering over their flapjacks and black coffee.

Both looked up as a shadow—or rather two shadows—blocked the open doorway. On the threshold stood a man whose clothes and bearing proclaimed him a tramp. Close at his knee, and surveying the partners with gravely inquiring interest, was a tawny-golden young collie dog; one ear bound up in a queer arrangement of splints.

On the way to the ranch house, Brean had skirted the edge of Number Three camp; modestly keeping out of sight of its busy workers. The sight of smoke curling from the foreman's chimney and the faint-borne aroma of coffee had made him change his plans. Perhaps he could get a satisfactory meal here, without risking ejection by facing the partners at the ranch house. Wherefore, he had made furtively for the shack; and now stood confronting the two he had sought to avoid.

For a moment the men at the table stared dully at the man in the sunlit doorway. The man in the doorway stared embarrassedly at the men at the littered table; and inhaled the smell of coffee and fried meat. The collie also sniffed appreciation of the goodly smells; and continued to eye the eaters with friendly gravity. It was Brean who spoke first.

"I say, you fellows," he said, dropping for once into the voice and manner that had been his birthright. "I have a really valuable collie, here. I am forced to part with him, because I have decided to abandon my hike through your state, and return East. He is sheep-broken. I know how worthwhile he will be on your sheep-ranges. Do you care to make me an offer for him? I was referred to you by my good friend and former schoolfellow, Carston, of the Beaulieu ranch."

The last portion of his smoothly spoken harangue was pure inspiration. True, an Englishman named Carston owned an adjoining sheep ranch. And Brean had chanced to hear his name. But never had he set eyes on the rancher; an odd reluctance causing him to avoid fellow-countrymen, in his present straits.

"Why didn't Carston buy the pup himself?" demanded Royce Mack, breaking the brief silence, as Joel glowered perplexedly at the visitor as though trying to place him in an elusive memory.

"He's full up, with sheep dogs," said Brean, glibly.

"So are we," grunted Fenno. "Say, where have I run across you before?"

"Perhaps at Carston's?" suggested Brean, trying not to quail. "But I was not in these hiking clothes then. I wonder you recognize me."

"Maybe," grumbled Joel. "But I doubt it. I'll remember, presently. I always do."

"In the meantime," urged Brean, with much jauntiness, "do you care to buy this dog?"

"No," replied Joel. "We don't."

"It's your own loss," smiled Brean. "I offered you the chance, because Carston told me to. I must be going. By the way," lingering at the threshold, "will you sell me a mouthful of breakfast? I shall be glad, of course, to pay a fair price for it. I hoped to get over to Carston's ranch house in time to eat. But I overslept. If it is any trouble—"

He hesitated politely.

"If you had kept your eyes and ears open, on your hike," supplied Mack, wondering at the British pedestrian's ignorance of the ranch-country's ways, "you'd know folks around here don't let a stranger pay for a meal. If an American had offered to, it'd have been an insult. Being foreign, I s'pose you don't know any better. Draw up a chair and eat. Stop at the stove and bring the coffee-pot along with you."

He spoke with no hospitality. Yet he was

almost fawningly friendly, compared with his partner, who continued to favor the guest with a deepening scowl of perplexity. Brean was glad he had shaved the beard which had been one of his salient marks when last he had met these men. Also that, this time, he had aban-doned his wonted tramplike speech.

Eagerly, yet with no show of his stark eager-ness, he drew up a rickety chair to the board; and began to eat. Nor did he abandon the table manners which, like correct speech, were his birthright. Royce, covertly watching, was im-pressed.

The collie lay down at Brean's feet. The pup was hungry. But he did not beg. This, too, impressed Royce Mack. Picking up a greasy lump of pork from the central dish, Royce tossed it to the pup. The latter caught it in mid-air— an easy trick his breeder had long since taught him. Then he proceeded to eat it,—not wolf-ishly, but with a certain highbred daintiness.

"What's his name?" asked Mack.

"Treve," said Brean, trying not to sound as if his mouth were chuck-full.

"Funny name for a dog," commented Royce.

"Not in my country," civilly contradicter Brean, pouring himself another cup of coffee.

"What's the matter with his ear?" pursued Mack.

"Torn in a fight," replied Brean, wishing devoutly there might be more eating and less talking at this meal. "I set it, as best I could. It's only makeshift. But the splint and the bandage must stay on, for a few days. After that the ear will be as good as new."

"H'm!" marveled Royce, noting the skill wherewith the bandage was applied. "You dressed it as neat as a doctor."

"Quite naturally," assented Brean, transferring two more flabbily cooling flapjacks to his plate. "You see I chance to be a surgeon."

At this statement and at the confirmation offered by the deft dressing on the ear, Joel Fenno's face took on new clouds of puzzlement. He felt he had almost cudgeled his memory into placing the visitor. Now, this new development sidetracked his processes. He was quite certain he had not met Brean in any medical capacity. He had been increasingly sure he had met the man under circumstances somehow unfavorable to Brean. But again he was all at sea.

"You say the pup is broke to handlin' sheep?" demanded Fenno, in hope of finding some clue to bring his thoughts back again to the right trail. "How old is he?"

"A year old, last Monday," returned Brean, rising as he spoke. "In my country, we begin to break them to sheep at four months. I am sorry you don't care to buy him. He is a bargain."

He paused for an instant, then resumed, as he started doorward:

"I must thank you for a good breakfast. I shall not forget your hospitality to a foreigner in disreputable hiking clothes. But, really," feeling for his pocket, "I should feel more comfortable and less like an intruder, if you would let me pay for what I have eaten."

Fenno's curt headshake and his partner's more vociferous refusal were interrupted by Treve.

Past the shack a herdsman drove a handful of lambs toward the marking yard. As the way was short, and as the Number Three outfit's only dog was a half mile away herding another and larger bunch of sheep, the man had undertaken to steer the lambs, singlehanded. He was making a ragged job of it.

At sound and scent of the approaching huddle of sheep, Treve leaped to his feet; queer ancestral instincts tugging at the back of his alert young brain. In all his eight months of life he had never seen nor smelt a sheep. But his Scottish ancestors, for a hundred generations, had earned their right to live by tending such creatures as these which came trooping past the shack. Something far stronger than himself urged the pup to action.

At a single bound he cleared the table and bolted madly out through the doorway, straight among the lambs. They scattered in every direction at his onset.

The shepherd yelled aloud in consternation. The lambs' wild bleating merged with Treve's wilder barking. The two partners, at these dire omens, jumped up; and dashed out of the shack, to witness the damage menacing their four-footed means of livelihood.

Lionel Arthur Montagu Brean stood, for one brief instant, frozen with horror. Then he bolted through the back window of the shack; and ran at top speed to the nearest patch of cover. Nor did he slacken greatly his rapid retreat until he had put something like five miles between himself and Number Three camp. Even then he did not come to a halt, but kept on at such pace as he could muster.

His haste and his continued flight were due only in part to the unmasking of his pretense that Treve was a trained sheep-worker. As he fled from the shack he snatched Joel Fenno's vest from the back of the rancher's chair.

During breakfast he had noted the presence of a broken old wallet in the inside pocket of this momentarily discarded garment. From the ill-fastened top of the wallet he had seen protruding the fringed edges of a little roll of bills.

And, as he fled, he took with him the price of his dog.

Meantime, the partners reached the shack's doorway just in time to see Treve come to a momentary halt as he eyed the far-scattering bunch of lambs.

Something else was clawing at the collie's heartstrings. Something he could not account for was striking into his young brain. Ancestry was gripping him; even as it has gripped scores of other untrained collies at their first sight of galloping sheep. This atavism takes a murderous turn, in some such dogs; but in a few instances it plays true to form.

Treve haited for only an instant. Then, like a furry whirlwind, he was off after the lambs. Working wholly by instinct, he flashed past three of them that were racing neck and neck. Then, almost without breaking his stride, he wheeled, sweeping the bleating trio ahead of him toward two more strays.

He bunched the five in some semblance of scared order, then darted away to the remaining strays, driving them, singly or in pairs, toward the nucleus he had formed. Again and again he tore around this nucleus, as it tried to scatter; welding it firm again.

When the last stray had been added to it, he set the compact bunch in motion. Brean was

somewhere back there by the shack. To Brean,
if to any one now, he owed allegiance. And to
Brean he resolved to drive his baa-ing and milling lambs.

Thus it was that the partners, in the doorway, saw the young dog round up the bunch and
bring it toward them.

"A little ragged in spots, his work is," commented Royce Mack. "But for a young dog it
isn't so bad. Maybe they train 'em ragged, over
in England. We might do worse than take him,
if we can buy him cheap. We're a dog short,
since that rattler got Zippy. Besides, the pup's
got a way with him that makes a hit with me.
We can easy train that roughness out of him."

He lowered his voice, and spoke with his lips
close to Fenno's ear; lest Brean catch his words.
Joel looked about; as, at a wide-arm shooing
from the shepherd, the lambs bolted into the
marking yard with the joyous collie at their
heels.

Treve, his job done, trotted into the shack with
them to rejoin his tramp-master. Royce patted
him in comradely fashion. To his own surprise,
he had begun to take a strong fancy to the
beautiful pup.

They did not find Brean in the hut. While
the partners were still wondering what had become of him, Joel Fenno discovered the loss of

his vest. And Treve's ears were assailed with language which would have done credit to Fraser Colt.

"Well," philosophized Mack, when the older man had sworn himself hoarse, "we've got the pup, anyhow. It's up to us to make him worth the fifty bucks that panhandler got with your wallet. The dog's yours. You've sure paid for him."

"Your money as much as mine," grunted Fenno. "It was from the ranch cashbox. I brang it over here to give Billings for that lumber he freighted to Number Three last week. He was due, past here, to-day, and—"

"Then it's *our* dog," amended Mack; feeling somehow happier for the knowledge. "Anyhow, we'll see whose he is. Suppose we match for him?"

Fenno glowered. He had bad luck when he and his partner matched coins for anything. Yet his sporting nature was roused by the suggestion. His glance fell speculatively upon the foreman's treasured lump of sugar on the bracket.

"Gimme your pencil," he ordered. "Mine is in my vest."

With the proffered pencil stub, he fell to work making regular dots on the cube of sugar.

Mack, after one questioning glance, saw his intent and grinned.

"Roll dice for him, hey?" he chuckled. "Good boy! Only we'll have to rub those spots off the sugar afterward. Moyle sets a heap of store by that trophy. He'll be as sore as a—"

"Roll, first?" asked Joel, finishing the transformation of a smudged lump of sugar into a spotty-looking and irregular die.

"No, you," said Mack. "Best two out of three. Let 'er roll!"

Treve had come back from a fruitless quartering of the room, for Brean. He stood inquisitively beside the table, as Joel prepared to cast the die. Treve knew well what the spotted object was. In early puppyhood his breeder's little daughter used to give him lumps of sugar to eat; until her father had caught her at it and had forbidden her to do it any more; telling her that sugar is bad for a dog's teeth and stomach. The pup had regretted deeply the loss of these delicious treats.

"Say!" snarled Joel, as he paused in the act of rolling the die. "I remember, now. I always remember, sometime or other."

"Remember what?" asked Royce, impatiently. "Remember you promised your dying great-aunt you'd never shake dice with any man named

Mack? Oh, roll it out, man! I want that dog.
He sure is—"

"I remember that slick English crook," went
on Joel, unheeding. "He's the tramp that pan-
handled us for grub, back at the house, last
year; and tried to steal the tobacco jar. I told
him, then, I'd put a bullet in him if he ever dast
show his face here aga'n."

Pettishly, cross at memory of the swindle, he
rolled the cube of sugar across the table. In his
ill-temper, he rolled it an inch too far. It
bounced off the table-edge.

But it was not destined to land on the floor.
In mid-air Treve caught it. In another second
he was crunching it, rapturously.

"And now we won't ever know what number
was on top," grumbled Joel, disgustedly. "Not
without we cut him open and see. We'll have
to match for the measly cuss, after all. And
you always win when we match."

"Nope," said Royce Mack, taking pity on his
disgruntled partner. "We won't match. Treve's
decided it for us; by swallering our only fair
way of deciding. He's OUR dog."

CHAPTER II: THIRST!

TREVE lay drowsing, in the early morning sunshine, in front of the Dos Hermanos ranch house. The big young collie sprawled lazily on his left side; his classic head outlined sharply against the warming sand of the dooryard; his tiny white forepaws thrust forward as if in a gallop; the sun's rays catching and burnishing his massive tawny-gold coat.

Treve was well content to sprawl idly like this. It had been a large night. Mack and Joel Fenno, and three of their men, had spent hours of it in rounding up a bunch of stray sheep that had butted their silly way out of the rotting home fold, after sundown, and had rambled off aimlessly down the coulée.

The sheep had been gone for hours and had traveled with annoying steadiness and speed before their loss was noted. Then, it had taken some time, through the dark, to overhaul them; and far longer to convoy them home.

The sheep might never have started upon their illicit ramble—assuredly they would never have proceeded along ten minutes of it—if Treve had been on the job. But the big young dog had gone with Royce Mack, in the buckboard, over to Santa Carlotta, for the week's mail; and had not gotten home until dark. It was only during his before-bedtime patrol of the outbuildings that he found the forced wattle; and realized what had befallen the fold's occupants.

He had dashed up to the ranch house. There, by his clamor of wild barking, he had brought the two partners out of doors on the jump. He led them to the empty fold and obligingly took up the scent there; tracing the strays far faster than his human companions could follow through the dense dark and over the rough ground.

Ahead of him, this morning, was another long day's work as soon as the partners should finish breakfast. In the meantime, it was pleasant to sprawl sleepily on the dooryard's soft sand.

Through the open door, rumbled the sound of voices. Being only a real-life collie and not a phenomenon, Treve could not understand one word in ten that reached his keen ears, as he lay there. But he did not need a knowledge of words to tell him the two men were quarreling.

Vaguely, Treve regretted this; not only as a highly developed collie always dislikes the sound of human strife, but because one of those men was his god. He did not like the thought that any one should be speaking unkindly to this deity of his.

However, he had heard quarrels, before, since he came to Dos Hermanos Ranch; and none of them had ended in any harm to his deity. So, he listened drowsily, rather than apprehensively.

To both the partners Treve was docilely obedient. Under their tutelage he had become one of the best herding dogs in that valley of herding dogs. But to only one partner did Treve grant the allegiance of his heart. Old Joel Fenno regarded all livestock as mere counters in his game for a livelihood. He neither liked nor disliked Treve. He worked him hard; and he saw that the collie obeyed orders. There the man's interest in him ended.

Young Royce Mack was different. By nature he was a dog-lover. Moreover, he "had a way" with dogs. Between him and Treve, from the outset, a deep friendship had sprung up. At every off-duty moment, Treve was at Mack's heels. He slept beside his bunk, at night; and usually lay beside his chair at meals He joined Mack, right joyously, on all walks or rides. In brief, he adopted Royce as his overlord; and gave him glad worship.

With disgusted grunts, old Fenno had noted the jolly chumship between dog and man. To him it was as absurd as though Royce Mack had made a pet of a horned toad. Yet never until now had he voiced any active objection. Fenno was a man of few and grudging words. To-day, however, he considered it high time to speak. He chose the breakfast table as the place for his rebuke.

"If that cur had been to home, where he belongs, yesterday afternoon," he grumbled, as he began his second cup of coffee, "them sheep wouldn't ever have got a chance to stray."

"If he hadn't been here, last night," said Royce, "we'd never have found them in a week. Besides, it wasn't his fault he was off the job, in the afternoon. I took him to Santa Carlotta with me. You know that."

"Sure, I know it," growled Joel. "Why wouldn't I know it? Cost me a night's sleep, didn't it? Oh, I *know* it, all right! But what I'm gettin' at is: Every critter in this outfit has got to earn his way; got to pay for his keep. If he don't, then he's got to stop eatin' our grub. Treve pays for himself when he works. And when he don't work, he's dead wood. Dos Hermanos Ranch can't afford dead wood. We don't hire Treve to go drivin' to Santa Carlotta in lux'ry and to traipse around on loafin' walks with you. Nor yet we don't hire him to snore in the bunk room, nights, when he'd ought to be on guard. If that's what he's goin' to do, the sooner we feed him a lump of lead, the better."

The old fellow returned to the task of demo

ishing his breakfast. He ate surlily and without gusto. He did all things surlily and without gusto.

Royce Mack did not speak for a moment or two. He had been waiting for this outbreak ever since the mischance at the fold. It was like old Fenno not to have blurted it in the first flush of the excitement; but to wait until he had marshaled his facts and had cooled down to normal.

Royce, too, had had time for preparation. Presently he made reply; schooling himself to calmness and even to an assumption of good humor.

"Treve isn't dead wood," he said. "If he'd never done another lick of work, since we had him, he'd have paid for a lifetime's keep by rounding up that bunch of strays, last night. You remember where he found them. And they were still traveling—still heading north. By daylight, they'd have been over the edge of the Triple Bar range. And you can figure what that outfit of cow-men would have done to 'em. We'd never have seen wool nor hoof of one of 'em again. The Triple Bar or any other of the cattle crowd wouldn't ask better than to shoot up a flock of sheep that strayed onto their range."

Joel Fenno kept on munching his food, interspersing this with noisy swigs of coffee. He said nothing. Mack resumed:

"Besides, we've got Zit and Rastus, for the regular herding and for night guard. That isn't supposed to be Treve's job. They're both born to it. They're little and black and squat and splayfooted and they can't be made homelier by galloping all day and every day, over hardpan, for hundreds of miles in the broiling sun. Neither of them has got Treve's brain or his looks. I don't want him turned into a splayfoot drudge. He earns his keep, good and plenty, here on the home tract. We agreed to that, long ago."

"*You* agreed to it," mumbled Fenno, his mouth full, his eyes glum. "*I* didn't. I haven't been jawin'. But I've been watchin'. An' here's where we come to a showdown. Till we got that cur, there wasn't any loafin' here. Since then, you go on silly walks with him, when you might be workin'. That comes out of *my* pocket. You let him sleep in the bunk room, like he was a Christian. The Dos Hermanos is a workin' outfit. No time for measly pets and the like. It's got to stop."

"I don't neglect my job, by taking Treve up into the hills or along the coulée for a tramp, Sundays," denied Mack. "Better do that, on my rest day, than play poker in the mess shack or ride over to Santa Carlotta and get drunk

on bootleg. He's my chum. If you don't like
him—"

"I don't. I don't like a hair of him. He—"

"Then figure out what his keep costs us; and
deduct it from my share of the profits, every
month. That's fair, isn't it?"

"No," denied Joel, sullenly. "It ain't. You're
makin' us both lose money by the time you waste,
learnin' him tricks and suchlike, and loafin'
around with him. Besides, it sets a bad example
to the hands. Yesterday, I saw Toni tryin' to
learn Rastus to shake hands. Tryin' to make
him do like Treve does. Nice stunt for a sheep-
wrastler, huh? Shakin' hands! It's got to
stop."

"If it stops, then I stop, too," said Mack.

He spoke without heat, but with much
finality. Fenno grunted as usual and pushed
back his chair from the table. Royce continued,
getting to his feet:

"I'm the only man who ever was able to get
on with you, Joel. I've stood your grouches
and your crankiness; because I figured those
grouches hurt you a lot more than they could
hurt me. And I've always tried to dodge any
squabbles with you. I'm still going to try to.
So I guess you'd better think over what you've
just said about our getting rid of Treve. If
Treve gets out, I get out. Not that I'm fool

enough to value a dog more than I value a man; but because when one partner begins handing out ultimatums, it's time for the other to quit. The ultimatum habit is a rotten one. If I gave in to the first ultimatum, there'd be more and more of 'em; till some day there'd come one that I'd have to fight over. So, the first ultimatum is going to be the last one. That's why I'm asking you to think it over and take it back. See you at supper time. So long."

Still holding in his temper, he left the shack; Joel Fenno staring after him in baleful speechlessness.

As Mack came out into the dooryard, Treve was off the ground in one leap; and cantering up to him; eagerly expectant of accompanying his god whithersoever Royce might be going. But Mack checked him.

"No, old boy," he whispered, stooping to pat the classic head. "Not this morning. He's riled. No sense in riling him worse, by us starting off to work, together. He'd figure we were going to waste half the day in chasing jackrabbits and learning tricks. Stay here. He's going down to the South Quarter this morning. He said so yesterday. He said, then, he'd need you to help Rastus drive that South Quarter bunch over to the Bottoms. I've got to pack the big truck across to Santa Carlotta for the freight we found there yesterday. It'd be good fun for both of us, to have you ride on the front seat with me, Treve, son. But—well, just now, he'd likely throw a fit if you took the morning off. . . . Lie down there and wait for him."

The dog obeyed. But he did so with none of his wonted gay alacrity. Naturally, he understood not a tithe of Royce's harangue. But he caught some of its drift, from the tone and from a scattered word or so that was within his experience.

Like so many lonely men, Mack had fallen into the habit of talking to this collie chum of his, during their long rides or hikes, as if to a human. The dog, in true collie fashion, had learned to read both voice and face; and to pick up the meaning of certain familiar words.

For example, he understood perfectly, now, that he must not accompany his god as usual, but must lie down and wait for his other owner's commands. This was ill news to the dog. His deepset dark eyes were full of wistful appeal, as he stretched himself reluctantly in the sand again and stared after the departing Royce.

Treve had not long to wait there, alone. In another minute Joel Fenno slouched out of the ranch house and stood on the threshold looking moodily down at him. The collie did not greet Fenno's advent with any of the exuberant joy wherewith he had hailed Mack's. Indeed, he did not greet Joel at all.

He lay, returning the man's look. Treve was ready to obey any command given him by this oldster or to do any work Fenno might assign him to. He recognized that as his duty. But duty did not entail an enthusiastic greeting to a man who had never yet lavished so much as a careless pat on his head or spoken a pleasant word to him.

Joel Fenno was wont to bolt breakfast and then to hustle busily off to the morning's tasks. But to-day he stood quite still, his brooding old puckered eyes scanning the dog; his ears strained for some expected sound.

Presently he heard the sound he had been awaiting. It was the starting of the truck's engine; down at the barn. Joel shifted his puckered gaze to the group of ramshackle adobe buildings.

Royce Mack was backing the big truck out of its cubby-hole. He swung it about and headed bumpily for the main road. Treve's own eyes and ears were at attention, as he saw Mack departing on a jaunt without his chum. He whimpered, low down in his throat; and peered longingly after the truck. Then with a sigh of resignation he turned again to face Joel.

As the truck vanished in a fluff of choky yellow dust, Fenno came to life. Stepping back into the shack, he scribbled a few lines on a crumpled paper bag; and pinned the paper to the deal surface of the table, where it must catch Royce's notice as soon as the younger man should come into the house again.

Writing was a tedious and grunt-evoking labor to Joel Fenno. He took a pardonable pride in his few literary productions. Now, he gratified such pride by bending over to reread what he had written. Half aloud he muttered the scrawled words:

"Mack, maybe I was too hot under the collar about Treve. Maybe he is a good chum, like you say. I aim to find out. I am going to let Toni take the bunch over to the South Quarter with Zit or Rastus to-day. And I am going to take a two-day camping trip down to the Ova and back. Last year this time the waterholes, down there had kept the grazing pretty good. If it is as good this year we can maybe save a couple of weeks rent money on the gov't grazing lands up on the peaks by going to the Ova first. It is worth a try. I ought to be back by to-morrow night. I am going to take Treve along for company. JOEL."

Fenno, for the first time in his sixty-odd years, was attempting wily diplomacy. And he was doing it very badly indeed. It did not occur to him that his partner might not accept, at its face value, this unprecedented taste of his for Treve's society.

True, both ranchers had had a hazy idea of investigating grazing conditions in the Ova, before shifting their flocks, as usual, to the government grazing lands on the slopes of the Dos Hermanos peaks, for the summer and autumn. But it was a trip any of their men could have made for them. It was unlike Joel to waste two busy days that way, in person. Royce could not well avoid wondering at it. This possibility, too, escaped Fenno's imagination. To him, his scheme appeared truly inspired.

He valued Mack's partnership. In a grouchy way, he was fond of the jolly young fellow. Royce was a hard worker and a good sheep man, Moreover, he had up-to-date ideas which more than once had been coined into money for the ranch. Fenno had no intention of breaking with so useful a partner.

At the same time, he had still less intent of letting Royce go on loafing and frittering valuable time away, as Joel deemed it, by making a pet of a dog. He regarded the romps and comradeship and long walks of the two, as a hustling financier might view a card game among his employees in the middle of a busy office day.

Time was money. Also, if Mack had any energy and inventiveness to spare, he might better place those at the service of the ranch than in teaching a cur to find his tobacco pouch or to catch food-morsels from the top of his own nose.

Joel had protested. His protest had been met by Mack's firm refusal to give up the collie. There was no sense wasting time in useless bickering. The one wise move was to get rid of the dog; and to do it in such a manner that Mack should not suspect his partner of doing it purposely.

Fenno's plan had been worked out, in swift detail, as soon as Royce had departed for the day's work. He would start on horseback toward the Ova. At some spot too far from the ranch for Mack to trace the deed, and lonely enough to preclude the chance of witnesses, he would stop; put a bullet through the collie; scoop out a shallow grave in the sand and bury him.

Then, the same evening Fenno would return to the ranch house, saying Treve had run away during their journey and that he had come back for him. Mack could prove nothing. According to Joel's elaborate calculations, he could suspect nothing. Treve would merely seem to have strayed from his human companion of the trip, and either to have lost his way home or to have been stolen by some Mexican or else shot by a passing cattleman. It was very simple.

Fenno made certain of his scheme's verisimilitude by ordering Chang, the cook, to put up two days' rations for him. Then, giving commands to Toni, he saddled his mustang for the lethal ride toward the Ova. At his imperative whistle, Treve ranged alongside the pony, and the two set forth.

The dog did not relish the prospect of a ride with Joel. True, almost every dog enjoys a walk or a ride with even a human whom he does not love. But Treve was aware of a queer distaste for to-day's jaunt. Perhaps he was warned by the sixth sense which puzzles so many collie-students. Perhaps the heat of the day and the glum company of Fenno made the outing seem less attractive than usual. Yet, obediently, even if not ecstatically, he loped along at the pony's side.

The mustang enjoyed the trip still less than did the collie. Fenno had no understanding of horses. He rode, as he did everything else; busily and unsparingly. He had no sympathy or sense of fellowship with his mount. To him, a horse was a machine which must be made to earn its cost and upkeep. He would have sworn derisively at any one who might have suggested to him the need of warming a horse's bit on an icy morning or of dismounting during a ten-minute halt or of easing his mount over the heavy going of the sands or tethering him out of draughts and in the shade rather than in wind and sun.

Horses understand such failings on the part of the men who use them. Thus, not a pony on the Dos Hermanos ranch bothered to lift head and to whinny when old Fenno clumped into the barn in the morning. Not one that did not toss back the head in fear of a fist-blow when Joel undertook to bridle him.

His mount, to-day, was a temperamental little buckskin, Pancho by name, whose devil temper and inborn mischief had never been trained fully out of him. Royce Mack understood Pancho and got good service from him, in spite of the buckskin's occasional phases of meanness. But Joel Fenno and Pancho had a steady hatred for each other.

Joel had chosen the buckskin for to-day's ride, because his own temper was still frayed from the night's work and the morning's squabble. Subconsciously, he yearned for something on which to vent his crankiness. He found himself watching for any trick or meanness on the part of Pancho which should warrant the liberal use of quirt and spur.

When a man is looking for a fight, Destiny is

prone to send one to him. Fenno had not ridden
for more than two hours, when Pancho saw, or
affected to see, something terrifying about a
jack rabbit that bounded out of a sage-clump in
front of the pony's nose.

Pancho went straight up into the air, wheeling half-way about, as he did so, and coming to
earth again, stiff-legged, in a series of spine-
jarring buck-jumps. The first of these banging impacts nearly unseated Fenno and wholly
snapped the ill-tied cord which strapped the
bundle of rations to the back of the saddle.

So occupied was Joel with the punitive values
of curb and quirt and heel that he did not observe the loss of his provisions and water bag.

Treve had viewed the advent of the jack
rabbit with pleased interest; foreseeing some
excitement in chasing the long-eared and longer-
legged bunny. But, instantly, the scrimmage
between man and horse offered far more excitement for him, and with less need for active
exercise. Wherefore, the collie stood, tulip ears
cocked and classic head interestedly on one side,
watching the battle.

Two or three times, it is true, he had to dodge
back in lightning haste, to avoid Pancho's flying
heels or crazy plunges. But, on the whole, it
was a most entertaining and lively spectacle,
wherewith to vary the tedium of the hot trip.

Nor was the collie's fun in it marred by any anxiety as to the outcome. Once or twice when Pancho had cut up like this with Royce Mack, the dog had been terrified for his god's safety; and had even sprung for the plunging pony's nose, until Royce had shouted gayly to him to stand clear.

But to-day, Treve could witness the fight with unmarred interest. He did not care, in the very least, whether Pancho should demolish Joel or Joel demolish Pancho. He had no liking for either of them. It was an enthralling spectacle to watch. And no personal feeling was involved.

The horse fought frantically. The man fought back with scientific fury. For ferocity and murderous brutality, he outbattled the beast.

In little more than a minute, Pancho gave up the conflict. Not that he was subdued, but because he found he could not hope to win this particular bout. He stood trembling and non-resisting; while the rider whaled him unmercifully. Then, at a harsh-voiced order, the mustang continued his journey; his mouth dripping blood-flecked foam; his coat a white lather of sweat and weals; his sides scored bloodily by the rowels.

Joel settled himself down into his saddle. Grimly. he was pleased with himself. He had worked off his sour temper, and he had won a victory. The dog, resignedly trotting along beside him, could have told him how far he had come from breaking his foe's spirit. For Treve could see the pony's eyes. And a devil was smoldering behind them. Their whites showed unduly. There was a hint of murder in their rolling irises.

Joel Fenno, smugly confident in his own horsemanship and in the victory of man over brute, would have sworn there could not be an atom of fight left in the sweating and trembling victim of his beating. Thus, for the billionth time in history, a man might have profited vastly had he known as much as did his dog.

Two hours went by. And another hour. Then, Fenno began to scan the distance for some shady spot where he might make his noonday halt, for a bite of lunch and ten minutes' rest.

There was no shade in sight. In fact it was the most shadeless season of a shadeless region in that semi-arid belt of shadeless country.

In Dos Hermanos County, except on the slopes and summits of the Dos Hermanos Peaks, the average yearly rainfall is but twenty-four inches. And more than twenty-one of those twenty-four inches fall between November and April.

Late May had arrived. The level ground—

most of it little better than hardpan—was beginning to dry to the consistency of friable clay. The lower foothills were losing the last of their verdure and beginning to assume their summer coat of khaki tan. True, in such lowlands as the Ova, the occasional waterholes, and like receptacles for rainfall, sometimes on wet years kept enough green grass alive to serve as temporary grazing ground for sheep; before the utter drouth of summer sent the sheep men to the government land high in the mountains, with their flocks, in search of grass to carry the livestock through until late autumn. But this was not a wet year.

Joel Fenno saw the arid sweep of ground; broken, perhaps a mile ahead of him, by an irregular ring of yellowish green. Here, by all signs, should be a waterhole. True, no shade was near it. But it might offer a chance to bathe his hot face and wrists in moderately cool water. The increasing heat of the day made this seem more and more desirable.

Fenno headed for the waterhole. His tired pony plodded along over the uneven ground with head adroop. Treve had moved from Pancho's right side, to his left; seeking such tiny patch of shade as the mustang's moving body might afford. The air hung dead and stifling.

The sun blazed down in a copper glare from the
pitilessly hot sky. Nature seemed dead and
blistering.

Joel's tough skin sweated drippingly. It was
the hottest day, thus far, of the year; and the
weatherwise man knew it was the first of at least
three scorchingly hot days. He was not minded
to continue the ride any farther than he must.
It would be well to do what he had come to do,
and then turn back toward the ranch.

This was as good a spot as any for his purpose. Here, at intervals, patches of soft and
easily-diggable sand cropped out through the
hardpan and rock. It would be easy enough to
gouge a space deep enough to bury the body of
a dog. Yes, and it would be best to do so, before
getting any nearer to the waterhole. The presence of water might well attract other wayfarers,
—men who might investigate a newly heaped
mound of sand, in the dead level. The burial
would better be here, a mile on the hither side
of the waterhole and on a trackless bit of ground.

Joel Fenno halted his mustang, and glanced
around to make certain he had the wide sweep
of swooningly arid country to himself. In that
pitilessly clear atmosphere, his keen old eyes
could have descried any moving object, many
miles away. Treve, still keeping in the shadow
of the pony, stopped and looked inquiringly up

at the man. It had been a long and fast and
steady ride, under the sickeningly hot sun glare
and over the ever-hotter hardpan. The dog was
glad for a rest.

Then, suddenly, his attention was caught by
Fenno's upraised voice. Joel, in the course of
his sweeping survey of the country behind him,
had chanced to drop his gaze to the hips of his
sweating and welt-skinned mount. He saw the
water bag and the bundle of rations were gone
from behind his saddle.

He was an old enough plainsman to realize
what this implied. It meant he must go hungry
until night—he who had ridden himself into
such a hearty appetite. It meant, too, that he
must do all his drinking from the muddy and
perhaps alkaline puddle of the mile-distant waterhole; and that thereafter he must travel through
the heat with unassuaged thirst until he should
get back to the ranch at nightfall.

Small wonder that he burst into a roar of red
profanity!

He knew well enough how the mischance had
occurred. His spine still ached from the buck-
ing of Pancho, four hours ago. It must have
been during that series of jarring bucks that the
water bag and the bundle had been loosened and
had tumbled unheeded to earth. It was Pancho's
fault—all Pancho's fault!

In a gust of wrath, he slashed the mustang across the neck with his quirt.

Now a horse is almost as quick as a dog to note a change in his master's mood. Even before the blow—even before the burst of swearing—Pancho had become aware of a slackening in his rider's wonted grim self-command. He had prepared, in his meanly uncertain mind, to take advantage of it.

Before the quirt had fairly landed athwart his neck, Pancho had left ground. This time he did not buck. Straight up in air shot his forequarters.

There was no warning of the outbreak. Moreover, Fenno had been sitting carelessly in the saddle; for the horse had been standing still. There was no scope for guarding against the trick. Scarce did the man's knees seek to grip the pony, in anticipation of any plunge the quirt blow might entail, when Pancho reared.

With the speed of light, the mustang flung his head and shoulders upward. In practically the same motion he hurled his tense body back; dashing himself to the ground, with his rider beneath him.

More than once, in former battles, Pancho had attempted this, with Joel. But, usually a fist-thump between the ears had brought him down on all fours again before the ruse was, complete. Failing to land such a punch, Fenno had at other times twisted out of the saddle and safely out of the falling body's path, before the pony could strike ground.

But, to-day, the outshot fist started its drive an instant too late. It grazed Pancho's ear. Joel slipped from the saddle; but again a fraction of a second too late.

Down crashed the nine-hundred-pound mustang, full on the helplessly struggling body of his fallen rider; pinning Fenno to earth on an outcrop of shale rock.

With a snort and a wriggle, Pancho was up on his feet again.

On the trampled ground behind him floundered a writhing and bruised man, who twisted like a stamped-on snake.

With all his might, Joel Fenno strove to get up. He knew something of untamable horses' temper; and he knew what must be in store for himself, should he fail to regain his feet.

But he could not arise. He did not know why. His legs refused to obey him. The fall, and the crushing weight that ground his back into the rock, had wrenched the spine. While his injury was not mortal or even beyond easy surgical cure, yet it had left his legs temporarily numb and useless. He was paralyzed.

The mustang celebrated his own release by a

thunderous circular gallop; the circle bringing him again toward the prostrate man. With lips drawn back from his evil teeth, and with ears flat, the infuriated pony charged. Here was the longed-for chance to revenge himself on the enemy who had scourged and roweled him and jerked his lips to ribbons with the curb chain! The devil that lurked behind the rolling eyes flamed forth in murder.

With an effort that wellnigh made him faint with agony, Fenno reached back to his hip for the service revolver he had strapped to his belt that morning for the killing of Treve.

Then, the agony of his mind made him forget the anguish of his body. In his tumble, the pistol had bounced from its holster. It was lying some ten feet away; impotently reflecting from its blue barrel and cylinder the glint of the noonday sun. For all use the weapon could now be to its owner, it might as well lie in the next county.

Down at the helpless cripple thundered Pancho.

The mustang's flashing forefeet were in air above the man; poised for the tearing beats which should stamp their victim to a jelly. Joel shut his eyes.

But the murderous hoofs did not reach their goal.

This because a tawny-golden body whizzed through the air, from nowhere in particular, but with the deadly accuracy of a rifle shot. A pair of snapping jaws sunk their teeth deep in the mustang's sensitive nose; while a sixty-pound furry body whirled itself so sharply to one side that Pancho's aim and velocity were deflected.

Down came the hoofs; but waveringly and scramblingly and not within ten inches of the fallen man. Before they could rear again, the grip on the nose was changed to a slash along the left side of the mustang's head. Under the pain of this, Pancho veered. A second slash veered him still farther from the crippled Joel.

Probably Treve had no clear idea why he dashed to the rescue of the man for whom he had no feeling except a vague dislike. While Pancho and Joel had fought upon more even terms, the dog had looked on impersonally, entertained by the spectacle, and with no impulse to interfere. But now that the man was down and helpless, somehow it was different.

To a dog, all men are gods. That does not mean they are his own particular gods or that he has any interest in most of them. But they are of the race which he and his ancestors have served and guarded and worshiped since the days when the new earth was covered with vapor.

and the Neanderthal man tamed the first wolf-cub.

So now, when Joel Fenno lay stricken and defenseless and the mustang turned on him in murder, the collie played true to ancestral instinct.

Pancho spun about at the dog that had balked his yearning to murder the man. Apparently the collie must be gotten rid of, before the mustang could finish the task of killing Fenno, with any peace and absence of interruption. Wherefore, the pony turned his attention to killing Treve.

But, in less than a handful of seconds, he found he had taken upon himself a job far too big and too dangerous for his powers. The dog entered rapturously into the sport. He was everywhere at once and nowhere at any particular moment.

He was rending the bloody nostrils of the mustang. He was nipping the mustang's hocks. He was slashing at the throat; he was tearing at face and chest and hips, in almost the same instant. With perfect ease, he eluded the flailing hoofs and the pony's wide-snapping jaws.

Joel Fenno forgot his own intolerable pain in the fascination of the combat. But, as suddenly as it began, the fight ended. The mustang had wit enough to know when he was bested. Bleed-

ing, smarting, confused, all the lust of battle
bitten out of him, he turned tail and fled. After
the first few yards of clamorous barking and
heel-teasing, Treve let him go and trotted back
to the groaning Fenno.

Gravely, inquisitively, the collie stood over the
man who had brought him here to shoot him.
Down into the tortured face he looked. Joel
returned the sorrowful gaze. with something of
terror in his own leathern visage. He was jolted
out of a lifetime's beliefs and theories. His
thoughts would not assemble themselves.

He tried once more to get to his feet. But his
legs were numb. He sought to wriggle along
on his stomach toward the mile-off waterhole.
There he could quench the awful thirst that had
begun to grip him. There, too, he might be
found by some passerby, seeking water on the
way across the arid waste.

But the pain of even the slightest motion was
more than his iron nerve could endure. With a
groan he gave up the attempt. Supine and panting, Fenno lay where he had fallen; the great
dog standing protectingly above him.

From time to time Treve would bend down to
lick the tortured face or to whine softly in sympathy. He knew the man was helpless and in
pain. But there was nothing he could do except
to interpose his own hot shaggy body between

Fenno's head and the terrific sun-rays. And even this may have been done by accident.

Thirst gripped Joel; tenfold more agonizingly than did the pain of his wrenched back. His mouth was parched and burning. His tongue had begun to swell. Burying his face—now sweatless and dryly torrid—in his hands, he lay and prayed for death.

When he looked up again, Treve was gone. An awful sense of loneliness seized the tormented sufferer. Blithely would he have given his share of the ranch, in return for the dog's comforting presence at his side. More blithely would he have given ten years of life for one drop of water, to ease the fever and maniac thirst that possessed him.

To few is it given to receive the granting of the only two wishes they make. But, presently, it was granted to Joel Fenno. He heard a patter of running feet. Toward him, from the direction of the waterhole, Treve came bounding. The collie's massively shaggy coat was adrip with water.

Up to the parched victim he trotted, and lay down beside Fenno's head. Greedily Joel dug both fevered hands in the dog's mattress of soaked fur, squeezing into his own mouth the drops of grimy water wherewith the coat was saturated.

Now, Treve had done no miraculous thing; although to Fenno it seemed a major miracle of brain and devotion. Indeed, the dog had done something absolutely normal and characteristic. Seeing Joel lie still, with his face buried in his hands, he had concluded the man was asleep; and thus was in no immediate need of the collie's services. Thus, the young dog had scope to think of his own needs.

For more than five hours, through the scorching heat, Treve had been running; without so much as a single drink of water to cool his throat. Collies, more than almost any other dogs, require plenty of drinking water. Now that he was at leisure to consider his own wants, Treve realized he was acutely thirsty.

His uncanny sense of smell told him there was water, somewhere ahead. Off he went to investigate. Finding the waterhole, he drank his fill; then, collie-like, he wallowed deep in the muddy liquid. Cooled and with his thirst assuaged, he recalled his duty; and galloped back to the injured man; lying down in front of him to await orders. That his soaked coat chanced to contain enough water to soothe the torment of Joel's fever-thirst, was mere coincidence.

Twice more, during that terrible afternoon of heat, the dog stole away to the waterhole to drink and to wallow. Both times he came back to the sufferer who waited so frantically to wring out into his own burning mouth the life-saving drops.

Even before the riderless Pancho came cantering home in late afternoon, Royce Mack had begun to worry. Returning early from Santa Carlotta, he had found Joel's note; and had read perplexedly between the lines. At sight of Pancho, he flung a saddle on another pony and yelled to two of his men to follow. Then he set off at top speed along the trail toward the Ova.

Dark had fallen, hours agone, when the bark of a collie came to Mack, on his plodding ride. Then there was a scurry of padded feet; and Treve was leaping and barking about Royce's pony. From a mile to one side of Mack's line of march, the night breeze had brought the collie his master's scent. He had galloped to intercept him and to guide him to where a half-delirious old man lay sprawled out on a hot rock.

At sight of the rescuer, Joel Fenno tensed his muscles and forced his face into its wonted sour grimness. But he could not keep his delirium-tickled tongue from babbling.

"Say!" he grunted, before Mack could speak. "We'll keep Treve, if you're so set on keepin' him. Not that he's reely wuth keepin'—except maybe sometimes. Let him stay on at Dos

Hermanos, if you like. He's—he's only part collie, though. He's got some of the breedin' of—of the ravens that fed Elijah. Let him stay with us. I don't mind, so long as he don't eat too much. . . . Now quit gawpin' like a fool; and help get me to a doctor! Why, that collie's got more sense than what you've got. Besides, he's—he's sure one grand water-dog!"

CHAPTER III: MAROONED!

ALL through the parchingly dry summer the sheep of the Dos Hermanos ranch had pastured on the upper slopes of the Peaks; far above the rainless and baking valley where the verdure was dead and where the short grass would not come to life again until late autumn should usher in the brief rainy season.

Here on the government grazing land of the lofty mountainsides there was good pasturage. Here, too, as far up as the end of the timber line, there was shade and there were tempered heat of day and coolness of nights; and there were brooks and springs and pools of cold water.

For a mere handful of dollars, paid to the government, the Dos Hermanos ranch partners and many another denizen of the valley could graze their sheep at will among the upland meadows and gorges.

Young Royce Mack and old Joel Fenno still kept their headquarters at the lowland ranch house during the hot spell, one or both of them riding up, weekly, into the cooler hill country to inspect the flocks and to see that their three shepherds were taking best advantage of the successive grass stretches.

When it was Royce Mack's turn to make this periodic tour of the mountain pastures, he always took with him the tawny-gold young collie, Treve. This companionship meant much to both dog and man. For the two were still inseparable chums.

Three little black collies, Zit and Rastus and Zilla, were permanently attached to the flocks; and worked, day and night, with the shepherds, in all weathers. But Treve's actual sheepdog work was more intermittent. True, in emergencies or in times of extra toil, he was impressed into service with the sheep. But, as a rule, nowadays, he was the ranch house's guard and the guard of the home-tract folds. He helped, also, in rounding up and driving bunches of sheep to the railroad, and the like. The routine duties fell to Zit and Rastus and Zilla.

Occasionally, for Mack's benefit, Fenno still complained of this favoritism shown to the big dog. But, since the day when Treve saved him from death under the broiling sun, on the Ova trail, he had privily accepted the collie as a privileged member of the ranch household.

This he did in grudging fashion, as he did all things. It was an ingrained trait of old Fenno's crusty nature to be grudging of anything and everything; from toothaches to legacies. But, to his own amaze and shame, he had become aware of an odd affection for the big young collie. This fondness he hid from Royce and from Treve himself under a guise of grumpy distaste.

So successfully did Joel mask his new liking for the dog that Mack had no suspicion his partner did not still regard Treve with the impersonal aversion which he felt toward all the world. As for Treve, the dog was as well aware of Fenno's new attitude of mind toward him as though Joel had spent a lifetime in cultivating his society.

A collie has a queer sixth sense not granted to all dogs. But even a street puppy has the instinct to know what humans like him and what humans do not. Treve, of yore, had known that Fenno had no use for dogs in general, nor for him in particular. Since their ordeal on the Ova trail and during Joel's brief convalescence from his hurts, the collie recognized that the old man had grown reluctantly to like him.

Formerly, Treve had obeyed Fenno, as part of his daily routine of duty. But never had he accorded to the oldster the slightest mark of personal friendliness. Nowadays, at times, he would stroll up to Joel, with wagging tail, and would thrust his classic nose affectionately into the old

fellow's cupped hand or would lay a white forepaw on his knee or come gamboling across to
greet him on a return to the ranch.

Such exhibitions of good-fellowship embar-
rassed the crochety Joel as much as secretly they
delighted him. For the first time in his sixty-
odd years, a living creature was proffering active
friendship to him. It did funny things to
Fenno's withered sensibilities.

When other humans were present at these
manifestations, Joel would thrust the dog aside
with a glower or a mutter of disgust. When no
fellow-human was in sight, Fenno would look
guiltily around him and then give Treve's head
a furtive pat and would whisper: *"Nice* doggie!"
He would do this with as keen a sense of self-
contempt as though he were picking a pocket.

Treve, with a collie's inherent love of mischief,
not only understood the foolish situation, but
seemed to take positive delight in shaming Fenno
by playful efforts to make friends with him in
the presence of Mack and the shepherds.

"You owe a lot to that dog, Joel," said Royce,
at dinner one day, as Fenno angrily shoved aside
the paw which Treve had placed on his knee.
"It's a wonder you keep on hating him. He
doesn't make friends with every one. And I
don't see why he keeps on trying to make friends
with you. He never used to. Why can't you

pat him or say 'hello' to him sometimes when he comes up to you like that?"

"I got no use for dogs," grumbled Joel, "nor yet for any other critter; except for the work we can get out of 'em. I got no time to go makin' a pet of any cur. One of these days, when he comes sticking that ugly nose of his into my hand or wiping his dirty forepaw onto my knee, I'm goin' to give him a good swift kick."

He glared forbiddingly at the collie. Treve wagged his plumed tail, unafraid; and thrust his muzzle into the cup of the forbidding old man's gnarled hand. Joel drew back in ostentatious aversion. But, somehow, he did not carry out his threat of a kick. Presently, when Mack chanced to leave the room, Fenno slipped a large hunk of meat from his own plate to the collie's dinner platter on the kitchen floor. He did it with the air of one poisoning a loathed enemy. But it was the biggest and tenderest morsel of meat in his noonday meal. And he had been waiting an opportunity to give it, unobserved, to Treve.

All of which was silly, past words. Nobody realized that more clearly than did Joel Fenno.

The endless hot summer wore itself out; but not until long after its drouth had worn out every trace of vegetation in the valley and the lower foothills; and had turned the once-verdant lowland world into a khaki brown lifelessness. Day after day, evening after evening, the mercury in the rusty thermometer on the Dos Hermanos ranch house porch registered anywhere from 110 to 120. It was weather to fray nerves and temper. Treve, under his heavy coat, sweltered and looked forward longingly to the occasional trips to the mountain pastures.

Then came late autumn; and on one of these mountain trips both partners went, instead of going singly. They took along Treve; and they took every man on the ranch except Chang, the old Chinese cook.

The time had come to drive all the sheep down from the mountain grazing grounds, into the valley ranges, for the winter. It was a job calling for the services of all available men and dogs.

Up through the foothills toward the towering heights of the mountains rode Mack and Fenno; the collie gamboling happily along in front of their ponies and halting at every few yards to investigate the burrow of some rabbit or groundsquirrel.

In front of the riders loomed the twin peaks of Dos Hermanos, rising into the very clouds. For more than three-fourths of the way up, there were lush forest and meadow. Then, the timberline halted abruptly; like the ring of hair that encircles a baldheaded man's skull. Above timber line, on each peak, was a smooth expanse of rock; crowned by snow.

The foothills were passed by; and now the indiscriminate green of the left hand peak, whither the riders were moving, took on a hundred irregularities. The brown and twisting trail upward, through rock-shoulders, could be seen in spots. So could the dense forests and the softer green of the cleared grazing lands. Adown the left peak roared the torrential little Chiquita River, broken in fifty places by cataract and cascade;—the river that is born among the mountain-top springs and is fed by melting snows from the summit.

By reason of the innumerable inequalities of ground and the erratic course of the rock-ledges, this mountian stream forms roughly a half-moon in its descent; and is joined and reënforced, three-fourths of the way down, by the Pico, a tributary rivulet from adjacent summit-springs; forming a "Y," that encloses perhaps five square miles of the wildest and most inaccessible section of the left slope.

By reason of the trickiness of the Chiquita River and of the narrower Pico, the sheepmen seldom lead their flocks into the "Y." Not only is much of the pasturage bad, but the streams are subject to sudden freshets from unduly swift melting of the summit snows. Thus, flocks venturing into the enclosure are liable to be cut off unexpectedly from the outer world or even to be swept to death in attempting to cross.

Wherefore the place is shunned by man and sheep. And as a result it long since became the winter haunt of such wild animals as spend the rest of the year on the inaccessible upper reaches of the left peak.

In another hour of steady riding, the partners had reached the lower plateau of pasturage on which they had told their men to have the Dos Hermanos sheep rounded up, this day, for the drive to the ranch.

There, on the rolling plateau, they found their flocks and shepherds awaiting them; the little black collies busily keeping the mass of milling and silly sheep in some semblance of formation.

The partners had left the ranch house while the big autumn moon was still yellow in the sky. The sun had barely risen when they reached the plateau. Within another half hour the long procession of woolly sheep and their attendant men and dogs were starting down the twisty trail toward the far-off valley;—the partners arranging to camp for the night among the foothills and to reach the ranch some time the next day.

For sheep in great numbers cannot be hurried unduly. Nor can their drivers insure against a score of senseless stampedes or side-excursions which delay the march to the point of utter exasperation. A sheep is probably—no, *certainly*—the most foolish and non-dependable item of livestock sent by Satan to harry an agricultural life.

"The patriarch, Job," spoke up Fenno, dourly, as he and Mack chanced to be riding side by side, after an uncalled-for scattering of a thousand of the sheep had delayed the line of travel for nearly an hour while Treve and Zit and Rastus and Zilla and the partners and the shepherds (named in the order of their importance in handling that particular crisis) had succeeded in getting them into line again and in preventing any wholesale scattering of the rest of the huge flock, "The patriarch, Job, in Holy Writ, got the name for bein' the most patient cuss in all the Bible. D' you know how he got that same reputation, Royce?"

"No," laughed the younger man, amused that his taciturn partner should choose such a time for theological debate. "If it's a riddle I give it up. How?"

"The Good Book tells us," glumly expounded Fenno, mopping the sweat from his leathern face, "the Good Book tells us Job owned 'seven thousand sheep.' But it tells us he had seven sons to handle the measly brutes, and a multitude

of men servants. So he could stay home an'
work at his trade of being patient and let his
boys and that same multitude of hired men rustle
the sheep. I'll bet $9 if he'd had only one lazy
young rattle-pated kid of a partner and three
numbskull Basque herdsmen and three or four
wuthless collies to help him work the sheep, he'd
never 'a' won the Patience Medal in his district.
He'd likely 'a' been jailed for swearin'. I—"

"Speaking of 'worthless collies,' " interrupted
Mack, who had been standing in his stirrups and
staring over the gray-white sea of sheep, "what's
become of Treve? Generally, when his work's
done for a few minutes, he trots alongside me.
You took him with you, didn't you, when you
rode back after that last bunch of strays? You
ran the bunch into the lot that Zit is handling.
Where's Treve?"

"Oh, likely he's barkin' down some gopher-hole
or tryin' to make Toni play tag with him, or
suthin'!" growled the old man, annoyed at
Royce's dearth of interest in the comparison
between Job and his partner. "He'll show up.
He always does. You waste more time worritin'
over that four-legged flea-pasture than any sensible feller would spend on his bankbook.
Treve's all right. He always is. It's a way he's
got. Fergit it."

But, oddly enough, Joel himself did not forget it. Indeed, presently he made excuse to ride back to speak to Toni; who was in charge of the rearguard of the flock. Out of hearing of his partner, he bawled lustily to Treve. But there was no answering scurry of white paws.

Nor, when the party made camp, at dusk, among the foothills, had the big young collie rejoined them. Joel Fenno scoffed at Mack's show of anxiety about the absent Treve. Yet, Joel discovered now that he had dropped his pipe, somewhere along the route; and fussily he insisted on riding back through the dark to look for it.

He was gone for three hours. On his return he grumbled at his failure to find the missing pipe—which, by the way, he had been smoking throughout his three-hour absence.

"Didn't see or hear anything of Treve, back yonder, did you?" queried Mack, from among the blankets.

"Treve?" repeated Joel, grouchily. "Nope. Never thought to look for him. Likely he's gone on ahead; and we'll find him at the ranch house. He's a lazy cuss. Likely he's scamped his work and trotted on home. Nope, I never bothered to look for him. It was my pipe I was huntin'. Not a measiy dog."

He cleared his throat contemptuously. His throat was rough and raw from repeated shoutings of Treve's name, during his three hours of futile hunt for the missing collie.

Treve was not at the ranch house, when the herders got there, next afternoon. Fenno was loud in derision, when Royce Mack insisted on riding back over the mountain trail in quest of the lost dog. But Mack went. And he found nothing.

Meanwhile, Treve was in serious trouble.

Toni and the other shepherds had grown unspeakably weary of the lonely mountainside life; and yearned for the ranch with its nearness to a town. The bunk house was a bare eleven miles from the 1,500-population metropolis of Santa Carlotta.

Thus, their work of driving the sheep down the trail, toward the valley, was marked with more haste than care. But for the presence of their two employers, they would have done the driving in a far more precipitate and slipshod way. At it was, at every possible chance, when Royce and Fenno were engaged elsewhere along the line of march, they sacrificed care to haste.

At one point, thanks to this over-hurrying, a large bunch of wethers, at the rear of the procession, bolted. They streamed backward, up the trail, and they scattered to every side of it in fan-formation. It was heartbreaking work to get them back. Fenno and Treve had gone to help Toni and the little black Zit in the thanklessly hard task.

"All here?" Joel had demanded, when the round-up of the strays seemed complete.

"All here!" glibly announced Toni; and Fenno rode forward.

Toni had been certain all were there;—chiefly because he wanted to believe so. Hence, he did not trouble to count the bunch of galloping wethers. He knew that both Treve and Zit had worked the underbrush and the upper trail, in search of the wanderers; and he knew both were absolutely reliable sheep dogs. Zit was back with him again. And Treve, presumably, had trotted ahead with Fenno. Toni knew Treve would not have given up the search while any strays were left unfound. The delay had been long. The Basque herder was cross and hungry.

Toni had been justified in his faith that Treve would not abandon the quest, while any strays still remained outside the flock. Treve was on the job. And that was why Treve was in trouble.

When, for some idiotic reason of their own, the several hundred wethers of the rear guard started to bolt, the foremost contingent of them went up the steep trail in a mad rush, well in advance of the rest. Up they galloped, along the twisting path, crowding and milling and jostling. Midway of their rush, a jack rabbit flashed across the trail; just in front of their leader.

At this truly terrifying spectacle, the leader shied with as much dread as might a skittish colt at sight of a newspaper blowing across the road. Into the underbrush he wheeled, continuing his flight at an acute angle to the trail, but bearing gradually farther away from it, as bowlder and thicket forced him out of his direct line.

After the manner of their breed, the remaining sheep of this advance band wheeled into the underbrush behind him. After the first few hundred feet, some of them balked at a narrow brooklet which the leader had crossed at a single jump. They turned again toward the trail, leaving the rest—forty-eight in all—to run on and to become hidden in the undergrowth.

Zit, following close behind, came to the brook. There, the scent veered to the left; and he pursued it; presently coming up with the contingent which had not crossed; and herding them skillfully back to the main body.

The forty-eight strays continued their onward and upward course, at last slackening their gallop to a trot and stopping now and then to snatch at a mouthful of herbage, but always resuming their journey, farther from the trail.

There was no sense at all in their doing so. This, probably, was why they did it;—being sheep.

Treve had gone after a half-score sheep that broke trail lower down the mountain. He rounded them up and sent them into the main flock. Then, scenting or hearing or guessing the presence of other sheep, higher on the mountain, he cantered up the steep slope to investigate. His straight line of progress brought him out on the track of the strays, a few rods to the right of the brooklet. He followed; only to catch the scent of Zit's flying feet, where they had passed by, a few minutes earlier. The scent proved that Zit had rounded up this particular bunch of strays, and that Treve's climb had gone for nothing.

Thirsty from his fast ascent, he stopped at the brook to drink. Here the sheep had arrived. Here, some had turned and had been overtaken by Zit. But here, too, Treve's scent told him, other sheep had crossed the trickle of water; and Zit had not followed this lot.

As he stooped to drink, Treve's nose was not eighteen inches from the opposite bank. There, the leader and his remaining followers had planted their feet as they bounded across. The scent was fresh. To the trained collie it told its own story. Zit had missed the clue because of following the remnant that they had not crossed. In following the stronger and nearer scent he had taken no note of the other. Treve himself might well have overlooked it, but for the chance of his stopping to drink.

Hot on the track of the escaped forty-eight wethers, the collie sprang across the narrow brook and up the hill after them. Bad as was the going and uncertain as was the runaways' course, it was a matter of only a few minutes for him to overhaul them.

They had just come to a huddled pause in their flight. Detouring, to avoid climbing a high ridge of rock which arose in front of them, they had followed this barrier of stone to rightward, with some idea of going around its end. But this they could not do. The ridge ended abruptly in a cliff that jutted out above the Chiquita River.

The Chiquita was in flood. This, because a spell of warm weather, had replaced a spell of snow and chill on the summit; sending millions of gallons of melted snow cascading down the peak. The Chiquita and the Pico alike were changed from modest creeks to turbulent torrents. Even the usually dry stream beds along the slope were now full of water, as in the case of the brooklet which some of the sheep had crossed and which others of them had avoided.

Thus, the venturesome leader of the wethers found his detour had been in vain. There was no space between the cliff and the roaring river; no path whereby he and his forty-seven followers might continue their aimless climb.

Bridging the stream, just in front of them, was an uprooted tree; undermined, years earlier, by some freshet which had cut the dirt from its roots. Athwart the river, at this narrow point, lay the huge tree. Its branches had rotted away or had been broken off by successive hammering of freshets.

But the trunk still bridged the current, its top resting on the edge of a high bank of clay upon the far side. The bark had long since decayed. Worms and woodpeckers and weather and rot had been busily at work on the exposed trunk, for decades, until it was but a sodden shell of its former self.

The leading runaway apparently had no great desire to tempt a ducking, through continuing his escape by means of so fragile a path as the rotted log. Hence, he paused as he reached it. And the others piled up behind him, milling and bleating and as uncertain as he.

It was at this moment that Treve came charging up the mountainside; sweeping toward them, with a thunder of barking.

The dog knew every phase of sheep herding. He knew how to herd and drive a flock of lambs as tenderly as a mother would guide her child's first steps. He knew the art of coaxing and soothing the march of a bunch of heavy ewes. But he also knew that a band of scraggy wethers, on the autumn roundup, can be dealt with in more tumultuous fashion, and that finesse is not needed in driving such strays back to the flock.

Wherefore, his furious charge, now; a charge planned to get the sheep on the run, in a compact bunch, and to gallop them back to the main body. But, unfamiliar with that part of the mountain, he knew nothing of the impasse which had halted them; nor of the log across the river.

At sound of the bark and of the oncoming rush of the pursuer, the wether-leader lost what scant discretion a sheep may have been born with. In fear of recapture and of fast driving down the mountain, he ran bleating out on the rotten log. Urged by the same fear, the forty-seven wethers followed him.

A sheep is not as sure-footed as a goat. But sure-footedness was not needed. Under the pattering hoofs the decayed surface of the log crumbled; leaving a soft and ever-deeper rut for the ensuing hoofs to tread.

Over the impromptu bridge scampered the

wether; to the safety of the far bank. And over the same bridge, in scurrying haste, stormed the other sheep.

Under their sustained weight and the incessant reverberating impact of their pounding hoofs, the rotted log was assailed more heavily than its feeble shell of resistance could withstand. Not with the usual cracking and rending, but with a soggily soughing sound, it gave way. Not a fiber of it was strong enough to crackle. But the whole bridge went to pieces as might a wad of soaked blotting paper that is wrenched apart.

By the rare luck that so often attends idiots and sheep, the leader and forty-six of his flock had reached the high clay bank on the far side, before the thick log collapsed.

Treve came whizzing up the slope to the spot where the crossing had been made. He arrived, just as the log went to pieces. Its punk-like sections splashed noisily into the torrent below. And with them splashed almost as noisily the last sheep that had attempted the crossing. This wether had hesitated and started to turn back as he felt the bridge sinking under him. The moment of delay had sent him headlong into the water among the log débris.

Down plunged the unlucky wether. Before his body struck water, his silly head smote against a pointed outcrop of rock that protruded above the churned surface of the river. The contact broke the sheep's skull, as neatly as could a hatchet-corner. Stone dead, the poor creature went bobbing and tossing and revolving, down the swirling current.

Scarce had the wether plunged into the Chiquita when Treve was off the bank, in one wild bound; and into the water after him.

It was not the first nor the tenth time that the collie had "gone overboard" to rescue a sheep. For there is no limit to the quantity and quality of mischances into which sheep can entangle themselves. Falling off bridges is one of their recognized accomplishments.

But never in his two years of life had the young dog found himself in a torrent like this. At his first immersion into it, he was bowled over, then sucked under water; then he was spun dizzily about;—all before he could get his bearings. Rising to the surface and taking instinctive advantage of the current, he shook the water from his eyes and struck downstream after the bobbing gray-white body of the sheep.

At the end of fifty yards—during which a whirling log had well nigh stove the collie's ribs in, and two successive eddies had pulled his head under water—he saw a twist of the erratic current pick up the sheep's body and sling it high on a patch of stony beach at a bend in the stream.

There it sprawled. And thither the collie fought his breath-tortured way. But when he dragged himself up out of the water and sniffed at the wet huddle of wool and flesh, a single instant's inspection told him he had had his hazardous swim for nothing. The sheep was dead.

Panting from his stupendous efforts, Treve started at a canter along the far bank of the stream, toward the forty-seven wethers that had crossed in safety. His sole duty, now, was toward them; and he realized it. He must get them back to the other side of the river and thence down to the main flock, a mile below.

The sheep had been grievously affrighted by the splash of the log and by the mishap to their fellow-imbecile. They were scattering, with loud bleats, through the rock-strewn underbrush. But they did not scatter far. After them, in front of them, on every side of them, swept a golden-tawny and loud-mouthed whirlwind; that gave them no peace until they consented to turn back from their four-direction flight and bunch themselves as he decreed.

Then, his strays rounded up and submissive, Treve undertook to get them out of their predicament. But this was a task beyond his collie brain. He did not seek to drive them across the tossing little river. The death of the one sheep that had fallen into the flood told him the futility of such a move;—even could he have forced them to the terrifying passage. He must find some better way to get back to the flock.

The river, in its descent, waxed ever wider. Moreover, its course continued steadily to travel farther and farther from the trail. Perhaps for this reason, perhaps by mere instinct, Treve began to drive his scared sheep up the mountain; keeping ever as near as possible to the stream; and watching for a safe way to cross. Again and again he tested its bottom in hope of a ford. But he found none. Nor was the river bridged, farther up, by any tree.

Still, he continued his climb, marshaling the forty-seven wethers ahead of him. The going was rough and the sheep were tired and rebellious. But he kept on. At the end of a few minutes he stopped. Or rather, he *was* stopped. He was stopped by the same form of barrier as had halted the sheep, in the first place, on the other side of the stream, far below.

A rock ridge, some twelve feet high, and with a front as precipitous as the wall of a room, loomed in front of him and his flock. It continued to the very edge of the stream and indeed for a yard or two out into the water; the current foaming around its base. There was no way of climbing it. Treve must needs follow, to the right along its base, for an opportunity to skirt it or else to surmount it at some place where the cliff should be lower and less precipitate.

So, to the right, he guided his weary captives and moved along the ridge's base. Presently, the roar of the Chiquita River died away behind them as they pushed forward through the rubble and thickets that fringed the bottom of the cliff. Nowhere did the cliff itself appear to be lower. Instead, it seemed to be sloping upward, gradually, to greater height.

The sheep became harder to drive. For hereabouts were wide clearings in the forest and underbrush. These clearings were lush with grass. Here, no flock had grazed; the herdsmen wisely sticking to the other side of the Chiquita. But Treve would not let the wethers loiter. The day was growing late, and the journey to the flock below was momentarily waxing greater.

Only once did the collie check his steady drive. That was when the front of the cliff opened wide in a split that had had its origin in some ancient earthquake. Here was an aperture, some six feet wide; the cliff-top meeting above it in a sort of Gothic arch, formed by the toppling of two crest bowlders against each other, long ago.

Leaving his fagged-out sheep to browse on the

grass, Treve explored this opening. Warily, he advanced into it. For his nostrils registered the scent of wild beasts here. But, as the scent was old and stale, he did not hesitate to continue.

Inside the arch was a cave, partly natural, partly caused by the juncture of fallen bowlders at the top. The cavern was about ninety feet wide, by some seventy feet deep; before the gradually shelving roof rock made it too low for the dog's body to wriggle onward. Its floor was strewn with rock-fragments and with the scattered bones of animals long since slain.

Here the wild beast scent was somewhat more rank than from the entrance. Yet here too it was stale. To all appearances this was the lair of some brute or brutes that used it only as a winter-time shelter. The fact did not interest Treve. He had come in here, hoping the opening might go all the way through the ledge and let him and the sheep out at the other side. As it did not, he went back to his wethers; rounded them up from their grass-munching and set them in motion, still skirting the ledge in the same direction.

A few rods farther, the cliff was broken again; this time by a spring that trickled out from a rent in the precipice and filled a little natural rock pool in the ground in front of it.

Another half-mile brought them within sound

of rushing water, again; and they emerged on the bank of the little Pico River,—as swollen and as turbulent as the Chiquita itself and as impassable. Both tiny rivers had their birth on the summit. Both flowed down, on opposite sides of the cliff which extended from one to the other. The two streams converged a mile below.

The sight of this new obstacle roused Treve to worried activity. Once more deserting his flock, he set off at a loping run, downhill, skirting the Pico. And at the end of a mile he came on the seething confluence of the two rivers. Thence he traced the Chiquita back to the ledge; after which, perplexedly, he ran on and rejoined the sheep.

To his collie mind, one thing was clear. Until the waters should subside, there was no possibility of leading his wethers out of this enclosure.

Here they must stay; and here he must look after them. It would have been the simplest sort of exploit for him to swim the river himself and get back to his master. But this would involve deserting the sheep;—which is the first and the most sacred "Thou Shalt Not" in all a trained sheep dog's list of commandments.

Having been wholly out of earshot from the trail, Treve did not hear the shouts of Fenno and, later, of Royce. Mack, following the path of the strays, on his return, two days later, saw where it had approached the brook and then where part of it had branched off again, back toward the trail. Hence, he missed the one chance of finding his chum. He knew no sheep would swim the flooded river. The bridging log was gone. Thus, he did not explore beyond the Chiquita.

The tally at the ranch proved the flock to be forty-eight sheep short. Both partners came to the somewhat natural conclusion that these must have encountered a group of cattlemen, rounding up their herds on the no-sheep section of the peak; and that the cowboys had destroyed them and their guardian collie. Such reprisals were not unprecedented in the eternal sheepman-cattleman war.

Mack would have made further search and would have quartered the whole mountain. But, before he could arrange to do so, the rains set in. The upper half of Dos Hermanos peaks was lost in deep snow. The lower half was a combination of quagmire and torrent. No, the search must be postponed till spring. Heavy-hearted, the partners set themselves to forget the collie they loved and the sheep whose loss they could not afford. It was not likely to be a happy winter at the ranch.

At first the marooned dog and his forty-seven sheep fared comfortably enough. The grass was lush. The water was plentiful. In that man-avoided loop of the two rivers, there were an abundance of rabbits and squirrels and raccoons and similar small game which any clever and energetic collie could catch with no vast difficulty.

Treve was miserably unhappy over his absence from Royce and from home. But he was far from starvation. And his herding job was reasonably easy. The first snows did not creep down as far as the ledge. Nor was the cold too intense to make outdoor sleeping comfortable. The larger forest creatures were taking greedy advantage of the fat autumn season of easy kills, farther up the peak. Not until driven down by cold and by dearth of game would most of them invade the ledge-and-water-girt loop between the rivers.

But, in another fortnight, rain changed to alternate sleet and snow. In one night the wool of nearly half the flock froze hard to the ground. But for a merciful sluice of warmer rain in the early morning, the victims must have stuck there until they starved. But the accident gave Treve his warning. Thus had a bunch of sheep frozen to the corral ground, one sleety night, the year before, at the ranch. Next night Treve had helped Mack herd them through the narrow gate into a covered fold. The memory had stayed by him, as well as the sane reason for the act.

And, this day, when night drew near, he shoved and coerced his wondering charges in through the six-foot opening of the cliff-cave he had explored. It was an ideal fold. He himself slept at the cave's narrow mouth;—perhaps less, at first, with an idea of guarding his flock than to escape their rank odor and jostling bodies. But, on the third night, he had good cause to be glad of his choice of a bed.

He was roused from a snooze, by the return of the lair's winter occupant. Starting up, urged by some warning that pierced his slumber, he confronted an indistinct form that approached in the darkness, not twenty feet in front of him.

The elderly mountain lion which, for years, had made his winter abode in the cave, had dropped down over the ledge, from his summer and autumn wanderings in the rich hunting grounds among the higher reaches of the peak. A warm reek of delicious live mutton assailed his hungry senses as he neared his home. Then, of a sudden, out of the doorway of the lair flashed something hostile and furious; charging straight at him before the lion could so much as crouch for a spring.

Treve carried the battle to the enemy, ere the latter knew there was such a thing as a foe between him and the sheep whose stronger odor had stifled the scent of the collie.

With hurricane speed he dashed at the approaching beast. The lion reared on his hind legs, spitting, snarling, swatting with both murderous forepaws. But, by reason of the attack's complete surprise and a season of heavy feeding and his advancing years, he was slow. The dog was able to dive beneath the flailing claws, slash the unprotected underbody, and spring to one side.

The lion swerved, to follow. But Treve was of a breed whose ancestors were wolves;—a breed whose brain never quite loses, at emergency, the wolf-cunning. A million times, in the world's earlier centuries, had panther and wolf done death-battle in prehistoric forests. Their warfare was a phase of the eternal cat-and-dog feud. Some native ancestral skill guided Treve, to-night.

For, as he swerved, he twisted back, with the speed of thought. The mountain lion lunged after him. The collie was no longer there. Instead, his white fangs had found the mark that instinct taught them to seek. They closed on the nape of the lion's neck, as the old cat shifted his head in pursuit of his dodging foe.

The lion thrashed madly about to dislodge the jaws that were grinding unrelentingly toward his spinal cord. He tossed the dog to and fro. He banged him against the ground and against the cliffside. Once his curved claws raked Treve obliquely, shearing to the bone.

But the dog hung on; ever deepening his bite into the neck-nape. He was knocked breathless. He was in torment. But he hung on. He redoubled the muscular pressure of his grinding jaws. It was his only chance. And he knew it.

Then, with a last frantic plunge, the lion flung him off. The dog's whirling body crashed athwart the cliffside.

Treve fell breathless and stunned to the ground; and lay there. The lion did not follow up his victory, but lay where he had fought. He twisted and writhed like a broken snake. That last irresistible fling had been his death-struggle. The collie's teeth had found their unerring way to the spinal cord.

When, at last—battered and bruised and bleeding—the collie staggered to his feet, the enemy sprawled inert and lifeless, ten feet away from him; and the cave was reverberant with the bleating of panic sheep.

On another night, two coyotes approached the cave. Treve stood his ground in the narrow passageway, resisting their lures to venture forth; that they might take him from opposite sides.

One of them, feinting a dash, in hope of drawing him out, ventured too close. The next moment he went howling back to his mate; a broken forepaw dragging limp.

The two marauders contented themselves with lurking out of reach for the rest of the night. In the dawning they set off in search of easier prey. Nor did they return.

Luckily for Treve, the wolves and the bulk of the other large beasts of prey had not yet crossed the rivers or come down over the ledge, for the winter. As it was, his labors were wearing enough; in leading his hungry flock to stretches of snow not too deep or too hard for them to dig through in search of grass.

Then dawned a morning when the temperature was many degrees below zero. It was the third morning of the first real ice-grip weather of the young winter. Another night or so of such awful cold would bring the hungry wolf-packs down from their higher hunting grounds; —down to where the scent of sheep would muster them to the slaughter.

On that morning the hollow, below the spring-trickle, was frozen solid. Perforce, Treve led his sheep afield in search of water. He led them to the Chiquita River, a quarter mile below the ledge. As they neared it, he left them and bounded forward.

To his amazed near-sighted eyes, there was a wide and solid bridge spanning the stream at this narrow point;—a bridge which, assuredly, had not been there when last he visited the river. It shone like white flame in the bitter cold sunrise.

The freshet had long since subsided. The freezing of the pools near the summit, for two nights, had made the stream sink still lower. Here, the queer trend of the water into a cataract, and the sudden visitation of the supreme cold had caused a phenomenon familiar to every one who has seen northern waterfalls in winter. An ice-bridge had formed over the shallow cataract.

Now, Treve had no method of knowing whether this seemingly firm bridge was strong enough to hold an army or too fragile to support a mouse. Nor did he stop to test it. Enough for him to realize that he and his sheep were no longer cut off from the world.

Wheeling, he bunched his flock, with clamorous barks and with flying feet; and fairly hurled them at the bridge. Laggards and cowards were nipped or hustled. Fearing their guard more than they feared the uncertain ice, the forty-seven wethers rushed the bridge; slipping and slithering across it, helter-skelter, singly and in twos and threes.

Over they surged, in safety; the big young dog driving them fast and mercilessly.

Early winter dusk had fallen. Royce and Fenno were entering the ranch house at the close of their day's chilly work, when a shout from Toni, at the barns, made them stop and turn around.

Up the meadow, from the direction of the foothills, a scarred and thin collie was driving a bunch of thinner and leg-weary sheep. All day and at a racking pace Treve had driven them; giving them no semblance of rest; keeping them at a gallop whenever he could urge their tired legs into such violent action.

Now, at sight of Mack, the collie left his detested charges to the oncoming Toni; and galloped ecstatically up to Royce; leaping on the dumbfounded man and licking his hands and making the icy air reëcho with his rapture-barks.

While master and dog were greeting each other, Toni counted the sheep and made report to Fenno.

"Where—where the blue blazes have you been, old friend?" Mack was demanding of the excited dog. "And where'd you lose all that flesh and get all those scars? You poor boy! Where you been?"

"Huh!" scoffed Joel, blowing his nose and

forcing his shaky voice to its wonted growl of complaint. "Best ask him what he done with that other sheep. There was forty-eight of 'em, when him and them disappeared. There's only forty-seven now. I'm wonderin'—"

"I'm wondering, too!" flared the indignant Royce, pausing in the petting of Treve, to whirl angrily on his partner. "I'm wondering what'd happen if some one should return a thousand-dollar roll of banknotes to you, that you'd lost. I'm wondering what you'd say to him. No, I'm not wondering, either. I *know*. You'd say: 'What became of the nice rubber band that used to be fastened around this roll?' Gee, but you're a grateful soul, partner! Lost forty-eight sheep; and Treve pretty near gets himself scarred and starved to death getting 'em back for you! And all you do is to kick because one of 'em's lost!"

He strode contemptuously into the house, whistling the collie to follow. But Joel Fenno surreptitiously laid a detaining hand on Treve's neck.

"Trevy," he cooed, hoarsely, bending low over the happy dog and petting him with clumsy fervor, "I—I reckon *you* understand, don't you? Lord, but I've missed you!"

CHAPTER IV: THE KILLER

THE rainy season was coming to an end—
the season as nastily disagreeable as it was
needful. Spring was at hand. And the folk on
the Dos Hermanos ranch rejoiced almost as
much as did their thousands of chronically damp
sheep and their soggy acres of mud-tormented
range land.

To Treve the winter had passed pleasantly
enough. He had had more time for cross-
country rambles and for jack rabbit chasing
than was at his command during the year's three
other and busier seasons.

The soaking rains bothered him not at all.
True, his mighty outer coat was often drenched
and flattened by the wet. But the queerly woven
and downy mist-hued undercoat served him as
well as could any mackintosh. It was waterproof
and all but coldproof.

The occasional snowfalls exhilarated him.
The glare and tingle of them went to his head
and made him frisk and roll in puppylike glee
and snatch up mouthfuls of the stinging white
flakes as they lay for a brief space on the sodden
or half-frozen earth.

True, hard snow-lumps had an annoying way of forming between his pads; so that he had to halt in his romps or his runs, every few minutes, to gnaw them out. But these were petty drawbacks. The snow, for the most part, was Treve's loved playfellow.

Royce Mack was as enthusiastic over the snowfalls as was Treve himself. They reminded him of the jolly winter sports in the Vermont hills he had left so far behind him. He and Treve used to tramp for miles through the glistening whiteness; just for the fun of it.

Joel Fenno had never in his long and grouchy life done anything "just for the fun of it." Fun had no place in his meager workaday vocabulary. Sourly he used to watch Royce and young Treve set forth together on their snow-tramps, in the rare hours of worklessness, that winter.

He grudged the idea of any energy not directed to the piling up of dollars and cents. Moreover, he had grown to care queerly much for the big collie that once had saved him from death. He was vaguely annoyed by the dog's evident preference for Mack; and the gay romps and rambles they enjoyed.

To Royce, the old chap grumbled loudly about the folly of wasting time in such fashion. He used to scowl in disgust at Treve and make as though to repel the collie's playful offers of friendship. Not to Royce or to any one else would Fenno have admitted that he had so far broken the crust of his own grouchiness as to entertain a genuine yearning for the comradeship of a mere dog.

Mack was deceived by Joel's attitude of lofty contempt; even though Treve was not. The fact that Joel ignored him or glowered at him, in public, did not offset to Treve the pleasanter fact that he fed him choice bits from his own dinner plate or patted his head with awkward furtiveness when Royce's back was turned.

One morning, as spring was dawning, the two partners sat at their sunrise breakfast, preparatory to starting out for a day of "marking," at their Number Three camp. Treve's usual place, at meals, was on the puncheon floor; to the left of Royce Mack's seat at the table. This morning, the big dog was absent.

"Where's Treve?" asked Fenno, with elaborate carelessness; adding, surlily: "It's good to have one meal in peace, without a measly cur to take away my appetite by scratchin' fleas and watchin' every mouthful I eat."

"I don't know where he is," Mack answered. "Around, outside, somewhere, most likely. These warm spring nights when we leave the doors open, he's apt to trot out, as soon as he's awake.

If it takes your appetite away to have him here
when we eat, I can tell him not to come in at
meals. He never needs to be told anything but
once."

Royce spoke, aggrievedly. Treve was his
chum, his loyal and loved comrade. It irked
him to hear Fenno's incessant grumblings at the
great dog's presence as a housemate.

"Oh, let him keep on comin' to table if you're
a mind to!" muttered Joel, ungraciously. "If it
makes a hit with you to have him spraddled out
on the floor beside you when you eat an' at the
foot of your bunk at nights and traipsin' along
after you all day—why, go ahead. We settled
that, long ago. I'd rather put up with it than
have you sore about it or bickerin' an' jawin' at
me all the time, because your purp can't be
treated like he was folks. I c'n go on standin'
it, I reckon. I used to figger that this outfit was
a workin' proposition; an' that every man and
every critter on the Dos Hermanos ranch was
s'posed to hustle all day and every day fer his
board and keep. But if it amooses you to keep
a dog that's just a silly pet an' to waste a lot of
good work-time playin' around with him—"

"Treve does his share of the ranch work, and
more than his share!" declared Royce. "You
know that as well as I do. And you wouldn't
have been here, grouching and whining, if he

hadn't saved you from dying, out on the Ova trail. Yes, and we'd have been shy forty-seven sheep, last fall, if he hadn't herded 'em safe home here, when they got lost up on the Peak. Oh, what's the use? We've been over all this a trillion times. Either say outright you don't want him in the house at meals and at night; or else quit nagging about it."

Joel Fenno rebuked this unwonted tirade from his pleasant-tempered partner by sinking into grieved silence. Surreptitiously, he hid under a slice of bread two tempting morsels of pork that he had been saving to give to Treve.

Seldom was the collie absent from meals, and Fenno missed him. He enjoyed feeding the big young dog on the sly, when Mack was not looking. The loveless, sour old man had never before made a pet or a chum of any dumb animal. He was unreasonably vexed that Treve should not be there to eat the bits of meat he had set aside for him.

As Mack wiped his mouth and got up from the deal table, Joel took occasion to slip the two fragments of pork into his own shirt pocket, on the chance of being able to give them to Treve, unnoticed, during the morning. Then he swore at himself for a slobbery old fool, for doing such a thing.

He and Royce left the house. As usual, they

made their way toward the ramble of adobe out-buildings which served as barn, garage, store-rooms, stable and "home-fold." As they neared this straggling group of shacks, two men came in sight, over the low swell of ground from the southward.

The men were mounted, and they rode fast. As they sighted Mark and Fenno, they left the trail-like road and cantered across the three-acre dooryard toward them.

At a glance, both partners had recognized the riders. They were Bob Garry, of the Golden Fleece sheep-ranch, five miles to southward, and Garry's foreman.

"I tried to get you boys on the phone," hailed Garry, as he drew near. "But you didn't an-swer. So we rode over. I—"

"Phone's been out of kilter, for three days," said Mack. "They're sending a man out from Santa Carlotta, to-day, to fix it. What's wrong?"

He noted both horses had been ridden hard and their riders' faces were grim.

"What's wrong?" echoed Garry. " 'Nough's wrong. We came over to see if he'd visited Dos Hermanos, yet. Has he?"

"Who?" snapped Joel; continuing crankily: "We don't hone for vis'tors. Not in a rush season like this. Who's due to come a-visitin'?"

"If you don't know," retorted Garry, nettled at the inhospitable tone, so rare in that region of roughly eager hospitality, "if you don't know, then it's a cinch he didn't come here. Your herders would have reported him, before now. He—"

"Who?" insisted Fenno, trying to stem the flood of angry garrulity and to glean the facts. "Who's—?"

"The Killer," replied Garry. "First one that's hit the Dos Hermanos valley, since—"

"Killer?" babbled Royce Mack, aghast. "Good *Lord,* man!"

He and Joel stared at the riders and then at each other, in slack-jawed dismay. Well did they understand, now, the grim look on the faces of Garry and his foreman. Well did they realize what was implied to all sheepmen by that sinister word, "Killer."

From time to time, throughout the annals of Western shepherding, flocks have been devastated by some predatory dog or wolf; whose murders have been wrought on a wholesale basis and have piled up a cash loss of many thousands of dollars, before he could be destroyed. Not a mere mischievous mongrel, which perhaps managed to kill a sheep or two and then was tracked down and shot; but a genuine Killer.

Such a Killer was the famed "Custer wolf" of

the Black Hills country, whose depredations cost more than $25,000 in slaughtered livestock, and whose killing, by Harry Williams, in November, 1920, was greeted by a local celebration which eclipsed that of Armistice Day. Such a Killer was the dread "black greyhound" of Northern California, with his hideous toll of slain and mangled young cattle and sheep.

Killers seem to be inspired by a devilish ingenuity which for a time gives them charmed lives and renders useless the cleverest efforts of ranchers and professional hunters to track and slay them. Tidings that such dog or wolf has begun operations in any particular region is cause for tenfold more alarm than would be the news of a smallpox epidemic. For it means grave loss to the community and to all the community's stockmen.

Small wonder that Royce and Joel gaped blankly at each other, on hearing Garry's announcement! Mack was the first to recover his tongue.

"Every time a lamb is missing or a wether gets gouged on a barbed wire," he said, with an effort at banter, "the yell of 'Killer' goes up. Most likely this is—"

"Most likely you're talking like a wall-eyed ijit!" cut in Garry. "Eleven of my sheep found, an hour ago, with their throats torn out."

"Huh?" grunted Fenno, with much the sound that might have been expected had he been kicked in the stomach.

"Eleven of 'em!" reiterated Garry. "Down in my Number Two range. I had a bunch of five hundred wethers and old ewes down there. My poor collie, Tiptop, was in charge of 'em. We found him with both forelegs broke and his jugular slit. He'd done his best. I c'd see that, by the way the soft ground was mussed up, all around him. But he's a little feller; and pretty old, besides. So the Killer got him. And then he got eleven of my sheep. Simmons found what'd happened, when he made his rounds, at sunrise. He came, lickety-split, to me. I phoned up and down the line; but the Golden Fleece seems to be the only ranch he came to."

"He didn't come here," said Royce. "We'd have got word, before now, if he'd done any killing at one of the outlying ranges. He—"

"That's the Killer of it!" commented Fenno, savagely. "I know. I've been in sections where one of 'em worked. Never visit the same place twice in the same month. Never go back to their kill. Clean up at one ranch to-night; then at another, twelve miles away, to-morrow night; then maybe a week later at one that's fifty miles away; then back next door to where they killed fust. No way to dope out where they'll land next. They're wise to pizen an' traps an' guns an' sich. Send out parties to track 'em, an' they give 'em the slip an' double back an' kill, right behind 'em. Put night guards on the ranges, an' next mornin' you'll find dead sheep not fifty feet from where the guards was posted. Killers are smarter than folks are. We're sure in for a passel of trouble—the lot of us. That's the way with luck!" sighed the old pessimist with the sorrily triumphant air of one whose worst fears are realized. "Yep, that's what I always say about luck. It's pretty bad, for a while. Then all at once it begins to get a heap worse. Now—"

"Well, I'm out to round up a posse of hunters," interrupted Garry. "That's the only hope. Post good shots everywhere, on every range; and then let a posse comb the country for the Killer's lair. Most likely he has a hide-out, somewheres along the foothills of the Dos Hermanos peaks, or maybe down in the coulée. And maybe, with the right men, we can root him out. Anyhow, with men hunting him all day and with the ranges close-guarded all night, he's li'ble to figger that this ain't a healthy region for his work; and he'll shift to somewheres else."

"You said just now that my partner is a wall-eyed ijit," drawled Fenno. "I'm not denyin' it. Lord knows he is. I found it out, a long while

back. But he's plumb sensible, compared to you,
Mister Garry; with your talk of trackin' down
a Killer or makin' the region too hot to hold
him. Why, that sort of a thing is meat an' drink
to a Killer! That's what a Killer likes better'n
to be 'lected Pres'dent. It gives him a chance
to amoose himself by gettin' the best of folks.
He'll run circles around your posse an' he'll toll
it into a swamp. He'll sneak behind your range-
guards; just like I said; an' they'll find a bunch
of killed sheep, next mornin', not fifty feet from
where they was standin' guard. You're wastin'
your time, a whole lot and you're losin' sleep.
No, sir, it's *you* that's the wall-eyed ijit;
not Royce Mack;—when you hand out that
line of chatter. Why, son, you couldn't even
strike the Killer's trail; let alone foller it!
He'll—"

"Maybe there's *three* wall-eyed ijits, then,"
spoke up the Golden Fleece foreman, "with you
for the middle one, Mister Fenno. 'Cause we've
found his trail, as plain as if it was wrote in big
print. Likewise we follered it. Follered it clean
to the main road; and lost it, there, on a ridge
of hardpan and rock that didn't leave any marks
like the wet ground did. Headed for the coulée,
I'll bet he was. It's a trail that ain't to be mis-
took for any other, neither."

"Huh?" grunted Joel, with reluctant interest,

"If it's a queer trail, maybe that'll help. Did—?"

"It's a queer trail, all right," said Garry. "It's a three-legged trail."

"A *which?*"

"A three-legged trail," repeated Garry. "Left front foot don't touch ground at all."

"A lame Killer!" ejaculated Mack. "That's something new."

"Maybe so. Maybe not," said Garry. "It struck me queer, first-off. But I got figgering on it. If it's a wolf or a coyote that's hurt its left front foot, that means it can't run as fast as it used to; and it can't run down its food in the hills. The only way it can get square meals is to slink down to the ranges and stalk a bunch of sleeping sheep. That's simple enough, ain't it? My foreman's right. We studied those tracks of the Killer, in the mud of the range and in the muck at the edge of the road. Three legs. I c'n swear to that. Left forefoot off the ground."

"Some sheep dog, gone bad, most likely!" ruminated Mack, half to himself. "I've read about such. And—"

"Nope," denied Garry. "Nothing like it. I thought of that, too. But it ain't."

"How d'*you* know?" challenged Fenno, ever eager for argument. "Can't a sheep dog hurt his left front foot as easy as a wolf can? Huh?

Tell me that! Is there anything in the Consti-
tootion that forbids a—"

"Sure he can," assented Garry. "Only, this
time he didn't. A dog that's spent his life running, thirty miles a day, over this country's
hardpan, after straying or bolting sheep—that
dog's feet gets as splayed as a cimmaron bear's.
A wolf's don't. A wolf don't have to run, except
when he wants to. And his pads don't splay, to
any extent. No more'n a house dog's feet splay.
These tracks was of feet that weren't hardly
splayed at all. So that's the answer to that.
. . . Well, we're wasting time. I wanted to
pass the word to you boys, and I wanted to see
if one of you or both of you would maybe join
up with the posse we're going to form. How
about it?"

Before either of the partners could answer, the
Golden Fleece foreman cried out and pointed
a stubby forefinger, dramatically. Around the
corner of the farthest outbuilding, from the direction of the coulée, appeared a bedraggled
figure.

The newcomer was Treve. His golden-tawny
coat and his immaculate white ruff and frill
were stained with mire and blood. Bloodstreaks
marred his classic muzzle and his jaws.

He was hobbling on three legs; his left forepaw dangling helpless in air.

The dog made straight for Mack and Fenno; his plumed tail essaying to wag greeting to his masters. He was a sorry sight. In his dark deepset eyes lurked the glint of half-shame, half-fun, which is the eternal expression of a collie that has been in delightful mischief and fears a scolding for his pranks.

After that first loud exclamation from the foreman, none of the onlookers spoke or moved; for the space of perhaps ten seconds. Frozen, wide-eyed, jaws adroop, they stared at the on-coming Treve.

In every brain raced the same line of glaringly simple logic. And in every brain was registered the dire word: "Guilty!"

Treve, ignoring the battery of horrified eyes, came limping up to Royce Mack, and stood in front of the younger man, gazing in friendly fashion into the whitened face and holding out for sympathy his sprained foreleg.

But, for once in his life, Treve received from his adored god neither sympathy nor a pat, nor any other sign of welcome. Royce simply blinked down at him in unbelieving horror.

As Mack gave no response to his overtures, Treve limped over to Joel Fenno, thrusting his bloodstained muzzle affectionately into the oldster's cupped palm. At the touch, a violent shudder wrenched Joel's whole meager body.

He did not withdraw his hand from the caress. But he turned his sick eyes miserably toward Bob Garry. In response to the look, Garry said curtly:

"The Killer's found; sooner'n I thought. I'm sorry, boys. I know what store you set by the brute. But there's only one thing to do. You know that, as well as I do."

There was no answer. Royce Mack took an impulsive half-step between the speaker and the wondering collie. Fenno did not speak nor stir. His sick old eyes were still fixed on Garry with a world of appeal in them. Garry spoke again; this time with a tinge of angry impatience in his tone.

"Well," he rasped, "I'm waiting to see it done. I reckon I've paid for my seat to the show. I paid for it with eleven killed sheep. And I don't aim to go from here till I make sure the Killer is put out of the way for good. We can settle, later, for the sheep of mine he slaughtered and for my good little old collie, too. But that can wait. Just now, the main thing is to see he don't do any more killing."

Neither partner answered. Garry laid a hand on the rifle he had strapped across his saddle-bow when he had started forth on the Killer-hunt. The gesture made old Fenno shake from head to foot as with a congestive chill.

Royce Mack, hollow-eyed and desperate, pushed the amazed collie behind him; and stood shielding him with his own athletic body.

"That won't get you nowheres!" sternly reproved Garry, noting the instinctive motion, and unstrapping his rifle as he spoke. "You know the law as well as I do. You ought to be thankful we've nailed him before he could do any more killing. It isn't once in a blue moon that a Killer is nabbed at the very start; before he c'n get away to the hills. We're plumb lucky. Now, then, will you shoot him; or do you want me to do it? Which'll it be? Speak up, quick!"

"Wait!" sputtered Royce, stammering in his heartsick eagerness. "Wait! This dog's my chum. He's never done anything like this, before. He'd never have done it, now; if he hadn't gone crazy, some way. I've read about sheep dogs 'going bad,' like this. It isn't their fault. Any more'n it's a human's fault, if he goes crazy. Folks don't shoot a human that's lost his wits. They shut him up somewheres and treat him kind; and then, like as not, he gets his mind back again. It's likely the same with a dog. I—"

"It's *you* that's lost your mind!" scoffed Garry, angrily, as he fingered his rifle. "If you haven't the whiteness or the nerve to shoot him, stand clear; and I'll do it, myself. He—"

"Wait!" implored poor Mack, the sweat running down his tortured face. "Hold on! Let
me finish. Here's my proposition:—I'll pay you
double market price on your eleven killed sheep
and on your dog he killed. And I'll put up a
thousand-dollar bond to keep Treve tied or else
in the house, all the time. I'll do this, if you
and your man will call it square and keep your
mouths shut about his going bad. I'm offering
this, on my own hook. My partner hates Treve,
anyhow. So I'm not asking him to share the
cost or the responsibility. How about it, Garry?
Is it a go?"

"It is—*not!*" refused Garry, his voice like the
scraping of a file upon rust. "I'm not in the
bribe-taking game. Besides, I'd feel grand,
wouldn't I, first time the cur sneaked loose and
began killing sheep again, all up and down the
Valley? Nice responsibility I'd have, hey? And
that's what he'd do. Once a Killer, always a
Killer. I'm clean s'prised at you for making
such a crack as that! Clean *s'prised!* Stand
clear, there! I'm going to put a stop to this
Killer danger, here and now. The law will uphold me. Stand clear of him, unless you want
me to take a chance at shooting him between
your knees."

He swung the rifle to his shoulder, as he

spoke. Then it was that Joel Fenno came out of his brief trance of dumbness.

"You're right," agreed Fenno, grumpily. "The law'll uphold you. But the law gives a owner the right to shoot his own dog, if he's willin' to. Royce, here, ain't willin' to. But I am. And I'm the cur's joint owner."

"Go ahead and do it then," ordered Garry forestalling a fierce interruption from Royce Mack. "Only, cut out the blab; and *do* it. I got a morning's work to catch up with. And I don't stir from here till the dog's dead."

"All right!" agreed Joel; a tinge of gruff anticipation in his surly voice. "That suits me. An' when you tell this yarn around, jes' bear witness that *one* of the Dos Hermanos partners was willin' and ready to obey the law; even if t'other one was too white-livered. Gimme the rifle. My own gun's up to the house."

He reached out for the weapon; and snatched, rather than accepted it, from Garry's hands. Hefting it, and turning toward Treve, he grumbled:

"I never did get the right hang of a rifle. A pistol's a heap handier. Got a pistol along, either of you?"

"No," said Garry.

The foreman shook his head.

"That's all right, then," cheerily remarked Fenno. "I—"

"You'll shoot Treve, through *me!"* panted Royce, shoving the collie behind him again; and advancing in hot menace on his detested partner. "It's bad enough to have—"

He got no further. Eyes abulge, he stared at Fenno.

Joel had caught the rifle deftly in both hands and was hard at work pumping the cartridges from its magazine. In clinking sequence they fell to earth. Three seconds later, he picked up and pocketed the shells and laid the empty and useless gun on the ground. Then he faced the loudly blaspheming Garry.

"I'll send the rifle back to you by one of the men," said he. "I'm not givin' it to you, now; for fear you may have a spare ca'tridge or two in your jeans. I was afraid maybe one of you had packed a revolver, too. That's why I made sure. Your teeth is drawed, friends. S'pose you traipse off home?"

"Joel!" cried Mack, overjoyed, incredulous. *"Joel!"*

The old man spun about on him; scowling, shrill with peevish wrath.

"What've I always told you about that dog?" he accused. "Didn't I always say he wa'n't wuth his salt? You've cosseted him an' you've

made much of him an' you've sp'iled him. Not
that he ever 'mounted to anything, to begin
with. An' now you see what you've brang him
to. Made a Killer of him! He—"

"I'm going to have the sheriff here, inside of
one hour!" the enraged Garry was declaiming,
unheeded, at the same time. "And after the
Killer is shot by an off'cer of the court, I am
going to bring soot agin you for impeding the
course of the law and likewise for stealing my
gun. Then I'm going to sue you both, in the
Dos Hermanos County Court, for the loss of
my sheep and—"

"Likewise," snarled on old Joel Fenno, still
haranguing his partner, "this comes of tryin' to
make a dog a c'mpanion instead of a beast of
burden, like the Almighty intended him to be.
I hope you're plumb sat'sfied with the passel of
trouble you've yanked down onto us, an'—"

"My foreman, here, is witness to it all," raged
on Garry, in the same breath. "He'll test'fy
how you d'prived me of my rifle, by trick'ry;
and then—"

"Don't go pirootin' off with the idee I put
Friend Garry's gun out of c'mission, jes' to save
Treve from the death he's deservin'," orated
Joel, to his dizzy partner. "I didn't crave to
have outsiders come here an' give me orders.
And if I help you hide Treve away somewheres

or ship him East to my nephew, before the sheriff gets here, it'll only be because—"

The advent of two new figures, around the corner of the barns, cut short the dual flood of oratory.

Toni, the Basque chief herder of the Dos Heimanos ranch, came into view. He was bent far forward under the weight of something that was balanced across his spine and which dangled lifelessly to either side of his ox-like shoulders.

Close behind him walked a smaller man, in soiled khaki and puttees; a repeating rifle slung by a bandolier athwart his back.

At sight and scent of the thing, carried by the big herdsman, Treve abandoned his puzzled efforts to make out what all the din and elocution were about. Wheeling, he bared his teeth and lowered his blood-stained head.

Then and only then did his human companions make out the nature of Toni's burden. It was the scarred and lifeless body of a giant gray wolf.

The partners, at the same time, recognized the slender khaki-clad rifleman who moved lightly along in the herdsman's wake. Twice, on his journeys, this man had stopped at the ranch for a meal. For hundreds of miles in all directions, he was known and admired.

For this was Eleazar Wilton, of the "Hunters'

and Trappers' Service," operated by the governmental Biological Survey;—one of the best shots in the West; and a huntsman who had done glorious work from Texas to northern Wyoming, in ridding the range country of predatory wolves. His fame was sung at a score of campfires and bunkhouses. He was a royally welcome guest wherever he might choose to set foot.

At sight of him, now, Bob Garry shouted aloud:

"Here's the man who'll do the job you tricked me out of doing! Cap'n Wilton, this dog has kilt eleven of my sheep! I call on you, in the name of the law, to put a bullet through his head. I'd 'a' done it myself; if these fellers hadn't fooled me out of it. He—"

"This dog, here?" asked Wilton in his quietly uninterested voice; as he strolled past Toni and up to Treve.

"Yep! That's the one!" trumpeted Garry. "See? He's still got their blood all over him. And his forefoot's bit and chawed where my collie died fighting him. There's other bite-marks on him, too. He—"

Royce and Fenno, by common consent, moved in front of their imperilled chum. But, before either of them could speak, Wilton interrupted Garry's harangue by stepping past the two part-

ners and laying his bronzed hands on Treve's
blood-streaked head.

There was greeting—almost benediction—in
the gesture. At the touch, Treve left off growling at the huge dead wolf which Toni was laying
on the ground, nearby; and glanced quickly up
at the stranger who had offered him this unwonted familiarity.

At what he read behind Wilton's steady eyes,
the collie's glint of suspicion softened to friendliness. His tail wagged, hospitably; and he laid
his cut head against the huntsman's khaki knee.

Meantime, Wilton was turning to the gesticu-
lating Garry.

"They 'fooled you' out of shooting this collie,
did they?" he asked. "Then it was the luckiest
bit of fooling done in Dos Hermanos County for
a long time. I was afraid of something like that
So I came on here, as soon as I could. I got
that double-sized herder to give me a lift with
the wolf; so we could get here quicker."

He nodded over his shoulder, as he spoke
The others, for the first time, took full cogni
zance of the wolf that Toni was stretching out
on the muddy ground.

The giant animal measured well over six feet
from muzzle to tail-tip. His hide was plentifully
scored with olden wounds and with very new
gashes. But it was Bob Garry who, with a gasp

of amaze, pointed out the beast's most striking peculiarity.

His left forefoot was gone.

It had been cut off, clean, at the ankle-joint. The injury had occurred long ago, for the skin and the hair had grown over the wound.

"Ever hear of him?" asked Wilton.

Nobody answered. Wilton continued:

"No, you wouldn't have been likely to hear. But, up in the Mateo country, there isn't a sheep-man or a cattleman that hasn't heard of him. I was sent up there, to get him. He had visited every range from San Mateo to Hecker's. Always they could trace him by his three-footed track. Must have been caught in a steel trap, years ago, and got loose by gnawing his foot off. He seems to have navigated faster on three legs than most animals can, on four. He was a 'lone wolf,' too. And he had all the sense of a dozen stage-detectives. Never tackled the same place twice in succession. Poison-wise and trap-wise. He could throw off pursuit as easily as any dime-novel Sioux. They sent me up to the Mateo district to get him. He fooled me, every time. Then he started south. The rains helped me track him. I suppose he didn't bother to confuse his trail or to double, on a long hike like that. More than a hundred miles, it was. And I could never catch up with him. Sometimes I lost his trail, altogether; and I'd pick it up, more by chance than by any skill."

A second time his hand dropped caressingly on Treve's head. The collie paused in the task of licking his own various flesh wounds and licked the caressing hand. Wilton smiled, rubbed clean his licked hand with his other sleeve, and resumed:

"Last night, at dusk, I lost the trail again. He was beginning to get cautious, once more. I figured that meant he was planning to stop and do some raiding. There was no use looking for tracks in the twilight. He couldn't be very far ahead of me. So I rode on. I rode till I got to the coulée, beyond here. It's a great place for any animal to hide out in;—with all those rocks and bushes. It struck me that would be just the lair for him to crawl into, daytimes; while he was ravaging this part of the world. Besides, it was right in his line of march. So I spent the night there; waiting for him. I was pretty sure I'd gotten in front of him; and that he'd stop there, to hide or else to sleep; before he went farther. Well, he did."

Again he paused, as if for dramatic effect.

"I watched, from before daybreak," he continued, presently. "No sign of him. I had crawled into a little niche between two bowlders, at the top of the coulée, just at its mouth. I couldn't miss him there. Then, about an hour ago, I got sight of him. He was pelting away, at top speed, on those three pins of his. And he wasn't using any craftiness, either. He was running, full tilt. And, not a hundred yards behind him, a collie was tearing along. This collie dog, here."

"They hunted together, hey?" exclaimed Garry. "I knew this cur was—"

"No," denied Wilton. "Dogs don't hunt with wolves. Coyotes do, but not dogs. The collie was hunting the wolf. He was after him, with every ounce he had. I take it the collie had been out on an early morning stroll, not far from his own home; when he got sight or scent of the wolf as he was coming this way from a kill And the dog gave chase. The wolf was all blood; so I knew he'd been at a bunch of live-stock, somewhere. The dog hadn't a mark on him. There was light enough for me to see that."

"Good old Treve!" applauded Mack. "But, Captain, if—"

"Wasn't the dog even running on three legs?" despairingly asked Garry.

"He was," admitted Wilton; adding: "And on the fourth leg, too. No lameness, then. I wondered, at first, why a Killer, like the three-legged wolf, should run away from a dog smaller and

lighter than himself. But I made a guess; and
the guess was right. Dawn had come. People
were likely to be astir. It was no time to be
caught in the open, in a fight. The wolf was
looking for cover. After he found it, there'd
be time enough to dispose of the collie. That's
wolf-nature."

"He—"

"The wolf got to the mouth of the coulée;
where another ten steps would hide him in the
undergrowth and the rock holes so safely tha'
no hundred hunters could root him out. He was
right below me. I drew a bead on him. But I
didn't shoot. Because just then, the collie over-
took him. And I saw the prettiest battle ever.
It would have been a crime to spoil it by a shot."

"Lord!" breathed Royce Mack. "Why wasn't
I there?"

"The wolf spun around on him," went on
Wilton, "and made a dive, wolf-fashion, for the
collie's foreleg; to break it. The collie was
going too fast to dodge, altogether. But he did
his best. And he got off with nothing worse
than a pinched left forefoot. Then the fun began. The old wolf was as quick as lightning.
But the collie—well, the collie was as quick as
—as a collie. I don't know anything quicker.
He got a slash or two; and once he was bowled
over in the mud and the wolf got a throat grip."

"But—"

"But the collie tore free, by leaving a handful of mattress-hair and skin in the wolf's jaws. And before the wolf could spit it out and get his jaws into action again, the collie had flashed in and gotten to the jugular. He hung on, like grim death; grinding those slender jaws of his deeper and deeper; while the wolf kept thrashing about and hammering him against rocks and against the ground; to make him let go. But the collie hung on. That's the collie of it. That's the thoroughbred of it, too. He knew he had the one hold he could hope to win by. And he held it. At last his teeth ground their way down to the jugular and through it. That's all there was to that fight."

"Treve!" babbled Joel. *"Trevy!"*

His unconscious exclamation went unheard in the hum of excitement.

"The collie lay down for a minute, panting," finished Wilton. "Then he got up and sniffed at the dead wolf. Then, before I had the sense to try to stop him, he limped off, in this direction. It seemed to me I remembered him, when I was at Dos Hermanos, last time. I got to wondering if he'd be shot, by mistake, when news came of killed sheep and when he was all bloody. So I hustled on here, after him. A dog, like that, is too plucky to let die."

"Mister Bob Garry, Esquire," drawled Fenno, sourly, as Royce bent in keen solicitude over his battered collie chum. "You was sayin' suthin', awhile back, 'bout having a mort of work to do, at your own ranch, this mornin'. Well, friend, the mornin's joggin' on. Here's your pop-gun. Here's your pretty ca'tridges. *Scat!*"

"You'll come to the house for some breakfast, won't you, Captain?" asked Royce, as the disgruntled Garry and his foreman rode off. "Chang can rustle you some grub, in no time. Come on, Treve. I want to wash out those bites of yours; and fix up your paw."

He set off toward the house, at Wilton's side. But Joel Fenno, behind their backs, buried his fingers lovingly in the collie's bloody and muddy ruff.

"Trevy," he whispered, the other hand groping in his shirt pocket, "here's some grand lumps of pork I saved out for you, from my breakfast. An'—an', Trevy, that Garry blowhard would 'a' had to shoot me as full of holes as these last year's pants of mine; before I'd 'a' let him git you. Yep—an' Wilton, too. Of all the dogs that ever happened, Trevy—you're that dog. . . . Hey!" he called grumpily after the departing Royce. "Here's your cur. Take him along to the house with you. He's jes' in my way, down here!"

CHAPTER V: A SECRET ADVENTURE

"THE only place where two can live as cheap as one," ruminated old Joel Fenno, pointing with his chewed pipestem, "is right yonder."

He indicated Treve, lounging on the puncheon floor in front of the group. Treve had awakened with some abruptness from a snooze and was scratching busily; driving his right hindfoot with great vigor and speed into his furry body in the general direction of the short ribs. On the collie's wontedly wise face was the grin of idiotic vacuity which goes with flea-scratching.

He was not looking his best or gracefulest or most sagacious, at the moment. Joel Fenno was sharply aware of his chum's absurd aspect. For the benefit of the ranch guest, he sought to forestall any unfavorable comment on the dog.

"Yep," he resumed, as Davids, the guest, eyed him in mild curiosity, "the only two, that can live as cheap as one, is not a spouse an' a spousess; but a flea an' a dog."

Davids smiled politely. Royce Mack had read this joke aloud to his partner, from a year-old copy of *The Country Gentleman,* a month before.

He forbore to encourage the old fellow's rare trip into the realms of humor, now, by so much as a grin. But Davids followed up his own civil smile by saying:

"I've been looking at that collie of yours, off and on, ever since I got here. He's a beauty. How's he bred?"

"They say there's beautiful things an' useful things," answered Fenno, surlily. "An' I've allus found the beautiful things is no use and the useful things ain't wuth lookin' at. Yep, Treve must be 'a beauty,' all right, all right. For he's no use to anybody. Jes' eats and snores and loafs; an' hunts fleas instead of sheep; an' tries to make busy folks romp with him. Likewise he succeeds in making 'em do it; so far as Royce, here, is concerned. The work hours my partner wastes in playin' and trampin' an' skylarkin' with that measly cur—"

"How's he bred?" repeated Davids, to stem the tide of Joel's chronic complaints against Mack and the collie.

"Bred?" echoed Fenno. "Who? Royce? All fired *ill* bred, when he has a mind to be. An' that's about all the time. He—"

"I mean the collie. What is it you call him? Treve?

"Treve? Bred? I don't—"

"He means," spoke up Royce Mack, from

boyhood memories of pedigreed animals, in the East, "he means, who were Treve's ancestors? We don't know, Davids. A queer sort of English tourist hobo came here and sold him to us. The man absconded with all the cash in Joel's vest and left the pup behind. As far as we know, Treve's pedigree began on the ranch, here. Why?"

"Because," said Davids, "he's a high-bred dog. What's more, he's the true show-type of collie. He's good enough to win a blue ribbon at any bench show in America. The hobo, most likely, stole him. Such dogs aren't left to roam at will."

Treve had ceased to pursue the wicked flea; or else his frantic clawing had dislodged the pest. For, with a lazy sigh, he resumed his nap on the cool puncheon. Stretched out there on his left side, silhouetted against the floor, he presented a picture to stir the heart of any collie-judge. The classic head might have been chiseled by a master-hand. The frame was mighty, yet as graceful as any greyhound's. The coat was unbelievably heavy and it shone like burnished copper.

Joel eyed the couchant dog with outward sourness of visage; but with inward pride that Treve should have won such praise from this Eastern engineer who had halted at the Dos Hermanos ranch for the night. It was part of Fenno's life-creed to maintain a continuous and universal grouchy disapproval of everything and everybody.

"Just what I've always said!" exulted Mack, at Davids' endorsement of his pet. "I've always told Joel the dog was good enough to go to any A. K. C. show. He's—"

"Yep!" snarled Fenno, "he'd make a show of us, all right. Why, most prob'ly they'd laugh him out of the place. Unless it was a flea-chasin' match. Then he might—"

"If I were you," put in Davids, addressing Mack and ignoring the peevish oldster, "I'd enter him for the big Dos Hermanos Show, up at La Cerra, next month. I was reading about it, on the way here. Quite a 'spread' on it in the Sunday *Clarion*. I'll leave my copy of it with you, if you'd like to glance over it. They're trying for a record entry. A big English judge is going to handle collies and one or two sporting breeds. On another page of the paper is a sort of primer for novice exhibitors; telling them how to enter their dogs for the show, whom to write to for premium lists and blanks, and all that, and how to make out the blanks. A lot of people don't understand how to do it. Take my tip and enter Treve at La Cerra."

"Huh!" snorted Joel, loudly.

"It's only about a hundred miles from here," pursued Davids. "You can make most of the trip by train; and get there in less than a day. Think it over. It'd be a fine thing to bring Treve home with a bunch of blue ribbons and maybe a big silver cup; and have all the papers printing his name. It's as much of a triumph for a dog to win first prizes at such a show as for a man to be elected to Congress."

Another derisive snort from Joel Fenno interrupted his homily and made Royce frown apologetically at the annoyed guest.

Now there was harrowing ridicule in Fenno's snort. But in the heart of Fenno an astonishing impulse had swirled into life. The snort was designed to frighten this yearning impulse to death. It could not.

Whenever any one looked or spoke approvingly of Treve, old Fenno had something of the thrill that might come to a man at praise of a cherished brother. While he girded at this feeling, as babyishly absurd, he could not check it. He loved the big collie; and he was inordinately proud of him. That others should admire Treve seemed in a way a sort of backhanded compliment to himself—to Joel who had never in his life been admired or complimented.

And now, at Davids' careless words, a glowing picture leaped into Fenno's dazed mental vision

—a picture of cheering throngs at the La Cerra show, all admiring and praising his victorious Treve. This and a crazy desire to take the collie there.

As if in contempt for his companions' chatter about a mere dog, Joel got up, presently, and sauntered into the house. He strolled through the room he and Royce Mack had assigned to Davids for the night. There on the floor, alongside the engineer's kitbag, lay the crumpled copy of the *Clarion*. Furtively, Joel pouched it and bore it to his own cubbyhole room. There, that night, long after the others were asleep, he crouched on his bunk and read and reread and sought to master the many bewildering bits of information as to the show and as to the mode of conducting dogshows in general.

Much was as Greek to him; until he figured it out with painful patience. Twice he flung the paper on the floor with a grunt of disgust. But ever that glowing vision of his chum's triumphs goaded him on. Through the silent hours he continued to wrestle with the details; as simplified for the benefit of novices.

Once, during his reading, he looked up, guiltily. In the doorway of his little room stood Treve; gravely inspecting him. The soft sound of rustled paper had roused the collie from his nightly slumber alongside Royce's bunk. He had

set forth to investigate. As Joel peered blink-
ingly toward him, Treve wagged his plumed tail
and came mincing forward; thrusting his classic
muzzle into the hand which Fenno instinctively
stretched forth.

"Trevy," whispered the old man, "how'd you
like to hear all them folks clappin' you an' sayin'
what a grand dog you are? Hey? Think it
over, Trevy. There needn't anybody know, but
you and me, Trevy. Royce has got to go to
Omaha, with them sheep, next month. He'll be
gone for two days before this show-date an' for
a couple of days after it. Nobody'll ever know,
Trevy. I'll tell the hands I'm goin' to run up to
Santa Clara to see about a bunch of merinos an'
that I'm totin' you along to herd 'em. I— Oh,
Trevy, we're a pair of old fools, you an' me! I
never thought I'd be such a dodo-bird as to waste
time an' cash on a dog. I'm gettin' in my dotage.
Granther Hardin used to think he was a postage
stamp, when he got old, Trevy. An' he used to
putter around, lookin' for a env'lope big enough
to stick himself to. They put him in a foolish
house. I reckon I'm qualifyin' for one, all
right, all right. But—you're sure a grand dog,
Trevy!"

The modernized old Spanish city of La Cerra,
at the westerly end of Dos Hermanos County,

had come to life in a rackety way, as it did once a year when the annual three-day show of the Dos Hermanos Kennel Association brought to town thoroughbred dogs and humans of all shades of breeding.

It was to this show, two years earlier, that Fraser Colt had been taking his collie pup when the latter's clash with a police dog in the baggage car had led to the temporary wrecking of one of his tulip ears; and when his resentment of Colt's kick had led his owner to hurl him bodily out through the car's open side door.

The memory of his own treatment at the hands —and boot toe—of the gross brute who had bought him on speculation and who had been taking him showward, rankled ever in the far-back recesses of Treve's brain. Which is the way of a collie. The harsh memory had been glozed over by two years of friendly treatment. Treve himself was not aware it existed. But it was there, none the less.

Joel Fenno, daily, had been more and more ashamed of his queer impulse to take Treve to the show. But, daily, also, the show-virus had infected him, more and more. Any one who has shown dogs will understand. Ever he visualized a more and more gorgeous triumph for his secret chum.

The first twelve miles of the trip were made in

the Dos Hermanos ranch's wheezy little car—the same in which Joel had piloted his partner to Santa Carlotta, the day before; when Royce set forth on his Omaha journey. Treve sat proudly beside the ever-more nervous Fenno, on the car's one shabby seat.

The dog was delighted at the jaunt, as is nearly every collie who is taken by his master on an outing. Instinctively, too, he felt Joel's grouchily suppressed thrill of excitement, and responded to it with a quick gayety. Apparently this was some dazzlingly jolly adventure he and his friend were embarking on.

At Santa Carlotta they took the spur line train for an eighty-mile run. Sixty of these eighty miles were across dreary greenish gray desert, flower-splashed, yet as dismal as the Mojave itself;—rolling miles of sick alkaline sand, skunk-infected, habitat of rattlesnakes—a waste strewn with sagebrush and Joshua trees. A dead and fearsome stretch; steel-hard of outline, shrilly vivid of coloring.

Then came the steep upgrade, over an elephant-backed mountain's swordcut pass; and a pitch down into the fertile valley whose nearest city was La Cerra.

Joel did not crate his dog; but sat on a trunk in the baggage car, with the collie curled up comfortably at his feet. The train-ride woke dim and not wholly pleasing memories in Treve. Something unpleasant had befallen him on such a ride. Once or twice he glanced up worriedly at the old man; only to be reassured by an awkward pat on the head or a grumbled word of friendliness.

It was so, too, after they had debarked and had found their way to the armory where the dogshow was in progress. As they entered the vast barnlike building, Treve's ears and nostrils were assailed in a way that made him halt abruptly in his stately advance at Fenno's side.

To him gushed the multiple plangent racket of hundreds of dogs barking in hundreds of keys. To a dog, even more than to a dogman, each bark carries its own translation. Treve read excitement in many of these barks that now yammered about his sensitive ears. In more, he read terror and loneliness and worried apprehension.

Also, the myriad blended odors of fellow-dogs rushed in upon him, dazing his senses with their incredible volume. It is through ears and nostrils that a dog receives his strongest impressions. And Treve was receiving more than he could assimilate.

His troubled, deepset eyes scanned Joel Fenno's gnarled face for reassurance. The oldster was wellnigh as confused and scared as his dog. He was a dweller in the lonely places. Crowds confused and frightened him. Yet he rallied enough to pass his hand comfortingly over the silken head of the collie and to mutter something by way of encouragement. Then man and dog marched valiantly down the intersecting aisles of barking or yelling or silently unhappy exhibits, to the section labeled "Collies."

There, Joel motioned Treve to jump up on the straw-littered bench that bore his number. He tied him; and tipped a lounging boy to get a panful of fresh water. The collie drank fever-ishly; but would touch none of the tempting meat scraps which Fenno produced from a greasy newspaper parcel for his benefit.

The great young dog did not cringe or shiver, amid this bedlam which tortured his sensitive soul and which was so hideous a contrast to his wonted life amid the sweet-scented silences. His head was erect. His dark eyes were steady. He was a good soldier. But—well, it was out of the question for him to swallow food, at such a place.

Joel looked about him. On either side of Treve's bench, and across the aisle, other collies were tied in their stall-like benches. Fenno counted eighteen of them, in all. Some were snipe-nosed and fragile. Some were deep of chest and massive of coat and had strongly classic heads, much like Treve's.

A few were snub-nosed and round-eyed and broad of skull. Old-fashioned types, these, and without chance of victory in any contested class.

Their like is seen at nearly every show. They are pets, loved by their masters or mistresses (oftenest mistresses), who think them wonderful. They are brought to shows in the futile hope that a blue ribbon or a cup may lend zest to their owners' pride in them. To a judge who is luckless enough to have a soft heart, these poor dogs and their cruelly disappointed owners are the saddest features of an exhibition which, at best, is never lacking in sad features.

Fenno stood, eyeing the dogs around him. He had a refreshing ignorance of everything which constitutes a collie's good or bad show points. All he knew was that Treve was the grandest dog on earth. He had come here to prove it to mankind at large. And the belief did not waver. Yet as he watched the handlers prepare their collies for the ring, he scowled. He had slicked Treve's glorious coat down smooth, with much water. He knew that humans are supposed to have their hair slicked down when they want to look their best. And he supposed it was the same with dogs.

But now he saw men currying their dogs with

expert touch; brushing the hair up and out; so that it should not cleave to the body and so that its texture and abundance might be fully seen by the judge. After watching this process for several minutes and catching sight of a collie poster on one of the benchbacks, Joel unearthed a mangy dandy-brush from his kitbag; and proceeded to fall to work right vigorously on Treve. The water had, for the most part, evaporated from the slicked coat. What was left of it made the coat and frill stand out with redoubled luxuriance as Joel brushed it upward.

Then Fenno scanned his neighbors, once more, for further tips in collie-dressing. He was vaguely aware that several spectators had paused at Treve's bench, as they drifted past. They were eyeing the dog in open admiration. This pleased Joel, but it did not surprise him. To him it seemed only natural that people should stop to admire such a dog. Then he heard one of the spectators read aloud to another from a gray-backed catalog he held:

" '217. *J. Fenno. TREVE. Particulars Not Given. Entered in Class 68.*'

"That's funny!" went on the reader, looking up from the catalog's meager information and studying afresh the collie in front of him. "That's mighty funny, Chris! Here's one of the best collies I've set eyes on. Class in every

inch of him. He'll give Champion Howgill Rival
the tussle of his life, for Winners, to-day. And
yet he isn't even registered. 'Particulars not
given.' It doesn't seem possible the owner of a
championship-timber collie, like that, shouldn't
know his pedigree and his breeder's name. 'Particulars not given.' Gee! That's the stock
phrase they use for mutts. This dog's a second
Seedley Stirling. It doesn't make sense. Who's
'J. Fenno,' anyway? Ever hear of him?"

"Some yap, out here, who bought the dog as
a month-old pup, I s'pose," answered the man
addressed, "and who doesn't know what he's
got. I'm going to hunt him out, before the
judging; and see what I can buy this collie for.
Maybe I can pick him up for a song. It's a cinch
his value will boom, after he's been judged.
Everybody'll be wanting him, then. I'm going
on a still hunt, right away, for J. Fenno."

"Meanin' me?" asked Joel, turning on him
with a sour suddenness that made the Easterner
recoil an involuntary step. "I'm Fenno. An'
I'm the man you've got to go on a still hunt for,
to buy this dog for a song."

"No offense," disclaimed the other, mistaking
Joel's normal manner for snarling displeasure.
"I like this dog of yours. That is," he hedged,
craftily, "I like him in spots. He's more good
than bad. I don't mind making you an offer for

him, if you've got the sense to sell him cheap. How about it?"

"I don't know how much cash you're packin' in that greasy old ill-fitting handmedown suit you're wearin'," replied Joel, with his wonted exquisite courtesy. "Nor yet I don't know what value you place on the mortgaged hencoop you live in, back home. But the whole price won't buy this collie of mine. Not if you throw in the million dollars diff'rence between your valuation of yourself and my valuation of you. Have I made it plain, friend? If I haven't, I'll try to speak less flatterin' and talk turkey to you."

Without awaiting reply he turned his lean back to the flustered Easterner. The move brought Fenno face to face with a stout man in vivid raiment.

"Selling that dog of yours?" queried the stout man, catalog in hand.

"Oh, *you're* looking for a bargain, too, from the 'yap,' are you?" snorted Joel. "Before the judge c'n tell him he's got a good dog? Well, the yap don't need to be told. He knows it. That's why he brang Treve here to-day. If your fat was wuth a hundred dollars a pound, you'd be a billionaire. But you wouldn't be able to buy my dog. Get that?"

He was about to turn away from the stout personage, as from his former interlocutor, when he noted the man was no longer looking at him. Instead, oblivious of the grouchy old hurler of insults, the stranger was once more studying Treve. In his plump face was a glint of perplexity, of struggling recollection.

Fraser Colt had an excellent memory. And the more he examined Treve, the closer he came to verifying a most improbable idea that had come to him, to-day, when first he caught sight of the collie reclining unhappily on the bench.

Back into his trained mind came the picture of a highbred collie pup, lying thus sorrowfully in Colt's stuffy kennel yard, some two years earlier, after Fraser had picked him up at his first master's forced sale. The dog's markings and facial expression were unusual. It seemed impossible. Yet—

Half-unconscious of his own gesture, Fraser Colt stretched out his hand toward Treve's shapely left ear. If there were sign of break or of ancient teeth-marks therein, the mystery was solved. If not—

Treve had lain resignedly in this place of turmoil, consoling himself by following with his sorrowful eyes the master who, for some unexplainable reason, had brought him here. Then, amid the million disturbing odors of the show, one special scent came to his nostrils in a wav to annihilate his heed of all the rest.

Suspiciously, his eyes clouding with half-formulated and long-sleeping recollections, he sniffed the heavy air. At the same instant, came the sound of a voice that was more than vaguely distasteful to him. Into his friendly heart sprang a righteous anger—but against what or whom he scarcely knew.

Then he saw Colt. And sound and scent and sight brought his dormant memories wide awake. He knew the man. Even as he would have recognized Royce and Joel, whom he loved —even as he would have recognized and loved them after two years of absence—so now he knew and hated the man who had maltreated him so abominably as a defenseless puppy. Into the soft eyes flamed red rage.

All ignorant of the emotion he had aroused, Fraser Colt had stretched forth his plump hand, confidently, to inspect the collie's left ear. The expert big fingers turned over the ear-tip. A glance showed Colt what he sought. There, faintly white, on the ear's pinkish underside, were the harrow-marks of the police dog's teeth. There, too, was a far fainter groove-mark where the plaster and splints had once remained for weeks on the healing ear. There could be no doubt.

This in less than a second. Before the big hand could be withdrawn, Treve had completed his recognition. More, he realized what liberty this loathed ex-owner of his was taking with him. The outstretched hand, too, was reminiscent of the brute blow that once had crashed against that mangled ear. And the dog's hatred flamed into life.

His white eyeteeth slashed murderously. Colt's thick sleeve and silken cuff were shorn, as by a razor-sweep. So little did cloth and silk deflect the slash that the eyetooth scored deep in the wide wrist; missing artery and major veins by a hairbreadth.

With a yell, Fraser Colt yanked back his hurt wrist. Yet swift as was his motion, it could not keep pace with the motion of the furious collie's head. And, before the hand was out of reach, Treve's front teeth had almost met in the fleshy heel of the thumb.

"You leave my dog be!" shrilled Joel, taking in only the fact that Colt had reached out and done some presumably painful thing to Treve, which the collie was trying angrily to punish.

He spoke too late. At the dog's assault, Colt's readily mislaid temper scattered beyond control. Still yelling with pain he kicked with all his might at the collie who ravened at him far over the pine footboard of the bench.

The kick was less well calculated than fervent. The fury-driven toe hit the top of the footboard;

shattering the wood to splinters. But it missed Treve. As the leg was withdrawn, Treve exacted tribute from the ankle of the loud-patterned trousers; and his jaws raked the man's shin, agonizingly.

But not until later did Fraser Colt have chance to note this latest hurt. For scarcely was the kick delivered when a lanky and wrinkled bulk had hurled itself cursingly at his fat throat.

Joel Fenno prided himself on his surly self-control. Yet when this big stranger kicked his beloved chum, self-control burst into a maniacal wrath that could find vent only in homicide.

He flung himself at the big man's throat; gouging, tearing, hammering; and all the while keeping up a gruesome whimpering noise from between his hard-clenched teeth; unpleasantly like the sound made by a rabid beast worrying its prey.

Back, under that crazy onslaught, staggered the unprepared Colt. His heel caught in a bench support, before he could rally his balance. And he pitched backward onto the aisle floor. Not once had Fenno relinquished his attack on the face and throat of his foe. Now, landing atop the squirming bulk, he drove his fists madly into the upturned visage. As Colt sought to fend off the flailing fists, Joel lunged at his neck with yellowed teeth.

Above them, lurching far over the edge of the bench, Treve tugged and struggled roaringly to free himself and to join in the carnage. Foam spattered from his back-writhen lips. Added to his own hate of Colt was the fact that this man was fighting with Fenno, whom the dog loved. With all his weight and all his might be strove to break free from his chain. A hundred dogs added their din to his.

All at once, the bystanders stirred from their momentary trance of amaze. As crowds came running to the scene of strife, fifty hands dragged Joel away from his enemy and lifted him, yelling and twisting, to his feet. Others helped Fraser Colt to rise. Still others hung officiously to the arms of both combatants, to prevent a resumption of warfare. Scores of voices vociferated and questioned and babbled. Every dog in the show took up the racket, with full-throated barks and howls. Every human jabbered. No human could be heard.

Presently, into the ruck, two policemen shouldered their way; followed by the show's superintendent. Out of the myriad simultaneous efforts at explanation and accusation, the police could gather only that a lantern-jawed old rancher had committed flagrant assault and battery upon Mr. Fraser Colt, a man well known to dozens present and vouched for by the superintendent. The rancher, presumably, was either drunk or insane.

His first madness dissipated, Joel stood trembling and sick; scared to the point of horror at what he had let himself in for; yet furious as ever at the assailant of his collie.

A policeman ended the uproar by taking hold of Joel's collar and propelling him through the milling crowd to the door of the armory and thence out into the street, where a commandeered automobile bore captive and captor to the police station a mile away.

Twice, on his forced progress through the armory and once during the horrible station-ward drive, Fenno tried to plead with the officer to let him make some arrangement for the comfort of his dog, before going to jail. But the policeman, every time, shut him up and would not let him peak.

Joel sank down in a miserable and all but sobbing heap on the slat bed of his cell. Not for himself was his woe. He foresaw a long jail sentence. In the meantime, what was to become of Treve? Who would feed him? Who would see he got back to the ranch? At the close of the show, would the beautiful collie be thrust out into the streets of this strange city, a hundred miles from home; to fend for himself—he who had always been so well cared for?

Worse yet, would he fall into the hands of the man who had kicked him—the man who seemed all-powerful there at the show—the man who had secured Fenno's arrest and who had, himself, gone scot free? He had kicked the collie, in the presence of Fenno. What might he not do to luckless Treve, now there was no one to protect the dog?

At the searing thought of his chum's defenselessness, Joel groaned aloud, rocking back and forth on his hard seat.

"An' it was all my own fault!" he mumbled, brokenly. "All my own foolishness! What'n blue blazes can I do? What—what *IS* there to do? Oh, Trevy, you trusted me! You was glad to come along with me. An' see what I've made happen to you!"

CHAPTER VI: DESERTED

A DAY earlier, Joel Fenno had been happily, if always grouchily, the master of his own actions.

To-day, Joel Fenno sat huddled miserably in a police station cell, at La Cerra, a hundred miles from home.

The man did not know how long he crouched there in growing mental torment, on the hard cell bench. It seemed to him a handful of centuries in duration. Actually, it was something under an hour.

Then a policeman came to lead him to the captain's room at the front of the station. Besides the captain, two other men were in the room. One of them was jolly and elderly. The captain treated him with grudging respect and addressed him as "Judge." The other was a lazy-looking chap, much younger, with a shock of red hair and a snub nose. The awesome police captain, apparently, was on comradely terms with him.

As Joel shuffled miserably into the private room, it was this red-headed youth who greeted him.

"Well, old-timer," he said, breezily, "it sure was one grand and wakeful little scrap while it lasted. I was in the gallery, looking at the chows benched up there. And I got a fine view of it. But I couldn't work my way through the crowd, till after you'd been gathered in. I thought they'd just turned you out of the place; till one of the bulls told me, a few minutes ago, that he'd cooped you. Then I hustled for Judge Brough and came here on the run."

He talked fast and with easy good-fellowship, undeterred by Fenno's sour glare. Scarcely had he paused for breath when Joel, ignoring him, turned to the uniformed captain in tremblingly eager appeal.

"Mister," he pleaded, "my dog got left alone there at that show. He's li'ble to starve or get lost or stole or hurt, without me to watch out for him. I—I'm kind of—kind of fond of him," he mumbled shamefacedly; adding in a more normal tone: "I got forty-one dollars in my pocket, here. It's yourn, if you'll see he's looked out for an' shipped back to the ranch, while I'm servin' my term. If that ain't enough, I'll write a check for—"

"You'll come around to court with me," interposed Judge Brough, "and write out a check for five dollars, for your fine. Then you can go and look after your own dog. I'm holding special court for your benefit, my man. Because this nosey reporter friend of mine is pestering me to. Come along. My car's outside."

"I—I don't—I don't just rightly understand!" sputtered Fenno, incredulous, as ever, that any such golden good luck could sift into his morbid life-lot. "I—"

"Gladden, here, was in the gallery," explained the judge. "Just as he told you. He saw it all. He gives me his word that you didn't tackle Mr. Colt, till Colt kicked your collie. Of course, that doesn't excuse you for breaking the law. But —well, I'm glad it was your collie, and not mine, that was kicked. I'm getting too old to punch my fellow-man. Come along."

In a trance, Joel Fenno trailed to the car, in the wake of Brough and Gladden. In a trance, he answered the Judge's few official questions, in Brough's chambers, back of the deserted court-room. He paid his fine, and then asked, uncertainly:

"C'n I go, now?"

At Brough's assenting nod, the old man set forth at a shambling run. Too long Treve had been left there, lonely and unhappy, among that mob of strange dogs and stranger men, and possibly at the mercy of Fraser Colt. He must get back to the collie as fast as a lanky pair of legs could carry him.

"Hold on!" called the reporter, hurrying after him. "Judge Brough says I can take you back to the show in his car. It's a couple of miles from here. Jump in."

Gladden had been sent to the dogshow, by his paper, *The Clarion,* in quest of human interest items that might brighten up the technical account of the exhibition. He was not minded to let slip this chance of getting more material for the most worthwhile human interest item the day thus far had produced. Wherefore, he stuck to the excited oldster.

During the drive to the armory, he fired adroit questions at the taciturn and worried Fenno; most of which the old man did not trouble to answer. But, from a word or two forced from Joel's overburdened soul, the lad gathered something of Fenno's dread lest harm had befallen Treve through Colt's ill-will.

"You can go to sleep over that, brother!" Gladden reassured him. "You and Treve, between you, managed to make Friend Colt one hundred per cent eligible for first aid treatment. Before I left, he had been helped across to the hotel and a doctor had been sent for. By the time Doc gets through stitching and bandaging him, Colt will be glad enough to stay in bed for the rest of the day and probably to-morrow, too.

He's in no shape to carry on a canine vendetta, just now. Sleep easy!"

Joel sighed in deep relief and turned upon his companion a look that, in a less forbidding old face, would have been classified as one of gratitude.

"You been mighty decent to me, young feller," he muttered, grudgingly, as though the effort at graciousness were physically painful. "An'— I'm thankin' you. Let it go at that.—Say! Can't this chuffer make his car move a wee peckle faster?"

"Not unless we want to go back to court again for wearing holes in the speed limit," said Gladden.

Joel sighed, rustily. Speaking to himself rather than to the reporter, he grumbled:

"I'd counted a hull heap on Treve's winnin' all them ribbon-gewgaws an' sich. Most likely the judgin's been goin' on while I was to the hoosgow. Luck couldn't ever hand me out a hundred p'cent parcel but there'd be sure to be a hole punched into it somewheres. I s'pose me an' Treve has got to lay away them grand hopes of our'n, like they was the pants of some dear dead friend; as the feller said. But if he could 'a' won just a single ribbon or a—"

"Buck up!" exhorted Gladden, who had caught

not a distinct word of the mumbled soliloquy but who saw the old man's first glow of relief was beginning to merge with his chronic gloom. "Buck up, brother. Jail's better than a lot of dogshows I've covered. It's a funny thing! I've covered every line of sport from cock-fighting to horse-racing. And I've found more bad feeling and less true sportsmanship in the dog game than in all the rest put together. More slams and knocks and poor losers and petty meanness than in every other form of sport, combined."

Fenno continued to fidget, unheeding. Less to distract the oldster from his worries than to air his own views, the reporter went on:

"I've figured it out. I mean the reason for the dog-game's unsportsmanliness. And I think I've hit on the answer. It's because there are so many women in it."

He paused, waiting for the exclamation which usually followed this pet speech of his. Fenno was deaf to the harangue. Undeterred, Gladden resumed:

"My wife says I'm a crank for thinking that. But it's true. In the old days we men were out fighting or fishing or hunting or doing other stunts that call for sportsmanship. The women were at home taking care of the house and the kids. During the centuries, men learned to be

sportsmen. They learned to lose gracefully and
to win modestly. They had to. They had thousands of years start on women in mastering
sportsmanship. It wasn't till a very few years
ago that women at large took any part at all
in sport. They had to learn it from the beginning. Or rather, they still have to. Most of
them haven't made much of a start at it
yet."

"Uh-huh," grunted the unhearing Fenno.

"Women don't take a general part in any
forms of sport, even yet," pursued the reporter,
"except dogshowing and tennis. At least those
are almost the only sports they've achieved any
prominence in. And look at the result! The
dog game is full of squabbles and backbiting
and poor sportsmanship. But for the A. K. C's
wise guidance it would have gone to pot, long
ago. As for women in tennis—well, maybe
you've read of the Mallory-Lenglen mixups and
others of the same sort. There couldn't be anything like that, on the same scale, in baseball
or pugilism or boating. Only in tennis. Because women are prominent in it. And in dog-
breeding-and-showing. Not that I'm knocking
women. It isn't their fault. Sportsmanship is
a thing that takes hundreds of years to acquire.
They've been at it for less than a quarter-
century. At that, they do fifty times better at

it than any man could hope to, in some purely feminine art he was just learning. And many of them are clean sportsmen—these women. Better than most men. But some few of them—"

"Say!" exploded Joel. "You tol' me that armory wa'n't but two miles away. We been ridin' in this open hearse for a—"

"We'll be there in a minute now," said Gladden, swallowing the rest of his oration. "It's just around that corner. Don't worry about your dog. He's all right. You won't even miss the collie judging. It won't begin for another half-hour. Plenty of time to— Here we are!" he finished, as the car swung a corner and stopped in front of the armory.

Joel scarce waited for the machine to halt; before scrambling out and making his way, at a run, up the steps and into the rackety building. Gladden followed as fast as he could; amusedly interested in the prospect of watching the grouchy old man when he should rejoin his belovèd dog.

This meeting was scheduled to be the most pathetic or the most humorous point in the story the reporter was planning. Would Fenno be as glum in that big moment as in the moment of his release from the cell? Gladden hoped so. He hated to think that the keynote of the story was to be spoiled by Fenno slopping babyishly over his restored collie chum.

Down the crowded aisles sped Joel; Gladden close in his wake. They reached the collie section. There Fenno came to a standstill with an abruptness that all but threw him off his balance and sent Gladden colliding against him.

Treve's straw-cluttered bench was empty.

It was the same bench, with the same printed number tacked to it; the same splintered pine footboard that Fraser Colt had kicked. But Treve was no longer there.

Gladden's trained reportorial eye fixed itself upon another detail of the deserted bench, a fraction of a second earlier than did Fenno's. The stout chain, affixed to the bench staple, was pulled to its full length and hung over the splintered top of the footboard. From the chain's snap hung a dog collar—broken. The collie's frantic plunges had at last made the decaying leather give way.

A man, working over a dog on the adjoining bench, glanced up at sound of Gladden's ejaculation. He noticed the reporter and the horror-petrified old ranchman. He addressed them, impersonally; though keeping a wary eye on Joel, as though fearing a fresh outbreak of assault and battery on the part of the newly released prisoner.

"He's gone," announced the man. "Kept lunging and tugging at his chain all the time the cop was taking you out. Kept it up afterward, too. All at once, the collar bust; and he was off after you, quicker'n scat. I made a grab for him as he went past me. But I missed him. I thought it'd be kind of neighborly to catch him for you. When I got to the front door, though, he wasn't anywheres in sight. The doorman told me the dog had gone whizzing out into the street, like greased lightning. No sign of him anywheres. That must 'a' been—le's see—that must 'a' been about three or four minutes after you was took away by the cop. Er—I'm glad to see you back," he ended politely, as Fenno did not cease from staring in blank despair at the empty bench and the riven collar.

Gladden made as though to speak. But he had no time to form the well-meaning words he was groping for. With a galvanic start, Joel wheeled and headed for the armory doorway. Gladden made after him, once more taxing his own young speed to keep close to the oldster.

At the front steps, he overhauled the ranchman.

"I'll phone the pound and then send word to the police to keep their eyes open for him," said the reporter, genuinely touched by the ghastly face of his companion. "And we'll advertise, too. Oh, we'll find him, all right! You mustn't worry."

Joel did not answer. Joel did not hear. All his days, he had lived in the open spaces and far from the peopled haunts of life. To him there was terror in the sight of such crowds as now moved past the armory. There was double terror in the spectacle of the thick-built city which harbored the crowds. He had a born and reared countryman's distrust and dislike for populous streets. To him they held mystery— sinister mystery.

Somewhere in these unfriendly and confusing and perilous streets his beautiful collie chum was wandering in search of the master who was responsible for his misfortune;—was seeking Fenno, wistfully and in vain, amid a million dangers.

A score of whizzing automobiles, flashing in and out, in front of Joel—the clang of trolley cars and the onrush of a passing fire-engine— all these were possible instruments of death to the ranch-raised collie who was straying out yonder, perplexed and aimless, hunting for the man who was his god.

Treve had crowded into two brief minutes more agonizing excitement and drama than had been his in the past two years.

He had met and attacked his olden tyrant. He had seen his master in life-and-death battle with that tyrant. Fifty-fold worse than all else, he had seen that cherished master overpowered and dragged away; and had had no power to fly to his assistance.

Small wonder the frenzied dog had hurled himself with all his might against the collar that held him back from battling for his master's release! Then, at last, the collar had broken; leaving Treve free to follow and to rescue the captured man. Down the aisle he tore; and out through the gateway and down the steps. It was in this direction they had taken Fenno. Treve had seen him go. And he ran by eye and not by scent.

But, when he reached the sidewalk and saw no trace of Joel, he reverted to first principles; and dropped his muzzle earthward.

Hundreds of people had traversed that stone pavement during the past minutes. But through the welter of scents Treve's keen nostrils had scant difficulty in picking up Joel Fenno's long-familiar trail. Rapidly he followed it;—but only for a yard or so. It led to the curb. There the policeman had bundled Joel into the car that was to bear him to the mile-off station. There, of course, the trail ceased. And there the dog paused, wholly checkmated.

After the fashion of his kind, he wasted no time in standing nonplussed. Instantly, he set off at a hand-gallop, nose to ground, running in a wide circle; in the hope that some arc of that circle might intersect Fenno's lost trail. It was a ruse he had employed a hundred times in seeking for strayed sheep. But always his questing nostrils, at such times, had inhaled the good clean smell of earth and herb. Now they were filled with the stench of spilled gasoline and of grease. They were baffled by the passing of countless feet and by the numberless and nameless reeks of the city streets.

Undeterred by the sickening strange odors, he continued his hunt; galloping in the broad circle he had begun. Head down, all his senses concentrated on the finding of the trail he sought, he was completing the circle when his nerves were jarred by a yelling voice just above him. There were menace and vexation in the voice. It was accompanied by a deafening blare. Instinctively, Treve shrank aside as he looked up to discern the dual noise's origin.

The sidewise move saved him from a hideous and too-common form of death. For, as he shifted his direction, a fast-going limousine's fender grazed his flank with such force as to send him rolling over and over in the filth of the asphalt roadway. The chauffeur, who had shouted and honked at him, yelled back a mouthful of oaths. But Treve did not hear them. Scrambling to his feet, jarred and muddied and breathless, he was barely in time to dart out of the way of a motor-truck that was bearing heavily down upon him.

The wide street was alive with these engines of destruction, all seemingly bent upon his death. Bewilderment swept the luckless dog's brain. For an instant he stood, glancing pitiably to left and right; trying to find a pathway of escape from among the tangle of vehicles.

Then the ever-ready wit of a trained collie came to his aid. This mid-street, assuredly, was no place for him. The sidewalk offered shelter, with no worse perils than the stream of passing pedestrians. Toward the sidewalk he made his way.

It is in such safety-seeking efforts that the average dog, in like conditions, becomes confused and is run over. Treve was not confused. With the skill and dexterity of a timber wolf he sped in and out of the traffic, timing his every step to a nicety; enacting prodigies of time-and-distance gauging.

In another few seconds he was on the sidewalk; nearly a block distant from the armory.

The collie was panting; but not from fatigue. He was panting through excitement and nerv-

ousness.   Light froth gathered on his lips and
tongue. His rich coat was one smear of muck
and mud. He was collarless. His aspect was
ferocious and disreputable. People made plenty
of room for him as he swung on down the sidewalk, nose to ground, still seeking Fenno's lost
trail.

His dangerous circling of mid-street had
failed to locate that trail. Collie-like, he knew
there was no use in casting back over the same
ground again. Henceforth, he must hunt on
mere chance and with nothing to guide him. It
was not a hopeful prospect. Fenno had left the
armory. That much Treve's eyes and nose had
told him. Fenno had walked as far as the curb-
stone. There his trail had ended.

Gallantly, the collie kept on, along his aimless
route, still sniffing the ground; pedestrians giving him the widest possible berth and turning to
look back apprehensively at him.

A man came briskly out of a store. So suddenly did he debouch onto the pavement that the
dog had no room to avoid him. The man felt
something collide glancingly with his knee; and
peered down. He beheld a huge collie; mud-
coated and bleeding from a graze on the
flank.

Panic possessed the newcomer as he recalled
the impact at his knee. By every law of fiction,

this was a mad dog. The dog, of course, had bitten or at least tried to bite him, in passing— which was also the way of fictional mad dogs.

The man, like most of the world, was actuated by what he had read, rather than by what he had learned, or should have learned, from real life experience. Hence, he did the one regulation thing that was to be done, under the circumstances. He screeched at the top of his lungs:

"Mad dog! MAD DOG!"

A hundred persons stopped and stared apprehensively around them. They saw a chalk-faced man clutching at his left knee with one hand while with the other he pointed dramatically at the harmlessly-trotting Treve. Again and again he waked the echoes with that imbecile bellow of "Mad Dog!"

Only a few times did he have a chance to warble the fool-cry as a solo. In a moment or so, voices from everywhere had caught up the shriek. The street reëchoed to the multiple howl. People ahead turned in fright as they heard it. Then they saw the mud-streaked and bloody collie trotting in their direction; and they scattered squawkingly to the refuge of shop doors or parked cars. (Two local newspapers, next day, printed strong editorials on the menace of allowing dogs to roam, unmuzzled, in the city.)

Treve was unaware of the furor he was creating. For all he knew, this sort of bedlam might be an ordinary phase of street life. In any event, it was no concern of his. And he padded unconcernedly on; still sniffing in vain for his lost master's footsteps.

His progress received a rude check, as a sharper note mingled with the looser volume of his pursuer's yells. Some born idiot had drawn a pistol and had opened fire on him. A bullet spatted the stone pavement just in front of him; a pin-tip of the scattered lead stinging his sensitive nose. Treve stopped, and looked back, in mild wonder.

Then, for the first time, he realized that everybody in the world was racing along at his heels; waving umbrellas or canes or any other weapon. One youth had even snatched up a half-full tin ash-can and was brandishing it above his head; while a halo of blown ashes sifted lovingly down upon him and blew into the eyes of those nearest him.

The pistol-wielder, luckily for Treve, chanced just then to be nearest the can-brandisher. He halted and took aim at the momentarily moveless dog. Providence sent an eddying breeze from heaven which gathered up a spoonful of ashes from the tilted can and whirled them blindingly into the marksman's eye. The bullet sped skyward.

A policeman, then another, appeared from no-where and joined the chase.

It dawned on Treve, belatedly, that it *was* a chase; and that he was its quarry. With no fear, but with a strong determination not to let these people catch him and thus prevent him from continuing his search for Fenno, the dog quickened his swinging wolf-trot into a hand-gallop.

One of the policemen was stopping at every third jump to rap for reënforcements. In response to these raps and to the clamor of the pursuit, a bluecoat rounded a corner, on the run, just in front of Treve. He made a noteworthy effort to brain the collie with his club. Treve saw the blow coming and he dodged it with perfect ease. Then, diving between the policeman's threateningly outstretched legs, and upsetting him, the dog continued on his way; though at a faster pace. Passersby, in front, gave him a world of room.

Pausing only at street crossings, to avoid passing motors, he fled at a mile-eating run; leaving the chase far behind. He was hot and worried and cruelly thirsty. Yet the sound of pursuit warned him not to slacken pace.

At last, this sound grew fainter. For no running men can hope to keep within hailing distance of a running collie.

Treve slackened speed. He glanced around

him. The houses had grown few and straggling. He was on the compact little city's out-
skirts. Ahead of him arose green foothills.
Toward them he bent his pavement-bruised feet.

Assuredly there was no sense in trying to find
Joel Fenno in that hell of unfriendly humans
behind him. There was no trace of the old man.
And Treve did what the wisest of lost collies
usually do. He headed for home.

On he went, until he had breasted the nearest
green slope of the ridge which divided the fertile valley from the desert beyond. Almost at
the summit, he found a little trickle of water,
from a hilltop-spring not yet dried by the approaching summer. There he paused; and drank
long and greedily. His thirst assuaged, he
stretched himself and clambered to the crest of
the ridge.

Pausing again, he lifted aloft his dainty muzzle; and sniffed. For perhaps two minutes he
stood thus, testing the breeze with quick, com-
prehensive intakes of breath. From side to side
he moved his head and forequarters; until presently he stood still; verifying the hint the air
had brought him.

Then, without a shadow of indecision in mind
or in gait, he set off down the desertward side
of the ridge. He knew the course he must take.

If perhaps this action of Treve's be scoffed

at, as nature-faking, there are a dozen authentic cases of the sort. How a collie can get his direction in the way just described, is past human knowledge. But that such direction *is* gotten in that way cannot be denied.)

Thus it was that the great dog began his hundred-mile homeward journey, across unknown land and guided solely by his mysterious sixth sense. Down the hill he went, never breaking that deceptively rapid choppy wolf-trot of his. In another half hour his feet had left the springy turf and ridges of the hill and were pattering across the prickling gray sands of the desert.

On he went; while the sun dipped past the meridian; on into sweltering afternoon. Here was no chance for thirst-quenching; no chance for adequate shade; no chance for anything but grim endurance. The collie's pink tongue lolled far out. His eyes were bloodshot from sand and from heat. The mud on his coat had caked and dried; as had the blood from the graze on his flank. He was suffering from thirst, from fatigue, from reaction. But he kept on.

At sunset, he had his first alleviation of discomfort. Trotting exhaustedly over the top of a gray sand dune he saw at its base, in front of him, a black and white animal, about the size of a cat. The animal saw and heard him. Yet it made no hurry to get out of his way. Skunks know from experience that few larger animals willingly take a chance of attacking them.

But Treve was as hungry as he was thirsty. All day he had been on the move; and he had eaten nothing. With express train speed he dashed downward, at this possible dinner. The skunk wheeled, bracing its four feet firmly in the sand; tail aloft.

But this was not the collie's first encounter with such opponents. Ten feet from the tensely waiting skunk, Treve leaped high in air and far to the left. Then, before the skunk could get opportunity to brace itself a second time, he veered as rapidly to the right; and slashed as he sprang. The skunk lay lifeless at his feet, its back broken. And Treve feasted in luxurious comfort.

An hour later he came to the railroad track. Here, it seemed, was surcease for his aching pads, from the teasing desert sands. Gladly he trotted along the ties, in the exact middle of the track. But after the first mile, the bite of cinders on his sore feet grew more unbearable than were the sand-grains. And he shifted from track to right-of-way.

Not five minutes later, the Limited came thundering past, shaking the earth and almost knocking him down by the suction of its nearby passage. Truly, those foot-cutting cinders had done Treve a good turn, by driving him from between the steel rails and out of the path of annihilation.

It was wolf instinct that guarded him from his next mortal danger.

In early dusk he was padding wearily along the sage sprinkled gray plain when something buzzed like fifty windblown telegraph wires, from beneath a sagebush directly in front of him. There was no time to dodge. Without stopping to plan his own action, he gathered his tired muscles and leaped; clearing the two-foot bush with several inches to spare. So instant-quick had been the move that the rattlesnake beneath the bush missed him by a clean six inches as it struck at his approaching bulk.

The great white desert stars came out in a black velvet sky. The torrid heat of day merged into a dampish chill which helped to assuage the collie's burning thirst. On he stumbled. Then his wornout frame took a new brace. From far off, the night wind brought him the craved scent of running water—the Dos Hermanos River.

It was two nights later when Joel Fenno came home to the ranch, after raking the city of La Cerra, hysterically, with a fine-tooth comb, for his lost dog;—after posting deliriously exorbitant rewards whose payment would have bankrupted him.

He halted the wheezy car at the gate and stumped up the walk. The dazed old man's spirit was dead within him. He hoped Royce Mack might not yet have gotten back from Omaha. He himself wanted to gather up some money and some clean clothes, before returning to La Cerra to continue the hopeless hunt.

As he started up the walk, something furry and cyclonic burst out of the house;—dashed limpingly down the walk to meet him and flung itself at his breast, barking ecstatic welcome to the wanderer.

"Treve!" gasped the unbelieving Fenno, chokingly. "Oh—oh, *Trevy!*"

That was all. But he gathered the gayly dancing collie into his arms in a bear hug that well-nigh crushed the victim's ribs.

The man's heart seemed likely to burst, from sheer joy and relief. He wanted to dance; or else to pray. He was not sure which. Then, of a sudden, he straightened himself and drew a long breath. Out onto the porch, from the living room, his partner, Royce Mack, was sauntering.

"Hello!" hailed Royce. "You've been to Santa Clara, Toni says. Treve must have gone on a rampage while we were both away. When I got back, this morning, he was lying at the door, all in. Cut and muddy and lame and—"

"Don't waste breath, gassin' about the measly cur!" rasped Fenno, with all his wonted grouchiness, as he fended off Treve's welcoming advances in much show of disgust. "Get busy an' tell me what prices you got for them sheep, down to Omaha. A business man's got no time to jabber dogtalk, when there's prices to be quoted."

"Say!" retorted Royce, nettled. "If I hated anything as much as you hate that grand collie of ours, I'd just bite myself and die of hydrophobia. Isn't there any heart in you for a dog like that?"

"No!" grunted Joel. "There ain't. Dogs is pests. An' this dog is the peskiest of the lot."

But in the darkness, he was furtively drawing a hoarded lump of sugar from his pocket and slipping it to the playfully eager Treve.

CHAPTER VII: THEFT AND UNTHEFT

"THAT cat of yours," commented Royce Mack,—as he paused beside the adobe shelf on his way into the kitchen of the Dos Hermanos ranch house, and addressed the slant-eyed Chang, who served him and Fenno as cook and handy man,—"that cat of yours must have more suction power than a three-horse-power gas pump. She draws up milk the way the sun draws up water. And what the skinny brute does with it all, is more than I can figure out."

As the young rancher spoke, he nodded critically toward a pinkish-grayish-white cat that crouched in morbid indolence on the edge of the high adobe shelf, alongside an empty tin dish. She was a forlorn and gloomy thing, of scrawny ludicrousness and nasty temper. Chang loved her, beyond words.

The Chinaman wiggled apologetically, as always he did when either of the partners said more than he could understand. His slitted eyes strayed protectingly toward his beloved cat. She looked like the kind of a cat a Chinaman like Chang might be expected to own and cherish.

Royce went on, in banter that his servitor took as solemn earnest:

"Twice to-day I've happened to see you fill that dish with milk. There must have been a quart of it, each time. It's barely noon and the dish has been emptied again. That makes half a gallon of new milk your rainbow-colored cat has absorbed, since breakfast. Why, man, that bag of bones couldn't *hold* half a gallon of milk! She must cart it off somewhere and sell it. Lucky for you that both our milch cows happen to be 'fresh,' just now. Or lucky for Mr. Fenno and me. Otherwise, we'd be drinking our coffee straight; and all the milk'd go to that miserable cat."

"She good cat," expostulated Chang, in his high voice. "Vel good catty. Catch mice. Catch lats. Keep house flee of 'em. Gland cat. Can't get um fat; no matt' how much eat. Not built fat. Just like Mist' Fenno."

A grunt of disgust from behind him made Chang spin about in apprehensive haste.

Old Joel Fenno had come padding up to the house for dinner, from one of the sheep pastures. He arrived at the kitchen stoop in time to hear his spare figure compared by the Chinaman to that of the scarecrow cat.

Though without normal vanity, Joel was not pleased. And the grunt would have been fol-

lowed by more vehement expressions of distaste
had not Chang scuttled nervously into the
kitchen, tucking the multicolored cat under his
yellow arm as he ran. Presently, out through
the doorway issued the sound of many pans clat-
tering. Dinner was in active preparation.

Joel poured water from a pail into a tin basin
on the stoop-floor; and began to scrub his dirty
hands with a lump of smelly yellow soap. Royce
had washed; and was starting into the house
when a scamper of galloping feet announced the
arrival of Treve.

The dog had been helping Toni, the chief shepherd, and the latter's squat black collie, Zit, in
No. 3 pasture, that morning with the manage-
ment of a new and fractious bunch of merinos.
But—as ever, unless he had orders to the contrary—the big dog had trotted home, promptly
at lunch-time. Always he lay on the floor, at
Royce Mack's left side, during meals; and occasionally a scrap of food from his master's plate
rewarded his presence.

Royce stooped to pat the dog, as Treve pat-
tered to the porch. The collie looked past his
master, up at the narrow adobe shelf which stood
fully four feet above the level of the floor. He
seemed keenly interested in that shelf. There
was a glint of mischief in his dark eyes. Joel
Fenno, gouging the soapy water out of his own

eyes, caught the dog's expression. Following the collie's quizzical gaze, Joel noted that the edge of the tin dish projected an inch or so over the edge of the shelf. In picking up the cat, Chang unconsciously had joggled it forward.

While Fenno still watched, Treve arose upon his hindlegs, his white forepaws resting lightly against the wall. Taking the edge of the tin dish daintily between his jaws he dropped to earth again; depositing the dish on the floor in front of him. Then, after a single disappointed glance at the empty receptacle, Treve walked away.

Royce Mack looked after him, with speculative amusement. Then an idea dawned on him. He picked up the dish and turned to the open doorway.

"Chang!" he called. "Fill this."

The Chinaman, delighted that his adored cat was apparently arousing so much interest in Royce, hastened to fill the dish to the brim and replace it on the high shelf. After which he returned to the kitchen to find the cat and bring her out to feast. Meantime, Joel Fenno snorted contempt at his partner's prodigal waste of milk and at his interest in a mere cat.

"Lord!" he exclaimed. "Ain't it enough for you to pamper that measly collie all the time, without dry-nursin' Chang's cat, too? Don't

you know, the more good milk she drinks the
fewer rats she'll bother to catch? She ain't wuth
her salt, now. You'll make her wuth even less'n
that if—"

He stopped abruptly his flow of chronic complaint. Treve had seen the Chinaman place the
refilled dish on the shelf. Instantly, and with no
hint of concealment or of snooping, the collie
trotted over to the wall, upreared himself again
and once more caught the edge of the dish in his
teeth. A second time he lowered it carefully
to the floor, not spilling a drop. Then he proceeded to lap appreciatively at its contents, his
pink tongue busily emptying the dish as fast as
possible.

The dog had an inordinate fondness for milk.
Indeed, it was because of this fondness and to
insure his cat from loss of her meals that Chang
had formed the habit of placing the milk dish
on the shelf, presumably well out of the dog's
reach. Finding it, empty, but upright, on the
porch floor, several times, the Chinaman supposed the cat had knocked it thither in jumping
on or off the shelf.

Chang appeared now, in the kitchen doorway,
a fatuous smile on his yellow face and with the
cat in his arms. He arrived just in time to see
Treve lift down the dish to the floor and begin
to drink.

The Chinaman's little eyes bulged. His nerveless arms let the cat slump to the ground. To him, the simple spectacle he was witnessing had all the earmarks of black magic.

This was not the first time he had suspected Treve to be a devil in guise of a furry dog.

He had thought it when the collie learned to manipulate the kitchen door latch with his forepaw and let himself into the house. He had thought it when Treve had sniffed disdainfully at a bit of tempting looking meat the Chinaman had drenched in carbolic acid solution with the idea of getting rid of him. The dog had sniffed, then stared coldly from the meat to its giver, and had walked off in icy contempt. (Not knowing it was the rank smell of the acid which revolted the dog, Chang had supposed Treve realized the meat was poisoned and that he knew who had poisoned it. Wherefore he forbore to try to poison him again; deeming such efforts useless.)

Chang had been even more assured the dog was a demon when once he chanced to see Joel Fenno—who blatantly and eternally professed dislike for the collie—surreptitiously slip Treve the choicest meat morsels from his own plate; and pat his head.

Now the Chinaman's last doubts were removed. It was not in nature that a dog could reach up, forty-eight inches, and lift down from a shelf a full dish of milk; setting it unspattered on the floor. It didn't make sense. The dog was a devil. It was not well to abide in the house with a devil. Yet the ranch job was one that Chang did not like to lose. Something must be thought up. Something must be done! Meantime, Chang retired into his kitchen.

Royce Mack was laughing loudly at his canine chum's exploit. Joel glowered at the placidly drinking dog.

"Gee, but that was clever!" Mack declared. "It took a lot of thinking out, too. Treve, you've sure got brains! So that's where all the cat-milk has been going! I wondered—"

"Clever, nuthin'!" grumbled Joel. "Any fool would have sense enough to steal food when he's hungry. He's stoopid. An' he's lazy, too. If I had my way—"

To shut off his partner's eternal invective against the dog, Mack passed on into the house, leaving Joel in mid-swing of his diatribe. Chang happened to glance apprehensively out of the window, a second later. He saw Joel bend over the lapping dog, a silly grin of admiration on his wizened face, and pat the collie's head in approving friendliness.

"Trevy," the old man was whispering, "it *was* clever of you. One of the plumb cleverest

things I ever seen you do. An' I've seen you do
a passel of slick things. You know more'n ten
humans an' a Chink, Trevy."

Treve wagged his tail vigorously at the praise
and caress. He even paused in his stolen meal
long enough to lick milkily the petting hand.
Joel grinned, resentless of the milk spattered on
his sleeve. Then, catching sight of Chang's
bobbing head, through the window, the old man
favored Treve with a glare of utter detestation;
and stumped into the house and slammed the
door.

When the partners had bolted dinner and, with
Treve at their heels, had gone back to work,
Chang repaired to his own cubbyhole room under
the roof. There, in front of his bash-nosed
Joss, he proceeded to burn a flight of faintly
perfumed prayer-papers, accompanying the process with certain pious "setting-up exercises"
before the idol.

To his Joss and to the spirits of his innumerable ancestors, Chang offered orisons for the
instant vanishing of that devil collie.

The dog's size and buoyantly noisy ways had
jarred him, from the first. Then the collie had
taken sinful pleasure in treeing Chang's dear
cat; and in making playful little rushes at her,
even when she sought refuge on her master's
thin shoulder. The uncanny wisdom of the dog,

had long ago completed the wreck of Chang's nerves. The big beast, assuredly, was a devil; and might in time be expected to wreak awesome torments upon the Chinaman himself.

Not a week earlier, on ironing day, Chang had burned a hole in the arm of Royce Mack's only silk shirt. To hide his fault, he had taken the ruined shirt out back of the stables and had buried it. Then he had gone smugly to his kitchen, prepared to deny with innocent smiles that he had ever set eyes on the garment.

Indeed, an hour later, he was in the midst of that convincing denial, when Treve frisked up to the credulous Royce, shaking merrily between his jaws the muddy and burnt shirt he had exhumed. Nothing short of a demon could have done that!

Yes, Treve must go. And Chang prayed fervently and burned many scented papers. Then, hoping, yet doubting, the efficacy of his devotions, he went down again to his kitchen.

Seldom is such immediate and complete answer vouchsafed to prayer-papers and Joss-genuflections as was granted to Chang.

Scarcely had he been puttering around the kitchen for three minutes, when a car stopped at the gate and a fat man in fine raiment came striding up the walk. Chang was alone in the house. Neither of the partners could be ex-

pected to return until supper-time. The Chinaman desisted from his task of dishwashing;
wiped his wet yellow arms on a drying flannel
shirt of Joel's, and shuffled forward to meet the
stranger.

Fraser Colt had come three hundred miles, to
claim his collie.

Recovering from his rough treatment at the
hands of Fenno and at the teeth of Treve, at the
Dos Hermanos dogshow, he had returned to the
show, next day, only to learn that collie and
rancher had departed.

To trace them had been a simple enough matter. In the back of every show catalog are the
names and addresses of the exhibitors. Thus,
to locate the owner of Treve was the work of a
minute. *"J. Fenno, c/o Dos Hermanos Ranch,
Dos Hermanos County."* That was the line at
the back of the book. And a score of people at
La Cerra knew the exact location of the partners' ranch.

A telegram had called home the bitten and
bruised Colt, on the second day of the show.
And the business involved therein had kept him
occupied for the next few months. But in the
first lull of work, he prepared to get back the
collie whose cash value would make worth while
any trouble involved in the quest.

By law, Treve belonged to Fraser Colt. Colt held the bill of sale whereby he had bought the dog, as an eight-month pup. He had lost him; and now had found him again. Any law-court on earth would uphold his claim to the collie's ownership.

So, with no fear of successful opposition he had come to the wilderness to recover his property. If Fenno should refuse, he could take the case to court and make the rancher not only give up the dog but pay trial costs. Several folk could swear to Treve's identity as the collie bought by Colt.

Then, when at last he should have the costly animal safe in his own kennel—well, it would be time to pay a little personal bill of his. At the thought, Colt was wont to glance at his bite-mangled hand and then swing his arm viciously; as though it already wielded a blood-flecked rawhide. Yes, there would be a sweet little hour of revenge for the way the dog had attacked him.

"I want to see Fenno," announced Colt, as the smiling Chang confronted him at the ranch house door.

"Not in," cooed the Chinaman. "And Mist' Loyce Mack not in. Not in till sup' time he come."

Colt did not reply at once. But neither did

he depart. Instead, he stood surveying the Chinaman's face, from between thoughtfully squinted lids.

Fraser Colt was a good deal of a scoundrel. He was a good deal of a brute. But his worst foe never doubted his queer power of reading human nature. Especially, could he read crookedness in the face of his fellow-man. He had an unerring eye for that quality—long possession of it having made him expert.

So now he was reading Chang as though the Celestial's usually inscrutable visage had been a printed page. Colt's alert brain was working fas..

He had come hither prepared for a scene of possible violence; perhaps for a long legal delay to follow it. And now appeared the chance for a short cut out of all that. If he could secure the dog without giving Treve's owners a chance to protest, then so much the better. Back at home he could register the collie under another name. If, in future, Joel should chance to recognize Treve at some show, there would be no redress for the rancher. The dog was Colt's. Chang was to be the means to this easy end.

As the Chinaman still wiggled nervously from one felt-slippered foot to the other, under the silent appraisal of Colt's eyes, the fat man drew forth a lump of bills; and began to riffle them.

Chang's eyes beamed admiration on the handful of money.

"Listen, Chink!" said Colt, at last. "There's a collie dog lives here. He's mine. And I want him. Get that?"

"Tleve?" quavered Chang, wonderingly.

"Yep. Treve. That's his name in the catalog. It wasn't his name when I had him. And it won't be when I get him back. He—"

"You want—you want take Tleve away—to take him away, so he not be heah no longeh, at all?" demanded Chang, dizzy with the speed wherewith his prayer-papers were paying double dividends.

"That's it," assented Colt. "And you're the man to help me. It's worth just—just fifty dollars to me to get that cur, without any fuss being made. To get him, quiet, and get him *away,* quiet. Want to earn that fifty, Chink? Nobody'll ever know."

Now, Chang was a man of much finesse. But this delirious prospect of having his prayer answered and of getting fifty whole dollars, to boot, drove him for once to simple directness.

"Yes-s-s," he simmered, ecstatically; his claw-hand outstretched for the money.

Into his moist palm, Fraser Colt laid a ten-dollar bill. The rest of the roll he pocketed.

"You get the other forty when I get my dog," said he. "Where is he, now? In the shack?"

"Nope. He out with Mist' Loyce Mack, Tleve is," replied Chang. "Not back till sup' time. At lanch house allee night, though," he added, consolingly.

"Good!" resumed Colt. "Now, let's you and me go into executive session. This thing ought to be easy to fix up. Do you get a chance at the dog, alone, any time;—when the others aren't likely to horn in?"

At supper, that evening, Treve lay as usual on the floor beside Royce's chair. He was more or less tired from a hard workday on the range, and he looked forward with joy to his own approaching supper.

Apart from such stray tidbits as Mack might happen to toss to him at the table, Treve had but one daily meal;—one big meal a day being ample for any grown dog and far better for his health and condition than is more frequent feeding. This one meal was always served to Treve on the kitchen hearth, by Chang, when the partners' supper was ended.

To-night, when Joel and Royce pushed back their chairs and lighted their pipes and Chang began to clear the table, Treve as usual arose and made his way to the kitchen. As a rule, his

supper was awaiting him on the hearth. But
to-night Chang had not placed it there.

As the dog turned toward the adjoining room
in surprise at the omission, Chang came scuttling
into the kitchen, laden with dishes. These dishes
he set down, then tiptoed back to the door and
shut it. From a cupboard he took Treve's
heaped supper plate and set it on the hearth
bricks.

The dog wagged his tail in appreciation and
followed the Chinaman to the hearth; his white
paws beating out an anticipatory little dance on
the puncheon floor. He neither liked nor disliked
this shuffling and queer-smelling Celestial. But
always he was keenly interested in the plate of
table-scraps Chang gave him at night.

Hungrily, now, he set to work on his supper.
Eating with odd daintiness, yet with egregious
speed, the dog became oblivious to everything
around him.

Chang stepped back to the cupboard and drew
therefrom a huge canvas bag and a length of
thin rope. Then, with an apprehensive glance
at the door of the adjoining room, he set ajar
the outer kitchen door and stole over to where
the collie was eating. Holding the bag and rope
ready, he came up behind Treve.

There were several prayer-papers and three
anti-devil charms in the bag. In one lightning

move, Chang slipped the sack over the unsuspecting dog's head and forequarters; jamming a double handful of the loose canvas, gag-wise, into the protestingly parted jaws of the victim.

Swiftly and dextrously the man trussed up his prisoner; pinioning his indignant struggles with wily twists of the rope. Then, in the same scared haste, and murmuring Chinese spells, he heaved the squirming burden over his shoulder; and ran staggeringly from the house.

Across the dooryard he ran and out into the road. There, though the load was heavy and restless, he continued at as rapid speed as he could, through the darkness, until he came to the bend of the road, a furlong beyond; where the coulée began.

Just beyond the bend waited a car with dimmed lights; a bulky man crouching beside it. With an exclamation of joy, Fraser Colt hurried forward to meet the burden-bearer.

Eagerly, he snatched from Chang the indignantly tossing bag, and heaved it into the tonneau. Jumping to the driver-seat, he pressed the self-starter.

"Hey!" squealed Chang, as the machine woke into motion. "Hey, Mist'! Fo'ty doll' I get, now. Gimme!"

He caught hold of the door, as he spoke, lifting himself to the running board.

"Sure!" pleasantly assented Colt. "You get what's coming to you, Chinkie."

As he spoke, he slugged his plump right fist to the point of the unsuspecting Chinaman's jaw; and at the same time stepped on the accelerator. The car lurched forward. The Chinaman lurched back.

On into the night sped the automobile, at as fast a pace as Colt dared to drive it along that bumpy twisting road, at the coulée-edge. Chang slumped, half-senseless, into a wayside clump of manzanita.

Colt had taken no foolish chances when he gave the Chinaman a fist-punch instead of the promised forty dollars. He was thrifty, was Fraser Colt. He was averse to unnecessary expense. He knew Chang would not dare betray him to Fenno or to Royce; and thus confess his own share in the kidnaping. With a smile of pure happiness, he drove on, not troubling to look back at his dupe.

Now, Treve was anything but a fool. When frantic struggles availed only to enmesh him the tighter and to exhaust what little air could still seep into the close-woven canvas sack—when his growls of wrath were smothered in the almost sound-proof bag—he sought the next expedient for escape.

By the time he had reached the gate, on

Chang's shoulders, the dog had rid his mouth of the stuffed folds of cloth which had been thrust therein as a gag. The first use he made of this freedom of teeth was to seize the nearest fold of canvas between his scissors-sharp incisors; and begin to gnaw.

Any one who has watched a mischievous puppy gnaw holes in a mat can imagine the power exerted by the skilled and mighty jaws of a grown collie; if put to such infantile use. By the time he was flung into the tonneau, Treve had worked a hole in the canvas, wide enough to permit his protruding nose to escape.

Wasting no time in vain howls, he wrought furiously and deftly on such portions of bag and rope as seemed to bind him most tightly. When it came to severing the twined rope, he resorted again to gnawing tactics. But with the rest of the bag, his curved tusks as well were brought into play.

Twice he heaved himself upright, only to find some part of him was still fast to the bag. Both times, he whirled about and bit fiercely into the trammeling folds or rope. He worked now with added zest of fury. For his nostrils had caught the hated scent of Fraser Colt, the man he detested above all the world. The man who had maltreated him and had fought with Joel Fenno, —the only unfriendly human the dog had known!

And he saw and smelt that his mortal enemy was in the seat just in front of him.

Too wise to risk attack until he should be free, he continued to rend loose his bonds. The car was jolting and bumping and rattling at first speed over the bad bit of climb in the trail-like road; rendering its driver deaf to the muffled sounds behind him.

Then, as Colt bent forward over the wheel, to negotiate a particularly tricky twist of the climbing road, something silent and terrible launched itself upon him from behind.

Sixty-odd pounds of furry muscular weight crashed against his fat shoulders. A double set of razor-teeth sheared like red-hot iron into the back of his fat neck.

With a yell, Colt threw back both clawing hands, instinctively, to fend off this unseen and agonizing Horror.

It is not well to abandon the wheel of a light touring car, just as one is driving around a right-angle pitch in an uneven road, by night;—the less so if the gully-sides of a steep coulée are within six inches of one's left wheel.

The left tire struck glancingly against a wayside bowlder. The impact twisted both front wheels sharply to the left. There was no hand at the wheel to correct the wrenching shift of direction.

Obliquely, the machine shot over the edge of the coulée and down its abrupt side. Ten feet farther on, the fender smote a scrub-tree. The tree was smashed. The speeding car turned turtle.

Before Fraser Colt was well aware of what had happened, the down-plunging car came to a jarring stop, then rose in air and fell on him, pinioning him beneath it. Treve was flung clear of the car and landed in a scratchy mass of greasewood. Beyond a bruise or so, both he and Colt were unhurt.

The man had been caught in the front seat-well of the topless little car; alongside and under the steering wheel. One side-door was jammed irremediably shut. The other had been knocked clean off. Through the aperture thus left, Colt began to squeeze his rotund bulk, to reach firm ground and to get free of the imprisoning car. But, as his head protruded, turtle-like, from its shell, something whizzed at it through the darkness; and two sets of teeth raked the fat face in a laudable effort to tear it off.

Back shrank Fraser Colt, screeching. Blocking the outlet as best he could with the torn seat cushion, he cowered in his tiny prison; while outside ravened and snarled the great dog who hated him.

Colt fumbled for his pistol. Somehow, in the

course of the wholesale spill, it had fallen out of his pocket. Once he reached out a tentatively feeling hand from behind the leathern barrier of cushion. Swiftly as he yanked it back, Treve's raking teeth were a fraction of a second swifter.

Around and around his barricaded foe whirled the roaring collie. Then, failing to get at or dislodge the man, Treve accepted the situation. He lay down at full length, alongside the car, as close as possible to the blocked aperture behind which the cramped and bleeding Colt was huddled.

Joel Fenno was awake at grayest dawn. He woke with a vague memory of unpleasantness. Then he located the cause.

Treve had strayed away after supper, the night before; and had not showed up as usual at bedtime. This was not the dog's habit. Always he was in the house and on his mat beside Royce Mack's bunk, before the partners went to sleep.

Royce had asked Chang if he knew what had become of their collie. Chang said he had given Treve his supper and that the dog had then strolled out of the kitchen, into the yard; and had not returned. Fenno had sneered ostentatiously at his partner's solicitude over the beast. But, secretly, he had worried.

Now, waking, he peeped into Mack's room.

No, Treve was not lying on his mat at the snoring Royce's feet. Joel dressed and went out into the dim morning.

A very few miles up the coulée was the southern boundary of the Triple Bar cattle range. Chris Hibben's Triple Bar outfit, like most cowmen, had no use for sheep ranchers or for sheepranchers' dogs. If, by any chance, Treve had strolled over their line and should be seen by any gun-packing puncher—

Joel set off at a worried walk, towards the coulée. The farther he went the faster he walked; the while cursing himself for a silly old fool, for wasting good sleep and good exercise on such a wild-goose chase.

At last, giving up the idea of squandering his energy by a trudge to the boundary of the Triple Bar, he stopped and made as though to turn back. As a salve to his feelings, he peeped over the wooded edge of the coulée, on the chance that Treve might be coursing jack rabbits somewhere along its dry bed. At the same time he bawled, perfunctorily:

"Treve!"

To his amaze, there was an answering bark, from somewhere along the coulée's upper sides, not a hundred yards ahead of him. Joel broke into a shambling run.

Around the sharp turn in the road, just in

front of him, appeared Treve. After a glance
of appeal at his master, and a pleading bark, the
collie turned and vanished into the chaparral
along the lip of the gorge. Joel knew enough of
the dog to read this plea aright. He followed,
and, at the road-turn, he peered once more over
the edge, along the general direction in which
the dog had disappeared.

There, before him, he saw an upside-down and
badly smashed automobile. Treve was mounting
guard alongside. From an opening in the in-
verted front section of the car, as Joel crashed
through the chaparral toward the wreck, appeared a blood-splotched and distorted face.

At sight of the face, Treve charged. The
head was withdrawn, and a doubled seat-cushion
was thrust hurriedly into its place. But not before Fenno had recognized the ample features
of Fraser Colt.

The old man stood, blinking down at the upset
car. Then his gaze fell upon a badly torn canvas
bag, lying nearby; a bag whose few remaining
bindings of rope showed sure signs of having
been gnawed asunder by teeth. Joel whistled,
long and low.

"I c'n understand how he cotched you, all
right, Mister Colt," said he, addressing the in-
visible occupant of the car. "Trevy c'n do 'most
anything, when he reely puts his mind to it. But

how *you* ever managed to ketch *him* is beyond me. He—"

"Grab your dog and help me out of here!" bleated Colt, feebly, his nerve gone. "I'll—I'll make it worth your while."

"Why should I butt in to help a dirty dog-stealer?" snarled Joel. "Tell me that, Mister. Why—?"

"I didn't steal him!" wailed Colt. "He's mine. He— Say, here's his bill of sale to prove it, friend!"

Cautiously, he shoved forth through a cranny in the cushions a crumpled paper. Joel picked it up and read it, at the same time mechanically ordering Treve back from an abortive charge at the disappearing fingers.

"H'm!" grunted Joel, after a long pause for thought. "The dog seems to b'long to you, all right. Selling him?"

"No!" whined Colt, in a last flare of spirit.

"All right," acquiesced Fenno, with something akin to geniality in his grouchy voice. "I'll drop around, in a day or two, and see if you've changed your mind. Nobody's li'ble to find you, down here in the chaparral, till then. Watch him, Trevy! Watch him, till I get back."

He started off, up the coulée side. A pitiful howl from the prisoner recalled him.

"Hold on!" wheedled Colt. "Don't leave me

here, with this rabid brute. I— What'll you gimme for him? I paid—"

"I'm not honin' to hear what you paid; or even what you *say* you paid," retorted Joel, scribbling a line or two on the bottom of the bill of sale. "I'll buy him from you for one dollar in cash an' for the priv'lege of taking him away; so you c'n crawl out an' get to a place where they'll fix up your car an' lift it to the road again. Take my bid or leave it."

Colt "left" it. He did so, right blasphemously. Joel said nothing, except: "Watch him, Trevy!" and strolled away. He had reached the road before Colt recalled him.

"Good!" approved Joel. "Lucky I got my fount'n pen, in this vest. Here's the bill of sale. Here's the pen. Here's the dollar. Sign under where I've writ that you've sold him to me. It'll keep you from comin' back to claim him ag'in In this neck of the woods, my word's better'n any stranger's, like yours. An' I'm p'pared to depose in court that you sold him to me of your own free will. If you try to steal him a second time, it'll sure mean jail for you. Not that you wouldn't be more to home there, than where decent folks is. C'mon, Trevy. Le's you and me go to breakfast. So long, stranger. There's a garage jes' up the road. Not more'n about nine miles. By-by."

As Joel and the collie neared the ranch house, Treve beheld the scrawny cat dozing on the kitchen stoop. In playful mischief, he rushed at her. The cat ran back into the kitchen, spitting blasphemously. Chang appeared on the threshold to learn the cause of his pet's fright.

One look at the approaching dog, and the Celestial grabbed up his cat and ran gibbering from the house. Nor did he stop in his headlong flight from the supposed devil, until he had left the Dos Hermanos ranch far behind him.

"We're out one good Chink," mused Joel Fenno to himself, as he and Mack prepared their own breakfast, at sunrise. "But we're *in* one grand dog. An' I'm figgerin' that's nineteen times better.

"Here, Trevy!" he called, slyly, taking advantage of Mack's momentary departure from the kitchen. "Here's a big hunk of fried pork for you—the kind you're always beggin' for. Ketch it!"

CHAPTER VIII: IN THE HANDS OF THE ENEMY

JOEL FENNO was wading almost thigh-deep in a billowing and tossing grayish sea. Here and there, near him, arose the upper two-thirds of other men—his young partner, Royce Mack; their chief herder, Toni, the big Basque; and the other Dos Hermanos shepherds.

The tossing gray-white sea was made up of sheep;—hundreds upon hundreds of milling and worried sheep. Through its billows, like miniature speed-boats of black and of red-gold, dashed Zit, the squat little black "working collie" and his little black mate, Zilla, and the glowingly tawny bulk of Treve.

The three sheepdogs had their work cut out for them. Drouth had come with an unheard-of earliness to the Dos Hermanos Valley, that spring. And, now, in the past week, fire from some herder's carelessly thrown cigarette had kindled a blaze in the tinder-dry buffalo grass, which a steady north gale had whipped into a very creditable little prairie fire.

The men of the Dos Hermanos ranch had fought back the crawling Red Terror, foot by foot; beating it to a sullen halt with brush, saving the ranch buildings by a cunningly managed backfire; and frantically digging and dampening shallow ditches in the path of the creeping scarlet line.

The ranch houses had been saved. The course of the fire had been deflected up the coulée. The dogs had been able, by working twenty-four hours a day, to hold in bounds the smoke-scared sheep.

But the range in many places was burned as bare of grass as the palm of one's hand. True, this area would bear all the richer verdure, later on. In the meantime, however, the innumerable sheep must be fed. And there was not grazing enough left standing to keep one-third of the ranch's stock.

Wherefore, the one possible recourse was adopted. Fully a month ahead of the usual time, the flocks were to be driven to their summer pasturage along the grassy upper slopes of the Dos Hermanos peaks.

This entailed much bustle and some confusion. For the ordinary preparations, to smooth the yearly exodus, had not been made.

Range pasture after range pasture had been denuded of its woolly popuiation. All the mass of sheep had been rounded up into the Number Three field; and now men and dogs were steering them toward the gateway, which opened direct on the trail they were to take for the hills.

An outsider, watching the scene, would have beheld merely a handful of excited men, waving staves and yelling and making uncouth and apparently unheeded gestures; and three panting and galloping dogs making crazy dashes through the tight-crowding multitude of sheep.

As a matter of fact, not one gesture of the men and not one step of the running dogs was without direct purpose. By degrees the sheep were bunched and headed for the wide-flung gateway, beyond which waited a shepherd.

At one moment, everything seemed hopeless confusion. The next, a disorderly but steadily progressing throng of sheep were headed for the open gate; and their leaders had begun to trot bleatingly out into the trail; started in the right direction by the shepherd who stood outside. The rest surged on in their wake.

By the time a half hundred of the pioneers essayed a scrambling rush from the trail, up a bank toward a burned and still smoking field beyond, Treve had cleared the pasture's high wire and had flung himself ahead of them; noisily yet deftly driving them back to the trail; rounding up strays; keeping the huddle in the right direction and giving wide berth to the gateway that continued to vomit forth more and more woolly imbeciles.

Treve had been far inside the pasture when the

sheep at last consented to head for the gate. In order to obey Royce Mack's shouted command to guide aright those already outside, he had been forced to leap on the backs of the tight-jammed sheep nearest him; and to run lightly along on a succession of bumpy hips, until he could spy an opening on the ground of sufficient size for him to pursue his race on solid earth instead of sheepback.

While Zit and Zilla continued to herd and drive forward the remaining foolish occupants of the field, Treve was here and there and everywhere in general and nowhere in particular; among the debouching and ever more numerous sheep that had hit the trail.

It was a time for lightning action—for incessant motion;—for the use of the queer hereditary sheepdog instinct. There was no question of merely obeying shouted orders, now, nor of following the direction of a waved hat. Treve was working "on his own." He was using his native genius as a herder; keeping that wild bunch headed aright and in the trail; and cutting short abortive efforts of the whole mass to cascade out on to the burnt fields on either side or to bolt for the smoking coulée.

His flying feet spurned the ground, scarcely seeming to touch it. His tawny-gold body flashed in and out; seemingly in ten parts of the trailside at once.

Then all at once the nerve-racking job was done. The whole flock was out of the gateway and safe on the trail; with Zit and Zilla weaving in and out, steering them straight; and the herdsmen in their places along the pattering ranks. Treve could change his flying zigzag gallop to a wolf-trot. He could even brush his panting muzzle against Royce Mack's hand as he trotted past the busy rancher.

Up the coulée-side trail moved the sheep; the myriad patter of their hoofs sounding on the rutted roadbed like cloudburst rain on a shingle roof.

Deep in the bottom of the coulée, to left of the twisting trail, the fire still snapped and flickered. Its smell and sight and smoke sent recurrent panic waves over the army of sheep. The three dogs seemed to know in advance when these efforts at bolting would begin.

Treve's white paws were grimed and sore from frequent dashes along the coulée-side; where he needs must run on the steep scorched bank paralleling the trail; turning back any loose edges of the gray-white flock that sought to scamper down the incline.

"Keep it up, Trevy," whisperingly encouraged

old Joel Fenno, as the collie whisked past him on
such an errand. "Another mile, an' the road's
due to shift to the right, away from this smoke-
hole. Then it'll be plain goin'."

Treve caught the low sound of his own name;
and wagged his plumed tail in reply, as he
ran on.

"Be past the coulée in a little while, now!"
sang out Royce Mack, to his partner. "The dogs
are holding them, great!"

"Yep," growled Fenno. "The two black ones
are. Treve's loafin' on the job, as usual. I'm
hopin' he won't do some fool stunt, when we get
to the crossroad, up yonder, an' hustle a bunch
of the sheep onto the Triple Bar range. I
wouldn't put it past the chucklehead."

Royce Mack did not answer, but hurried on
to his own new place in the tedious procession.
Fenno had touched on a theme that worried
him. Not that either Royce or Joel really
thought Treve would "do some fool stunt," at
the spot where the trail crossed the road that led
to the Dos Hermanos peaks, nor at any other
place or time. But both of them dreaded that
bit of crossroad territory, which bordered the
Triple Bar range.

The Triple Bar was a cattle outfit. Like most
other aggregations of cattlemen, its men held

sheep and sheep ranchers in sharper abhorrence than they held rattlesnakes and skunks.

More than once had a serious clash been narrowly averted, between the Dos Hermanos partners and Chris Hibben of the Triple Bar, their nearest neighbor to the north. It was understood, without need of words, that any Dos Hermanos sheep or sheepdog, setting foot on the Triple Bar range, would be courting swift and certain death.

To-day the continued reek of smoke and the crackle and smolder of fire, in the coulée below them, served to fray the sheep's bad nerves and to deprive them of what little sense they had. The work of the dogs and the shepherds grew increasingly difficult, as the trail mounted high and higher alongside the burning gorge.

At length, in front, appeared the open space at the coulée-head; the space where ran the road toward the peaks; and beyond which stretched the Triple Bar range.

The foremost dozen sheep caught sight of the cleared space. Perhaps with an idea that it signified an end of their smoky and terrifying climb, they bolted frenziedly toward it. Those behind them followed suit. A veritable tidal wave of sheep surged galloping toward the clearing; deaf and blind to all coercion.

Springing on the backs of the close-packed runaways nearest him, Treve tore forward to head off the stampede. He reached ground in front of the onrushing wall of sheep, at a spot where the bank rose high on the right side and where the pit-like top of the coulée fell in almost sheer precipice for fifty feet on the left.

Wheeling to face his panic-charges, Treve barked thundrously. But before he complete the bark or the wheel, the sheep were upon him. Unable to stop their own gallop and pushed on resistlessly by those behind, the front line smote against the whirling collie with the force of a catapult.

Knocked clean off his feet, Treve rolled writhingly to one side, to avoid being trampled to death. Over the coulée-lip he rolled; and crashed down the steep side of the gorge.

He landed on his back in the midst of a brushfire, at the bottom; breathless and half-stunned. Joel Fenno cried aloud, as he saw the dog reel over the cliff-edge. He ran forward, kicking aside the encumbering sheep that tangled his progress. He reached the lip of the gorge just in time to see the dog come charging up the precipitous slope, his beautiful coat smeared by soot and with sparks still crackling here and there in it.

Gaining the summit, Treve wasted not a second; but forged ahead toward the front of the stampede. He was too late.

The few seconds of leeway had permitted the galloping sheep to reach the clearing, unchecked. The two black collies were far behind, with the main flock. Nor were any of the men far enough forward to stem the rush. As a result, the first hundred sheep struck the cleared space at a speed which they could not check. Across the narrow highroad they hurled themselves blindly, shoved on by those behind them.

They crashed into a tall barbed wire fence on the far side of the road;—the boundary fence of the Triple Bar. They hit it with the impact of a battering ram. The front rank were ripped and torn on the jagged wires. But their weight and their blind momentum sagged the wire and snapped the nearest worm-gnawed post. A whole panel of fence gave way; falling obliquely backward, almost onto the grass. Through the gap and over the bodies of their wire-entangled comrades, swept scores of sheep. On they rushed; scattering into a ragged fan-shaped formation as they found themselves in the open range.

Joel Fenno went green-white with horror. Mack groped feebly for a gun at his belt. But, as usual, his gun hung forgotten from a peg in his bedroom. Indeed the whole party could not muster any weapon more lethal than a staff. The shepherds involuntarily came to a dazed standstill.

But Treve did not hesitate, for the space of an instant. Hurdling the sheep which struggled in the strands of wire, he cleared the low-slanted broken panel and sprang into the forbidden range of the enemy. His singed coat almost sweeping the ground as he sped, he bore down upon the hundred strays.

The boundary range of the Triple Bar was perhaps two miles wide by three miles in length. Dotted along its expanse numbers of cattle were grazing. Also, entering through a gateway, three-quarters of a mile up the field, rode Chris Hibben.

Fate had brought Hibben to this especial field at this especial minute, during his leisurely tour of inspection of the Triple Bar herds.

Hibben pulled his pinto pony to a standstill. Open-eyed and open-mouthed he sat staring; unable to believe what his goggled eyes told him.

There, inside the road-end of his sacred range, cavorted something like a hundred detestable sheep! There, too, among them, galloped an equally detestable dog! The thing was impossible!

To add insult to injury, a panel of his barbed wire was down; and men of the loathed Dos

Hermanos ranch were disentangling from it still more sheep; while two herdsman were seeking to steer something like a billion other vile sheep aside from following their brethren into the field!

All this, in almost no space of time, did Chris Hibben see. Then back to him came his senses and with them his flaming temper. He whipped out a heavy-caliber pistol and struck spurs deep into his pinto.

Down the field, like a cyclone, came the infuriated cattle king; whooping, Comanche-fashion, and brandishing his drawn gun.

Meantime, in other parts of the field, other things had been happening. It was mere child's play for Treve to round up and turn his runaways. It was the work of almost no time. Driving them headlong, he put them at the gap in the fence. Sharply checking their repeated tendency to loosen the close bunch into which he had welded the scattered hundred, he sent them at top speed toward the gap.

Through it he hustled them, just as the wire-tangled sheep had been cleared therefrom. Back into the mass of their fellows, Treve galloped the loudly baa-ing runaways. Then, collie-fashion, he whizzed about and stood midway in the gap, to prevent their doubling back.

He had worked fast and he had worked well.

Mildly, he was pleased with himself. He glanced from one to the other of his two masters for a word of approval. But no such word was spoken. Aghast, dumbfounded, Joel and Mack were gaping at the oncharging Chris Hibben.

Toni, the chief herdsman, had presence of mind to grab Treve by the ruff and to yank the indignant collie back from the fence gap, out onto the neutral ground of the road. As he did so, one of the restored runaways exercised his inborn traits of idiocy by breaking from his subdued mates and scampering again through the gap, into the field. To avert capture, he continued to run, even after he had achieved his escape. Others made as though to follow. But the shepherds beat them back.

Treve noted the single sheep's flight. It outraged all his native prowess as a herder that he should be held ignominiously by the scruff of the neck while such a thing went on. Twisting suddenly, he wrenched free from Toni's careless grip; and rushed back into the field after the stray. Toni snatched belatedly at the golden swirl of fur that flashed past him. So did Joel Fenno.

The sheep, hearing his pursuer behind him, veered to the left; making for a right-angle niche that indented one edge of the side fence, perhaps a hundred yards from the gap;—a sort of alcove; where cattle had formerly been herded in bunches of two or three, to pass on through a gate whose place had since been taken by the high barrier of wire.

With Treve not three feet behind him, the sheep reached this cul-de-sac; discovered that it led nowhere; and turned to get out of it. At his first shambling step he rolled heels over head in a somersault; a .45 bullet drilling him clean.

Chris Hibben had gone into action. As soon as the hard-ridden pony had brought him within range, he had opened fire. His first bullet found its mark; but—as he himself knew—more by luck than by skill. For, only in motion pictures and in Buffalo Bill shows can a man hope to take any sort of accurate aim from the back of a jerkily running pony.

Moreover, this pinto of Hibben's was but half-broke. At sound of the shot, the pony swerved, spun about on the pivot of his own bunched hind-legs; and then sought to get the bit between his teeth and run away. Failing, he resented curb and spur by a really brilliant exhibition of buck-ing.

Enraged, and by no means intending that his prey should escape or that the wizened old Fenno should complete his rheumatic run across the corner of the field in time to save the collie,

Hibben sprang to earth, flinging the reins over his pinto's head.

A trained cow-pony will stand for hours if the rein is thus flung. But the pinto was not yet well trained. Also, he had been bewildered by the shot and by the spurring, into a forgetfulness of all he had learned. He set off at a panicky canter, the loose rein catching in his forefoot and snapping.

Unheeding, Chris Hibben ran forward to the niche where Treve was standing in grieved amaze above the body of the slain sheep. Halting just within the outer opening of the alcove, Hibben leveled his gun, using his left forearm as a rest; and pulled trigger.

He was not twenty feet from the motionless dog; and he was a good shot. Yet he missed Treve by at least six feet. This by reason of a fragile old body that hurled itself against him from behind.

Joel Fenno had made the last few rods of the distance between the gap and the indented niche in something like record time; his stiff muscles stirred to incredible power by the imminent danger of his chum. The others from the Dos Hermanos ranch, Royce Mack among them, were still standing stupefied and inert. Joel struck up the pistol arm and in the same move banged his own full weight against the broad back of the cattleman. The result was a lamentable miss; and the saving of the collie's life.

The impact and the heavy-caliber pistol's own recoil, knocked the gun from Hibben's hand. Chris turned, cursing. His left elbow caught Fenno in the chest and knocked the little old rancher flat. Then Hibben stooped to regain the pistol.

But he was met and driven backward by a flamingly wrathful mass of fur and whalebone strength that smote him amidships, in an effort to seize his throat. Treve, seeing his loved master knocked down, had left his post beside the dead sheep and launched himself like a vengeful avalanche upon Joel's assailant. Here lay his first duty; and he wasted no time in fulfilling it.

Hibben staggered backward, clawing at the furious brute which sought to rend his throat. In the same instant, a scream of mortal terror from Joel Fenno was taken up by the far-off group at the gap. At the sound, Treve forsook his prey and spun about to face the slowly rising Joel. Hibben, too, forgot his own danger, in the stress of that shriek; and turned to look.

The drouth and the eternal smell of smoke had gotten on the nerves of the three hundred cattle pastured in the field. To-day, the inrush of the strange and repellent-smelling grayish creatures upon their territory had agonized those raw nerves to frenzy. On top of all this, the scent of fresh-spilled blood had the effect that so often it has on overwrought range cattle.

Something like fifty white-fronted Hereford steers suddenly lowered their horns and, by common consent, charged that blood-reek. In other words, Joel Fenno, in trying to get up, had seen coming toward the alcove-space a tumble of lowered heads and express-train red bodies. Though he was a sheepman, he knew what a cattle charge meant. And he screamed horrified warning to his fellow-human in that death-trap.

Old cattleman though he was, Chris Hibben stood frozen to stone at the sight. Then he glanced toward the alcove fence behind them. Seven feet of close-meshed barbed wire—coyote-proof, bull-tight, horse-high. No man might hope to scale so bristling a stockade. Hibben himself had ordained that fence in the days when this end of the range had been given up to calves, and when wolves and rustlers abounded.

Subconsciously, the two men stood close beside each other, as they faced the thundrous charge. Their hands met in a moment's tight grip. Treve did nothing so professionally melodramatic. He saw the peril quite as clearly as did Joel or Hibben. But his duty was to avert it; not to stand supine or to make stagey gestures. In the wink of an eye, he was off on his gay dash toward the on-thundering bunch of blood-crazed steers.

Treve had had no experience in driving cattle. But his wolf ancestors had known crafty ways of their own, in dealing with wild cows. Into their descendant's wise brain their spirits whispered the secret, now; even as Treve's collie ancestors had told him, from the first, how sheep must be herded.

Tearing along toward the galloping phalanx of horned and lowered heads, the collie burst into a harrowing fanfare of barks. Straight at the mad steers he ran; barking in a way to rouse the ire of the most placid bovine. Nor did he check his flying run, until he was almost under the hoofs of the foremost steer—a mighty Hereford which ran well in advance of his crowding companions.

To the lowered nose of this leader, Treve lunged; slashing the sensitive nostril; and then, by miraculous dexterity, dodging aside from the hammering hoofs. Not once did he abate that nerve-jarring bark.

The hurt steer swerved slightly, in an effort to pin the elusive collie to earth. The dog swerved, too—barely out of reach of the horns. As he dodged, he slashed the bleeding nostril afresh.

It was pretty work, this close-quarters flirting with destruction. The fearless dog was enjoying the gay thrill and novelty of it as seldom had he enjoyed anything.

Under the repeated onslaught, the steer definitely abandoned his former course; and set about to demolish the dog. But Treve, always a bare inch or two out of reach, refused to be demolished. Indeed, he ducked under the lumberingly chasing body and flew at the two nearest steers that pressed on behind their leader. The nose of one of these he slashed deeply. The second steer of the two was too close upon him for such treatment. Treve leaped high in air, landing on the back of the plunging animal, and nipping him acutely in the flank before jumping off to continue his nagging tactics.

That was quite enough. The steers had some definite object, now, in their charge. Following their three affronted leaders, the whole battalion of them bore down upon the flying collie. Forgotten was their vague intent to charge the alcove space and trample the blood-soaked earth around the dead sheep. There was a more worthy object now for their rage.

Treve noted his own success in deflecting the rush. Blithely he fled from before his bellowing foes. But he fled at an increasing angle from the direction in which first they had been going.

The steers hammered on in his wake. He kept scarcely five feet of space between himself and their front rank. Head high, plumed tail flying, he galloped merrily along, barking impudent insult over his shoulder; and leading the chase noisily down the field.

Treve was having a beautiful time.

Nearly a mile farther on, he tired of the sport. His ruse had succeeded. Putting on all speed, he drew away easily from the wearying cattle; made a wide detour and trotted back to his master. The winded steers had had quite enough. Finding at length that the dog had swiftness they could not hope to equal, they shambled to a halt. One by one they stopped staring sulkily after their tormentor; and fell to cropping grass. Steers are philosophers, in their way.

Treve found Joel and Hibben standing with the herdsmen at the fence gap. They were waiting only for his return to lift the broken-posted panel to place again, as best they could.

"If you're still honin' to shoot him, Mister Hibben—" began Fenno, sourly, as Treve came up.

"I—I left my gun back yonder," muttered Hibben, in reply, his tall body still shaking as with a chill. "And, anyhow— Say, put a price on that collie of yours! Don't haggle! Put a price on him. If I c'n help it, no such grand dog is going to have to live with a passel of sheepmen, no longer. He—"

"This here's only a dog," gravely interrupted Fenno, "a no-'count dog, for the most part. But we-all don't aim to humiliate him by makin' him 'sociate with cowboys an' steers and such-like trash. He ain't wuthless enough for that. So long, neighbor! We'll be on our way, now. Any time you want to reform an' buy a nice bunch of sheep, jes' give us a call. C'm'on Trevy!"

CHAPTER IX: HIS MATE

WHEN Treve saved Chris Hibben from a peculiarly hideous death under the hoofs of Chris's own Triple Bar steers, he did more to patch up a truce between the Dos Hermanos and the Triple Bar outfits than could a score of peace conferences.

From the beginning, throughout the West, sheepmen and cattlemen have been mortal enemies. Seldom has this eternal feud blazed hotter than between Chris Hibben's cattle ranch and the nearby Dos Hermanos sheep ranch of Joel Fenno and Royce Mack.

Ever there had been a grim understanding that a sheep or sheepdog straying over the line into the Triple Bar range was a sheep or sheepdog killed. More than once this understanding had been justified.

Then, too, a year before, a bunch of six yearling beef cattle had strayed through a fence gap and down the coulée into Number Six camp of the Dos Hermanos. There all trace of them was wiped out;—except that Toni and the other Dos Hermanos herdsmen varied their dreary

fare of tinned goods and tough mutton by a pro-
longed fresh-beef debauch.

Then had come the day when Treve unwit-
tingly played the rôle of Dove of Peace by turning a cattle stampede and saving the dismounted
Hibben from being trampled into the next world.
After which Chris gave terse command to his
cowboys that the pesky Dos Hermanos sheep
could come along and chew the barbs off the
wire of the Triple Bar home corral if they chose
to; and if need be they were to be escorted back
in safety and in cotton wool.

Nor did Hibben stop there. From that one
briefly terrific moment of the turned stampede,
he had seen what a collie could accomplish with
cattle. He saw more. He saw that two or three
well-trained collies could do the work of a dozen
cowboys. Yes, and they could and would do it
on board wages and without threats of going on
strike or complaints about the grub. Nor would
they vanish on pay-day and show up a week
later with delirium tremens. It would be a tre-
mendous saving. Anyhow, the experiment was
worth trying.

It was not Hibben's custom to do anything
rashly. Thus he planned to begin in a small
way; by the purchase of a single collie. If that
first dog should do the work satisfactorily it
would be time to buy more. With this in view

he surprised the Dos Hermanos partners, one evening, by riding across to their ranch-house. Mack and Fenno were sitting on the handkerchief-sized porch, smoking a before-bedtime pipe. At Royce's feet lay Treve.

On sound of Hibben's approach, the big collie was awake and alert. Down the path he dashed, to meet, and if need be stop, the intruder. Then, recognizing the man he had rescued, the collie drew aside and let Chris proceed up the path to the porch.

"Evening," said Hibben, stiffly uncertain of his welcome.

"Evening," replied Mack, with cold civility, while old Joel Fenno sat still and scowled mute query.

"Have you eaten?" went on Royce, in the time-honored local phrase of hospitality.

"Yep," said Chris; adding: "Not cawed mutton, neither."

He caught himself up, belatedly recalling that he was at peace with these sheepmen; and he hurried on to ask:

"Will you boys set a price on that collie of yours? Nope, I'm not joshing. I don't know how such critters run in price. But I've got a couple of hundred dollars in my jeans, here, that I'll swap for him."

"Treve's not for sale," was Royce Mack's curt

retort. "We told you that, the day he kept your steers out of your hair. He—"

"Hold on!" purred Joel, smitten with one of his rare and beautiful ideas. "Hold on, Friend Hibben. Trevy ain't for sale. Just like my partner says. Not that he's wuth any man's money —not even a cattleman's. But we've got kind of used to his wuthless ways and we aim to keep him. But if you're honin' for a collie, I c'n tell you where to get one. Always s'posin' you're willin' to pay fair for a high-grade article. I c'n give you the *ad*dress of the feller who used to own Treve."

"That's good enough for me," returned Chris. "The feller that bred this dog of yours sure knew how to breed the best. I'll hand him that much. And it's the best I want. Who is he and where does he hang out?"

"Wait," said Fenno, with amazing politeness, as he heaved his rheumatic frame up from his chair and pottered away into the house. "I've got his *ad*dress in here. I'll write it down for you."

With as near an approach to a grin as his surly leathern mask could achieve he made his way to his own cubbyhole room. There he dug out the battered gray catalog of the Dos Hermanos dogshow to which he had taken Treve. Riffling its pages, he came to the list of exhibitors' names at the back. One of these he jotted down with a pencil stump on a dirty envelope and returned with it to the porch.

The name he had found and scribbled was "Fraser Colt." After it he had copied the man's address, from the catalog.

It seemed to Joel the acme of refined humor to steer this once-hostile cowpuncher up against the man of all others who seemed most likely to cheat him. Judging from his own experience with Colt, he felt reasonably certain the dog-breeder could be relied on to whipsaw any trusting customer; especially when that customer was so far distant as to make it necessary to buy, sight unseen.

Royce Mack gave a low whistle of amaze as Fenno showed the name and address to him, on the way across the porch to hand it to Hibben. Then Mack choked back a half-born expostulation. He remembered the loss of sheep after sheep at the hands of the Triple Bar outfit. He saw no reason to spoil his partner's joke.

A week later, in response to a letter of inquiry, Chris received word from Fraser Colt that the latter had no full-grown and trained cattle-herding collies in stock, just then; but that he had an unusually promising thoroughbred fe-male collie puppy which could readily be taught to work cattle, since both her parents had been natural cattle workers.

As Mr. Fraser Colt was closing out his kennels and moving East, Mr. C. Hibben was at liberty to avail himself of this really remarkable chance for a bargain, by purchasing the puppy in question ("Cirenhaven Nellie") at the ridiculously low price of seventy-five dollars; payable in advance. If this generous proposition interested Mr. C. Hibben, would Mr. C. Hibben kindly forward his check (certified) for the above sum; along with shipping directions? If, on the contrary, Mr. C. Hibben was a mere "shopper" or was inclined to haggle, this letter required no answer.

Now Chris Hibben could no more have been cheated or overcharged on a consignment of beef cattle than could a bank cashier be hoaxed by a leaden half-dollar. But, on the subject of dogs he was woefully ignorant. Moreover, there was a curtly self-assured and businesslike tang to the letter, which impressed him. Besides, hadn't the Dos Hermanos outfit a wonder-dog, acquired from the same man? Surely it was worth the gamble.

Chris sent the certified check, as soon as he could get it from the Santa Carlotta bank.

A week later arrived a matchwood crate, containing the collie pup. Hibben himself motored across to Santa Carlotta to bring home his purchase. His homeward road led past the Dos Hermanos ranch. He saw the two partners washing up, on the steps, preparatory to supper. Beside them stood Treve; mildly tired and more than mildly hungry after a long day on the range.

Chris turned in at the gate and hailed Fenno and Mack, pointing with pride to the crate.

"Oh, you got her, hey?" said Joel, with much interest. "I'll come out and have a look at the pup. Fraser Colt sure knows a collie. Pretty near as intimate as a vivisector is due to know the smell of brimstone. This dog will be a treat to see."

"I'll save you the trouble of comin' out here," called back Hibben, lifting the crate and its light burden out of the truck. "I'll fetch her up there, onto your stoop. I haven't even had a chance to look at her yet. We'll have an inspection bee. I want your opinion of her."

As he talked, he was carrying the crate along the path. Joel astounded Royce Mack by going out to meet him and by carrying one end of the box up the steps. Joel was not wont to lend an unasked hand.

On the porch floor the crate was set. Hibben undid its crazy catch and opened its door.

Slowly, uncertainly, a half-grown collie pup stepped out and stood before them.

Hibben nodded appreciatively. He was no dog judge. But he could see that this was a really handsome puppy. Her coat was dense and long. It was a rich mahogany in hue; save for the snowy chest and paws and tailtip. An expert might have found the pretty head too broad and the ears too large and low for show-purposes or even for a show brood-matron's career. But the newcomer was decidedly good-looking. She seemed not only intelligent but strong.

Joel puckered his forehead. The unaccustomed smirk fled from his leathern face. The joke was turning out to be no joke at all. This strikingly handsome youngster appeared to be well worth seventy-five dollars.

Mack was loud in his praise. But, like Fenno, he could not reconcile the pup's excellent value with his own theories of Colt.

"Yep," pursued Hibben, "that's Cirenhaven Nellie. A beauty, ain't she? I'm sure your debtor for sickin' me onto that Colt chap. I wish now I'd ordered a couple more of 'em."

Treve had watched with keen interest the opening of the crate. Now he came forward eagerly and touched noses with the bewildered pup. His plumed tail was wagging in friendly welcome.

"He won't bite Nellie, will he?" asked Hibben, a trifle anxiously.

"No," answered Royce Mack. "Man is about the only animal that mistreats the female of his race. Treve's making friends with her. See, Joel? He's making more friends with her than ever he's made with any of the range collies. He acts like he knew she was helpless and that he had to protect her. He—"

Mack broke off in his lecture. The new puppy had begun to move about, on the porch, with a queer wariness. Now, coming to its edge, she did not observe that there was a two-foot drop to the yard below; and she was stepping out into space when a quick intervention of Treve's shaggy shoulder turned her back to confused safety.

"Hold on!" exclaimed Joel, suddenly. "I knew there was a catch in it, somewheres. An' her eyes have a funny look, too! Watch me."

He struck a match and held it scarcely an inch from the puppy's wide eyes; twitching the flame back and forth in the windless air, so close to her unflinching pupils that the lashes were all but singed. Nellie did not so much as blink.

"Blind!" diagnosed Joel, with grim satisfaction. "Stone blind. I knew there was suthin' queer. There was bound to be. Been blind always, most likely, if she's only six months old. Hibben, you're stung all the way acrost the board. Your Cironhaven Nellie couldn't ever be learned

to herd anything—without it was the three blind
mice the feller writ the song about. You're
seventy-five dollars in the hole!"

The poor blind pup seemed to sense the ridicule in his tone. She shrank back a little in
her groping approach toward the speaker. Instantly, Treve licked her face reassuringly, as
though he were comforting a scared child. The
big dog had known instinctively that this newcomer was afflicted and unable to look after herself. And his great heart had gone out to her
in loving protectiveness.

Now, before Joel had fairly stopped speaking,
the sensitive Nellie shrank even more appealingly
against Treve's shaggy side. For Chris Hibben
was waking the echoes with a salvo of profanity
that shook the house. Fenno listened with real
interest to the outburst. He had the air of one
who is acquiring many new and valuable words.
As Chris paused for breath, Joel said sancti-
moniously to Treve:

"Best run indoors, Trevy. You're learnin'
language that won't do you no reel good. You've
been brought up by a couple of God-fearin' sheep
men. This blasphemious cattle talk is new to
you. Best run away till he—"

A sharp gesture from Hibben interrupted him.
The cattleman whipped out his heavy pistol and
leveled it at the hapless little female collie as she

crouched shivering and frightened before him.

Nellie had had bruisingly terrible experience with Fraser Colt's brutal rages. To her, the sound of an angry voice meant a fast-ensuing kick—a kick her blind eyes could not tell her how to avoid.

Treve, too, understood Chris Hibben's volley of fury; and he understood the deadly gesture which was its climax. In an instant he was ready for what might follow.

"Stand clear!" bawled Hibben, dropping his pistol muzzle to cover the quivering Nellie's head. "You boys tolled me into gettin' this cur. Now you boys c'n have the job of buryin' her an' of mopping up your stoop. Stand clear, I said! And haul Treve out of the way; unless you want me to drill him, too."

For the tawny gold collie had stepped quietly between Chris and the puppy. Steadfastly, his mighty body guarding the cowed little Nellie, he was gazing at the furious cattleman.

Hibben took a stride nearer his victim. With his free hand and one booted foot, he thrust Treve sharply from between him and Nellie; leveling the pistol afresh as he did so.

Now, it was not on the free list to lay menacing hands upon Treve; to say nothing of booting him. The thing had never before been done. Added to his natural resentment was his keen urge to save Nellie from the fate he fore-read in Hibben's glance and in the leveled pistol. Once before had he seen the man fire that pistol; and he had seen a Dos Hermanos sheep fall dead from its bullet.

Before Chris could shoot, a furry thunderbolt launched itself on him; iethal as a flung spear; silent with concentrated wrath.

Under that fierce impact the unprepared Hibben reeled back; his finger spasmodically pressing the trigger as he threw both arms up to shield his menaced throat.

The bullet rent a splintering hole in the porch roof. The marksman, in his staggering retreat, slipped off the edge of the top step and bumped backward to earth; with a thud that knocked the breath out of him.

Scarce had his lean shoulders touched ground when Treve was on him; ravening for his throat.

Mack watched, dumbfounded. Joel, quicker-witted, yelled to the dog. Reluctantly, Treve quitted his prey; and in a bound was back at Joel's side; while Royce Mack with profuse apologies was helping the sputteringly infuriated Hibben to his feet.

Joel surreptitiously picked up the fallen pistol from the floor and pocketed it. Then he turned to look at Treve, who had left his side and had moved across to Nellie.

The puppy, frightened out of all self-control, had bolted. Her blundering rush had brought her up against the house door with a force that knocked her down. Now, shaking all over and moaning softly, she crouched with her head hidden in the angle of porch and door.

Above her stood Treve; his eyes fixed on Hibben in cold menace. The big dog knew well that it was not permissible to attack a human; least of all a human who was the guest of his two masters. Perhaps swift death might be the punishment for his deed. But he did not falter.

His body shielding the wretched puppy, he stood there, tensely ready for Hibben's next assault. Joel Fenno read the dog's purpose and his thoughts; as he might have read those of a fellowman. The collie was playing with possible death, to guard something that could not defend itself. Fenno's gnarled old heart gave a queer twist.

"Trevy!" he breathed, under cover of Hibben's loudly truculent return to the porch.

At sound of Joel's voice, Treve shifted his stern gaze from Chris to the old man. And in the collie's sorrowful dark eyes, now, was an agony of appeal. So might the eyes of a mother be raised to the doctor who alone could save her sick child.

Joel Fenno's thin lips set tightly. His old

eyes were slits. He was about to do the fool-
ishest thing of his career. The saner half of
him told him so and reviled him scathingly for
it. But sanity went by the board, in face of that
awful pleading in his belovèd dog's eyes.

"Hold on, friend!" he interposed, as the cursing Hibben peered murderously about the floor
for his lost pistol. "You'll stop temptin' Providence to swat this shack with lightin', as a punishment for that string of hellfire words you're
bellerin'; and you'll listen to me. You paid
seventy-five dollars for this poor sick puppy
you're tryin' to kill. Well, I'm buyin' her off'n
you, for seventy-five dollars. Get that? *I'm
buyin' her!* Now shut up an' stand quiet-like,
while I traipse indoors and git the cash for you.
. . . I'm doin' this out'n my own pocket!" he
snarled at the thunderstruck Royce. "Not out
of the partnership funds. Josh me all you like.
I don't care a hoot for your blattin'. I've—I've
took a sort of fancy to the pup."

Five minutes later Hibben was driving away;
grumbling but appeased. Joel, awkward and
shamefaced, was guiding Nellie's questing nose
to a saucer of bread and milk. Royce Mack was
looking on, bereft of speech and incredulous.
Treve, too, was looking on; a glint of utter contentment in his deepset eyes. Joel addressed his
blank-faced partner, glumly:

"Now l s'pose you'll be makin' my life rotten by hect'rin' me 'bout this! Well, I done it to show you there c'n be another dog on this ranch as wuthless as your mis'ble Treve. At that, I doubt if she's as wuthless as what he is. She ain't lived so long on the same ranch with *you.*"

Followed the first peaceful, not to say beautifully happy, time that Nellie had ever known. From the moment Fraser Colt had discovered her blindness—and thus her absolute uselessness —she had been kicked and maltreated and made to feel that her only use in life was to serve as a vent for her breeder's ill-temper.

Colt had continued to feed and lodge her, only in the well-founded hope of cheating some one into buying her. He and his kennels had been permanently disqualified by the American Kennel Club for crooked dealings. So, as he was forced to go out of the dog business, anyway, he had no fear of reprisal, in selling the blind puppy to some novice.

Under decent treatment now, Nellie's brain and spirits bloomed forth. Swift to learn and coming from a breed that has more than normal intelligence, her progress was amazing. Ever beside her, to fend off trouble and to show her the way, was Treve. With unfailing patience Treve watched over her and trained her. Joel

looked on with secret admiration and patiently
contributed his own quota to the wise training.

Nellie could never hope to see. But, with
almost miraculous intuition she learned to find
her way about. A collie's ears and nose are more
to him than are his eyes. Nellie's absence of
sight intensified tenfold her power of scent and
of hearing.

She could track either of the partners for
miles, nose to earth; nearly always forewarned
in some occult manner to avoid obstacles in her
path. She was even, in a small way, of help to
Treve in rounding up sheep. And ever that
strange instinct—a sort of sixth sense—developed more and more, as her brain and experience
developed.

Around the house she was the sweetest and
most loving of pets; though her real adoration
and slavish worship were lavished on Treve
alone. She was his shadow. And to her he accorded a tender friendliness which he had re-
frained haughtily from bestowing on the splay-
footed little black range collies.

It was nearly six months after the coming of
Nellie that the blizzard struck the Dos Hermanos
region.

In that southerly and semi-arid stretch, snow
was a rarity. Heavy snows were practically
unknown in the lowlands. Storms, which whit-

ened the Dos Hermanos peaks and slopes, fell usually as rain in the valley. But now, in mid-February, came a genuine blizzard.

It caught the ranch totally by surprise. The various bunches of sheep were grazing wide; as usual at that rain-flecked time of year. Out of a softly blue sky came a softer grayish haze. Two hours later the blizzard was roaring in full spectacular fury.

Every man and every dog was pressed into service. Floundering knee-deep through drifts, the partners and their herdsmen and Sing Lee, the new Chinese cook, sought puffingly to drive the scattered and snow-whipped sheep to places of shelter.

The dogs, half-submerged in the floury snow, staggered and fought their way in the teeth of the blast and the stabbing cold. Their pads were tight-packed with painful snow-lumps. There was no time to stop and gnaw these torments out. The dogs drove on, limping, unresting.

It was a madly busy three or four hours. Men and dogs alike were blinded by the whirling tons of snow. There was no such thing as following a scent, with any accuracy, through that smother. Nor could a voice be heard, fifty feet away, in the screech of the gale.

Spent, dizzy, numb, the partners came back at last to their snow-piled home. The storm had

ceased as suddenly as it had begun. Already a
watery sunshine was beginning to glisten on the
ocean of snow that spread everywhere.

"All safe except the bunch on Six Range,"
reported Royce breathlessly as he and Fenno met,
near the gate. "It was touch-and-go, with the
whole lot. But those got tangled up somehow in
the blizzard and bolted. Treve and I worked for
two hours to find them. But it was no good.
They've stampeded over the rock wall of the
coulée or else over the cliff into the river.
Either way, they're goners. In a storm like
that they—"

He stopped short. The dazzling white snow
around the house was darkened by a shifting and
huddling mass of dirty gray. The partners
squinted their snow-blurred eyes to see what the
phenomenon might mean.

There, encircling the house and pressing
against it for warmth in a world of pitiless
cold, swarmed something like three hundred
sheep.

On the porch—worn out and panting, her pink
tongue lolling—slumped Cirenhaven Nellie.

Nellie had followed Treve, as ever, into the
welter of blizzard, in pursuit of the stampeded
Number Six flock. Presently she had caught the
scent on her own account; and had held it.
When Treve had been lured aside in quest of a

handful of strays that had turned back from the main stampede, Nellie had plodded heavily on.

The scent of the main body of sheep had by this time become too badly obliterated by snow-swirl and cross-winds, for even Treve to pick it up. He could not scent Nellie's own tracks through that hurricane of whizzing snow which blotted out each footstep as fast as it was made.

But to Nellie the elusive scent was still strong enough for her preternaturally keen nose to follow it more or less correctly. When this was at times impossible, her uncanny instinct—the instinct of the trained blind—carried her on. Slowly, wearily, yet unfaltering, she kept up the quest.

She came staggeringly upon the sheep, at last, as they wavered on the precipice edge of the coulée—as they waited for some leader to be insane enough to fling himself over the brink; so that they might follow. Nellie ran nimbly along the slippery cliff-edge; forcing them back with bark and nip; just as one panicky wether was gathering himself for the downward leap.

Back she drove them, huddled and bleating and milling; rounding up the exhausted beasts and heading them away from the coulée. She had no faintest idea where they belonged; or whither to guide them. All she knew was that she was sick and suffering and that she stood in dire

need of getting home. Her Hour was close
upon her. So homeward she drove the flock;
unaware that she had achieved a bit of tracking
that no normal-eyed sheepdog could have hoped
to copy.

Next morning, Chris Hibben started for Santa
Carlotta, to direct the unloading of freight for
the Triple Bar. The snow was too deep for a
car to get through it. So Hibben rode his
strongest cow-pony;—a pony that made heavy
enough going of it through the drifts. As Chris
neared the Dos Hermanos ranch house, a man
came running out of the kitchen and hailed him
excitedly.

The man was Joel Fenno. Never before had
Hibben seen the old chap excited. Fearing something might be amiss in the house, the rider dismounted, tossed the bridle over his pony's head
and waded up the walk.

"What's wrong?" he demanded, as he came
face to face with Joel.

"Nuthin's wrong," Fenno assured him, his
mouth twisted in an effort to grin. "Ev'rything's grand—and 'ev'rything' incloods a bunch
of three hundred sheep that Nellie yanked out'n
the blizzard yest'd'y, for us. That dog sure paid
her board yest'd'y. She—"

"Say!" interposed Chris, none too graciously.
"Did you stop me, when I was in a hurry, just

to tell me Nellie had been wastin' her time by roundin' up a lot of mangy sheep? I'm glad-der'n ever that I sold her to you, if that's all she's fit for. Now if it'd been a bunch of good cattle—"

"She's fit for suthin' else," returned Fenno. "That wa'n't why I high-signed you. I wanted to show you the suthin' else she's fit for. C'm'on in."

He led the way into the kitchen. There, behind the stove, was a big box, half full of soft rags. In the box lay Cirenhaven Nellie, reclining comfortably on her side. At sound of Joel's step her tail gave a lazy wag or two, by way of welcome. But at sound and scent of the stranger behind him, her tail ceased to wave, and her lip curled in menace. For Nellie was on guard again.

This time she was not guarding silly sheep. She was guarding eight squirming gray-brown atoms, that nuzzled close against her furry body.

The baby collies were no larger than plump rats. But the way they wriggled and drank proved them none the worse for their mother's gallant exploits of the preceding day.

At a gentle word from Royce Mack, the collie mother dropped her tired head back on the bed of rags and suffered the outsider to draw near and gaze. Hibben stood looking curiously at the snuggling family in the box. Treve crossed the kitchen and stood beside Mack, his head on one side, gazing down at his babies. It was Joel who broke the silence.

"Eight of 'em!" he proclaimed. "An' they take after their ma. For ev'ry one of 'em is as blind as a cowman's int'llects. But in another nine days the hull eight of 'em is due to git their eyes wide open. That's when they'll commence to take after their pa an' be a credit to a sheep ranch. How many of 'em d'you want us to save out for you—at seventy-five dollars per?"

CHAPTER X: THE RUSTLERS

THREE miles to eastward of the Dos Hermanos ranch runs the Black Angel Trail. Far to northward it has its beginning. It cuts the state from top to bottom, like a jaggèd swordstroke. Up above the Peixoto Range it starts; and it runs almost due south across the Mexican border.

Nearly a century ago this trail was blazed. Of old it was the chief artery between the north counties and Mexico. The state roads and the railways have long since taken its place; and have diverted from it the bulk of traffic. Bumps and dips and narrow cuts between canyonsides render it impassable to motor car or to other modern vehicle.

But in spite of all this, the grass does not grow over-thick in the Black Angel Trail. No longer a main highway, it is a mighty convenient byway. Burro trains still traverse it. So do cattle drovers and shepherds. So do less reputable forms of traffic. It has great advantages over the thronged and town-fringed state roads, for the driving of livestock as well as for the transporting of goods which are best moved with no

247

undue publicity. Sojourners of the Black Angel
Trail have a way of minding their own business.
The law seldom patrols the backwater route or
takes cognizance of it.

Along this trail, from southward, one day in
earliest spring, fared a bee caravan, five wagons
strong. Each wagon carried full complement of
hives.

The only noteworthy detail of the procession
was that it numbered several more grown men
than can usually find time to accompany such a
caravan. The chief work of the bee route can
be done by women and boys; leaving most of the
men of the family or community to attend to the
crops at home.

Every year, these bee caravans are loaded with
hives, as soon as the fruit blossoms in the south-
ernmost corner of the state have been despoiled
of their honey-making possibilities. Northward
move the caravans; following the various blossom
seasons; and camping in likely spots along the
way, to let their bees ravage whatever blooms
happen to be most plentiful at that place and at
that time.

There is a regularly marked-out rotation of
blossom-ripening, in one section of the state
after the other. And this rotation the bee-
keepers follow; thus gathering the choicest honey
everywhere and all season long.

The five-wagon caravan halted and pitched camp in a sheltered arroyo, a few miles from the borders of the Dos Hermanos ranch. It was the first year a bee outfit had done such a thing. But then it was the first year the new almond orchard of the Goldring ranch, a mile to east of the arroyo, had put forth any profusion of blossoms. Thus there was nothing remarkable about the occurrence.

Indeed when Royce Mack rode back from collecting the mail at Santa Carlotta, and told his partner about their temporary neighbors, old Joel Fenno did not deem the news worth so much as a grunt of comment.

Instead, he glared dourly at Treve, who had trotted homeward alongside Royce's mustang.

"That cur," he railed, "is gettin' wuthlesser an' wuthlesser ev'ry day of his life. Here I go an' train poor little blind Nellie to work sheep with him; an' this morning I took her along to help me shift that Number Four bunch to Number Five. It was a two-dog job; 'count of the twist by the coulée an' 'count of some of the bunch bein' new. I took her and Zit. What d'ye s'pose? She wouldn't work with him! Acted like she didn't know how. An' no more she did, I reckon; her havin' worked only with Treve and only knowin' his ways, an' all that. I couldn't do a thing with her. Only that she's blind an' that she was most likely doin' her best, I'd 'a' whaled the daylights out'n her. An' where was Treve, all that time? Where *was* he, I'm askin' you? He was pirooting over to Santa Carlotta, along of *you;* pleasurin' himself an' holiday-makin', while there was work to do; —the measly slacker!"

"It wasn't Treve's fault," rejoined Mack, wearily. "I took him along for comp'ny. I didn't know you were aiming to shift that bunch till to-morrow. You said—"

"Took him 'long for comp'ny?" gibed Fenno. *"Comp'ny,* hey? You got plenty of comp'ny here, without no useless dog traipsin' after you. Ain't *I* 'comp'ny,' if comp'ny's what you're honin' after. Ain't I?"

"Yes," said Mack, briefly. "That's why I took Treve."

Leaving his glum partner to digest this cryptic speech, Royce stamped off to the back steps to wash up for dinner. Left alone with Treve, the elder partner lost his disgusted glower. Glancing furtively after Mack, he drew something from his pocket.

"Trevy!" he called under his breath.

The big collie had been following Royce out of the room. At the whisper of his name he halted and turned quickly back. Tail wagging and eyes full of eager friendliness to the old man

who had just been denouncing him so harshly,
he came up to Joel and sniffed interestedly at the
hand extended to him. In the palm was a
crumby and none-too-clean fragment of cake.

It was the final morsel left from a surrepti-
tious visit to the bakery, the last time Joel had
gone to Santa Carlotta. Guiltily, the old man
had bought a whole pound of stale jumbles. He
had bought them for Treve's sole benefit; and
he had been doling them out, secretly, to the
delighted collie ever since. It was the first
present of any sort he had purchased for anybody or anything, in all his sixty-odd crabbèd
years.

"Here you are, Trevy!" said Joel hospitably,
as the collie made a single dainty mouthful of
the offering. "An' when we go to town, next
time, I'll see can I git you some pound cake.
Pound cake is dretful good. You'll sure relish
it a whole lot, Trevy. Mighty few millionaires'
dogs gits to eat pound cake, I reckon. Then—
Say, Royce," he broke off, snarlingly, as he
caught the sound of his partner's return, "call
this durn cuss out onto the stoop with you. He's
tromplin' dust all over the clean floor. Dogs
don't b'long in the house, anyhow. You've got
him pampered till he's no good to no one. He
thinks he's folks. Take him outside!"

"I forgot to tell you," said Royce, coming

into the room, red and shining from his wash, "I met up with Chris Hibben, over at Santa Carlotta. He was coming out of the sheriff's office; and he was mad as hops. He says thirty of his beef cattle were run off the Triple Bar last night. Three of his cow-ponies were lifted right out of the home corral, too, he says."

"Strayed, most likely," suggested Joel, with no sign of interest in his neighbor's mishap.

"Chris says not," denied Royce. "He says they were lifted. Says it's rustlers."

At the ominous word, Joel Fenno's crooked brows twitched. Nobody in the sheep-and-cattle country, in those days, could hear the name "rustlers" without a twinge. In spite of watchfulness and in defiance of all law, livestock thieves had not yet been stamped out. They worked, as a rule, in gangs and with consummate cleverness. Their system of theft might vary, as occasion demanded. But whatever the system chanced to be, it had a way of circumventing the best efforts of ranchers.

It was easy for crafty and organized bands to lift large or small bunches of livestock from a vast range; to drive it to the nearest safe hiding place; and thence run it across the border or sell it to some dishonest wholesale butcher's agent. There was much money in such an enterprise;—much money and occasional death. For the captured rustler expected and received short shrift. The Black Angel Trail was the local livestock thief's route to wealth.

Long and disputatiously the Dos Hermanos partners talked over the news; Fenno as usual discrediting its truth and Royce increasingly impressed by it. The conference ended with an arrangement to send word to every herder on the Dos Hermanos ranch to keep strict guard for a night or two, and to carry a shotgun.

"Treve," said Royce, at bedtime, as the collie prepared to stretch himself as usual on the rag mat at the foot of his master's bunk, "you've got to do guard duty to-night. It's outdoors for yours. There are too many sheep in the home fold, just now, for us to take any chances. The other dogs are out on the range; and they've got to stay there while this scare lasts. All but Nellie. She's no good, Joel says, except when you can work with her. It's up to you to keep an eye on the fold. Outside, son! *Watch!*"

Treve did not catch the meaning of one-tenth of his master's harangue. But he understood enough of it to know, past doubt, that he was expected to stay away from his cherished rag mat that night, and stand guard over the house and the stable-buildings and the adjoining fold. He sighed discontent at his banishment. Then obediently he went outdoors and lay down with a little thump on the corner of the porch;—a post whence he could see or hear or scent anything going on in the clutter of outbuildings and yards in the hollow directly below.

His little blind mate, Nellie, came forward from the door-mat which was her usual bed and walked across the porch to him. Mincingly she came; her mahogany coat fluffing in the faint breeze. She touched noses affectionately with the big golden dog. Then, crouching, she danced her white forepaws on the boards, excitedly, tempting Treve to a romp.

But Treve was on duty, and he knew it. He resisted the temptation for a scamper and a mock battle in the soft dust. He lay still, merely wagging his plumed tail in recognition of the inviting dance. Failing to lure her mate into a frolic, Nellie lay soberly down beside him, her graceful body curled against his mighty shoulder

She loved to romp with Treve. Always he was as gentle in his play with her as with a weak child. With her, alone of the ranch dogs, would he unbend from his benign dignity. But since he would not play to-night, it was next best to cuddle close to him and to join in his vigil.

The long nights were a stupid and lonely time to Nellie, out there by herself on the porch. It made her happy, now, to have Treve's companionship in the hours of dark.

The two collies dozed. Yet they dozed as only
a trained watch-dog knows how to; with every
sense subconsciously alert. A little after midnight both their heads were lifted in unison, and
both sets of ears were pricked to listen.

Along the road beyond the ranch-house gate
came the pad-pad-pad of a slow-ridden horse
that wore no shoes.

This, by itself, was not a matter for excitement. Both collies knew the ill-kept road was
public, and that passersby were not to be mo-
lested. Thus, they did not give tongue, nor do
more than look up and listen as the horse padded by.

The night was close-clouded; though there was
a moon behind the banks of gray vapor. There
was light enough for even a human to detect
dimly any objects moving at a reasonable distance. To Treve's night-accustomed eyes there
was no difficulty in making out the figures of
horse and rider as they passed the gate.

The man was sitting carelessly in the saddle.
His face was turned toward the house, on whose
porch-edge the two silent collies were wholly
visible to him. He watched them a moment or
so, and they returned his gaze.

Then gradually his horse carried him past and
on a line paralleling the outbuildings. Treve's
eyes followed him, but only in the mildest in-

terest, as an incident of a quiet night. Nellie's uncannily keen nostrils sniffed the rider's unfamiliar scent, as the breeze bore it to her.

Then, of a sudden, Treve got to his feet; his hackles bristling. Dutifully, Nellie followed his example.

The rider had jogged on for more than a hundred yards. But at the far end of the outbuildings he had halted his horse. Dismounting, he took a hesitant step toward the palings which separated the ranch from the road. Instantly, both dogs were in motion. Running shoulder to shoulder, they bore down upon the man to resent the threat of intrusion.

Now "Greaser" Todd was anything but a fool. Hence the deservedly high place he occupied in his chosen trade. He knew dogs. A man in his line of business must know them and know them well. Of these two dogs he had gained casual knowledge, not only on an earlier ride past the ranch, but from chat with one of the herders whom he had managed to engage in idle talk that day. Thus, he was not silly enough to suppose he could hope to climb the paling undeterred.

But he had no desire to climb it just then. His plan was to get the dogs down here, well away from the house and from any possibly wakeful occupant thereof. Moreover, their dash would unquestionably bring forth any other of the ranch dogs which might be quartered around the fold.

As Treve and Nellie ran silently toward him, Todd sprang to the saddle again and set his mount in motion. The two collies came alongside, just inside the paling, as Greaser touched heel to his horse. He was grateful that they had advanced in silence, instead of barking in a way to disturb weary sleepers' rest. He was a most considerate man, was Greaser Todd.

As he cantered off, he drew from his saddlebags two objects, each about half the size of a man's fist, and tossed them over the paling at the angrily dancing collies.

The two flung objects were hunks of cooked meat; savory and alluring. One of them, on its downward flight, would have hit Treve in the head had not he flashed aside from the strange missile. It struck against a sloping stone and bounced back again through the gap between two palings into the dust of the road. There it lay, out of his reach; unless he should care to go all the way around to the gate and retrieve the tempting food. There Fenno found it next day.

The second bit of well-aimed meat fell to earth directly in front of Nellie's quivering nostrils. Lightly fed and perpetually hungry, she pounced upon the titbit; guided by her powers of scent. One gulp and she had swallowed it.

Treve was of two minds as to the advisability of waking the echoes with a salvo of barking by way of farewell insult to the intruder, or to go around and get the delicious-smelling meat that had rolled so provokingly out of his reach. The man was gone. His horse's light hoofbeats were dying away, up the coulée. The logical thing to do now was to get that generously-given meat and devour it.

Already, Nellie was beside the palings, thrusting her slender nose through the gap, in quest of the food she could smell but could not get. Being blind, she could not know, as did Treve, the futility of pushing her nose through one paling-gap after another in the hope of finding a space wide enough to let her jaws close on the meat.

But as Treve set off, along the inner side of the fence, on his errand of retrieving the fragment of cooked food, she seemed to understand his purpose. For she trotted eagerly alongside him; her shoulder as ever touching his, in order to guide her steps.

Treve had not gone twenty feet when he felt her swing away from him, in a lurch that almost upset her. Halting to let her catch up with him, after her supposed stumble, he saw Nellie stagger sideways a step or two, then curl back her lips from her teeth and come to a shivering stop. She moaned once in stifled agony; then collapsed in a furry heap on the ground.

Full of keen solicitude, Treve ran over to where she lay. As he gazed worriedly down upon the pitifully still little body, a trembling shook him from crown to toes. Not for the first time was the great collie looking upon Death.

His adored little mate was dead;—stone dead. How or why she had been stricken down so suddenly—she who just now had been so full of life and of pretty, loving ways—was beyond his knowledge. But grief smote him to the depths of his soul.

Long he stood there above her; now and then touching her still little body or face with his nose, as if entreating her to come back to him. Then, whimpering as no physical pain could have made him whimper, he turned and fled to the house.

Even as man in dire distress turns to his God for aid, so did the heartbroken collie turn now to his two human gods.

Bounding up on the porch, he scratched imperiously at the locked door; whining and sobbing in stark anguish of heart. Perhaps these humans could bring back to life the dear mate who had meant so much to him.

Fiercely impatient in his grief, he scratched the harder at the door panel; crying under his breath and quivering as in a death-chill.

After an eternity came a slumbrous and cross voice from Royce Mack's room.

"Shut up there, Treve!" commanded Royce, angry at being wakened. "Shut up, you fool! No, you can't come in! You're spoiled—pampered—just as Joel said. You'll stay outside, as I told you to. Shut up!"

Mack rolled over, as he finished shouting his peevish order, and sank again into slumber, worn out by his long day in the open.

Treve shrank back from the door as though his master's angry reproof had been a blow. Hesitant, he crouched there. He had turned to his god in his moment of heartbreak. And his god had refused to come to his aid.

Then, an instant later, the collie's ears were raised in new eagerness. A soft, if stumpy, footfall was crossing the kitchen floor. Joel Fenno opened the door and slipped out onto the porch, in sketchy attire, closing the door behind him.

"What's the matter, Trevy?" he whispered. "What's wrong, old sonny? Hey?"

Treve caught him by the hem of his abbreviated nightshirt and tugged at the garment, frantically; backing off the steps and seeking to drag Fenno after him. Joel gave one sharp look at the quivering dog; then nodded.

"I'll take your tip, Trevy," he whispered, disengaging his shirt from the hauling jaws. "Wait!"

He tiptoed indoors. But Treve was content. He knew the man would rejoin him.

In less than a minute Joel came back. He had yanked on his trousers and had stuck his feet into a ragged pair of carpet slippers. Under his arm he carried a loaded shotgun. In a trouser pocket were stuck four buckshot cartridges and a flashlight.

"Now, then," he bade the dog, "come on!"

Treve waited for no second bidding. He wheeled and made for the outbuildings. At every few rods, he would pause and look back to make sure Fenno was following.

"All right!" grumbled Joel, as if to a human companion. "All right! I'm a-comin', Trevy. I heard Royce call you a fool, jes' now. Maybe it's me that's the fool for trailin' along with you. And then ag'in, maybe not. You ain't given to actin' like this. Besides, with all this rustler-talk—"

He stopped short. Treve was no longer leading him on. The dog had halted at the fence edge, and was standing there, looking downward in drooping misery at something small and dark that lay at his feet. Joel pressed his flashlight button.

Almost instantly he released the pressure. But not before he had seen Nellie's lifeless body and had taken cognizance of her writhen lips. Her attitude and her convulsed mouth told their own story.

"Pizen!" muttered Joel, aghast.

His first sharp thought was for Treve. He went over to the disconsolate collie and felt his head and jaws.

"Nope," he said. "She was the only one that got it. If it was strong enough to git her as quick as that, it'd 'a' got you, too, before now. An'—an', Trevy, I'm thankin' Gawd it didn't! I'm a-thankin' Him, reel rev'rent!"

The old brain was working and working fast. Now that the Dos Hermanos ranch was at peace with the Triple Bar outfit, there was no neighbor who would poison any of the collies. The only person to do such a damnable thing must be some one who desired to get the ranch guards out of the way in order to rob the place.

Rustlers!

Joel listened. Except for an occasional bleat or stir in the nearby fold, no sound broke the awesome stillness of the early spring night. The collie stood statuelike above his dead mate, his sorrowful dark eyes fixed on Joel in dumb appeal.

"We can't bring her back, Trevy," said Fenno, gently, caressing the bowed silken head with rough tenderness. "Only the good Gawd c'd do that. An' in His wisdom, He don't ever do it no more—nowadays. . . . *He* knows why. *I* don't. We ain't so lucky as them folks in Bible times. . . . But maybe we c'n git the swine that killed her, Trevy!"

There was a fiery thread of menace in the old voice, a note that made the collie lift his drooping head and turn toward the rancher. Just then, blurred and from far off, came a scent and a sound. They were indistinguishable to gross human senses. But Treve read them aright.

The sound was of three cautiously-ridden horses. The scent was of men;—one of them the man who had loitered beside the fence and flung the meat that had killed Treve's mate.

The dog stiffened. His teeth bared. Deep down in his throat a growl was born. He remembered; and now he understood.

This was the man who had somehow done Nellie to death. It was directly after he stopped there, on the far side of the fence, that she had died. Red rage flamed in the dog's heart and eyes.

"Quiet, Trevy!" breathed Joel, at sound of

the low growl. "Hear suthin', do you? Quiet, then, an' wait! . . . Huh! Royce Mack called you a fool, did he? Called *you* a fool! In the mornin'—"

He fell silent. To his own straining ears now came the faint beat of muffle-hoofed horses. Nearer they came and nearer. Joel gripped his shotgun and peered through the high fence palings.

Presently, in the dim light, he was aware of three mounted men and two more men on foot, coming toward him from the direction of the coulée.

At the same moment one of the three riders spurred forward from the rest. Drawing his horse alongside the high fence, he vaulted lightly from the saddle, coming to earth on the inner side of the palings.

As his feet touched ground, something hairy and terrible whizzed at him through the darkness; awful in its murderous silence. Before Greaser Todd could get his hand to his knife or shove back his mysterious assailant, Treve's mighty jaws had found their goal in his unshaven throat.

The rustler crashed to earth, the mutely homicidal collie atop him; the curved white eyeteeth grinding toward the jugular.

"What's the matter, Greaser?" queried the

rider behind him, hearing his leader stumble and fall. "Bootsoles too slippery?"

As he spoke, he, too, vaulted the palings and dropped to his feet in the yard. One of the unmounted men was climbing the fence in more leisurely fashion, his head appearing now over the top.

As calmly as though he were shooting quail, Fenno went into action.

One barrel of his shotgun was fired point-blank at the rustler who had just landed in the yard. Wheeling, he emptied the left barrel into the head of the climber.

There was a panic yell from the road; then pell-mell a scurry of hoofs and of running feet. Slipping two new cartridges into the breech, Joel Fenno climbed halfway up the fence and fired both barrels down the road into the muddled dust-cloud that was dashing toward the coulée.

Royce Mack, still drunk with sleep, came staggering and shouting down from the ranch house, his flashlight playing in every direction. At the edge of the outbuildings he slithered to a dumbfounded halt.

The arc of white radiance from his flashlight illumed a truly hideous and incredible scene. Athwart the fence top, like a shot squirrel, sprawled an all-but headless man. On the ground, just inside the palings, lay another slumped figure.

Somewhat nearer to Mack knelt Joel Fenno, his gun on the earth beside him. He was stanching the blood of a third man—a man whose throat was that of a jungle beast's victim.

Beside him, tense and raging, and held in check only by Joel's crooning voice, towered the huge gold-white Treve.

"I reckon we c'n save this one of 'em, Royce, long 'nough for the sheriff to git his c'nfession," airily observed Joel, continuing his first-aid work. "I pried Trevy loose before he got to the jug'l'r. With Trevy standin' by, to prompt him like, the feller's due to talk all the sheriff wants him to. Me an' Trevy will see to that. As f'r them other two—"

"What—what the—?" sputtered Mack, stupid with horror.

"Trevy's a 'fool,' all right!" scoffed Joel. "Jes' like I heard you call him, awhile back. He tries to be more like you all the time. Likewise he s'cceeds. Now run an' phone for the sheriff. Me an' Trevy has had a busy night. It's up to *you* to do the rest of the chores."

CHAPTER XI: THE PARTING OF THE WAYS

TREVE lay on the porch at the Dos Hermanos ranch house; his classic head between his little white forepaws; his mighty gold-and-white body like a couchant lion's. A casual passerby would have said the dog was asleep. A dog-student would have known better. Seldom do collies sleep in that picturesque pose. Usually they slumber asprawl on one side.

Neither were the collie's deepset sorrowful eyes shut. They were looking wearily across the heat-pulsating miles of ranch land. Nor were they alert, as when the big dog was on guard. There was perplexed worry in their soft gaze.

Things were happening at the ranch; things Treve did not understand. Yet his collie sixth sense told him there were change and confusion in the air as well as in the words and voices of his two masters. These two masters were often at odds. The dog long since had ceased to let himself be stirred by their incessant and harmless quarrels.

But they were not at odds, nowadays. Indeed, there was a new civility—almost a sad friendliness—in their manner toward each other.

We humans often grope for the solution to

some baffling mystery which eludes our sharpest
intelligence, and whose key, could we but master
it, lies within easy reach of us. So with Treve.
The key to this disturbing new ranch development lay within six inches of his nose, in the
form of a newspaper which had fallen from the
porch rocker to the dusty floor.

Had Treve been able to read type—as he
could read human nature and weather signs and
danger to the Dos Hermanos flocks—a front
page news item in that paper might have told
him much. The paper was the Santa Carlotta
Bugle. The item had been written by the
Bugle's proprietor, himself, in his best florid
style. The proprietor, by the way, chanced to
be the managing editor, the city editor, the reportorial staff and the printer of the paper. Also
the business-and-advertising manager and office
boy. The *Bugle* was a one-man sheet.

His front-page article ran:

"Dan Cupid has been making a spring round-
up of the ranch country, this season. We have
had glad occasion to announce no less than four
engagements and two marriages, in the Dos
Hermanos Valley, during the past three months.
We now take personal pleasure in retailing the
latest romance from that garden spot of our fair
state.

"Mr. Royce Mack, younger partner of the popular sheep-ranchers, Fenno and Mack, of the Dos Hermanos Ranch outfit, is about to marry Miss Reine Houston, the lovely and popular and talented Fourth Grade teacher at the Ova school.

"Miss Houston's gain is the loss of the Dos Hermanos Valley; as the young couple plan to leave this section (which so aptly has been termed 'God's Country'), and to settle in the far and effete East, upon a well-stocked Vermont dairy farm which was recently bequeathed, along with a considerable cash legacy, to Mr. Mack, by his deceased maternal uncle.

"The nuptials, we understand, will occur at the bride's parental home in Dodge City, Kas., early next month. Miss Houston expects to leave Ova, Friday, to go home for her final wedding arrangements. Mr. Mack, we learn, will follow the first of the week."

There was more of the article, including a stanza of machine-made poetry, with a highly original reference to two hearts that beat as one. But no more is needed to explain the atmosphere of impending change which had begun to grate upon the collie's nerves.

For a long time this change had been coming. Treve had trotted across to Ova, evening after evening, for weeks alongside of Royce's pinto.

He had lain boredly on a rug in a stuffy little boarding house parlor, while his master forgot him and everything else in chatting with a plump girl who smelt annoyingly of lily-of-the-valley perfume. A girl who said at the outset that she didn't care much for dogs and who asked if collies weren't supposed to be treacherous.

Treve had known from the first that she did not like him. This bothered him not at all. For he didn't like her, either. Her pungent lily-of-the-valley perfume was as distressing to his sensitive nostrils as would be the reek of carrion to a human nose. Moreover, she was not the type of human that dogs like. Also, she took up too much of his master's attention.

Intuitively, Treve realized Mack was not as fond of him as once he had been and that the man was not the jolly chum of yore. It grieved the sensitive collie. He sought wistfully to draw Royce's attention more to himself and less to this painfully-scented outsider. But it was all in vain.

Royce Mack was blindly and deliriously in love. The world, for the time, contained for him only one person. That person was far more like an angel than a mere woman. And she exhaled in some occult way a faintly angelic perfume from her garments.

Sheepishly, Mack told his partner of the engagement. Joel's reply was a grunt which implied nothing or anything. Fenno made precisely the same reply, a week afterward, when news came to Royce of his comfortable legacy of cash and of pleasant farmland in southern Vermont.

Risking monotony, Joel had achieved a third grunt when Mack went on to inform him of the projected eastward move. This move meant a breaking up of the partnership. Mack could not run a dairy farm in Vermont and also a ranch in the West.

Joel came out of the silences and out of a maze of calculations long enough to make an offer for Royce's share of the Dos Hermanos. The offer was as meager as was Fenno himself; but it was as reliable. Too foolishly happy to barter, Mack closed with it. Thus, in another three days, Joel Fenno was to become sole owner of the ranch.

Both men had evaded the question of Treve's ownership. The collie belonged jointly to them. Yet he was not included in the list of land, buildings and livestock set forth in the bill of sale.

From the first, Mack had regarded the dog as his own, and had made Treve his particular chum. Joel had scoffed at such folly, and had pretended to hold the collie in utter contempt. But Treve had grown to be everything to the gnarl-souled oldster. For the first time in his sixty-odd warped years, he had learned to care about some living creature. It was with a twinge that he saw how much fonder the dog seemed to be of Mack than of Fenno's unlovable self.

Now, at the possibility of parting with his loved dog-comrade, his heart was as sore as a boil. Wherefore, as usual, he held his peace on the theme so close to him; and he was outwardly the more savage in his comments on Treve's worthlessness.

Treve lifted his head from between his paws, and stared down the road toward the coulée. His trained ears not only caught the rattle and chug of an approaching car, but they recognized it as a car belonging to the ranch.

Presently, the dusty runabout rounded the bend, a furlong beyond. Royce Mack was driving it. At his side sat a plump and slackly pretty figure in billowy white. Treve was too far away to catch the reek of lily-of-the-valley. But he knew it would assail and torture his keen nostrils soon enough.

The dog got to his feet, with a bark of welcome. He was about to lope forward to meet the car and escort Mack to the house, when Joel Fenno, hearing the bark, stumped out of the kitchen doorway behind him.

The old man had come from work, with Treve at his heels, a half-hour early that day. Now he reappeared from his bedroom, crossly uncomfortable in his store clothes; his neck teased by a frayed collar-edge and further girt with a ready-made tie of awesome coloring. If his bulls-eye emerald scarfpin had been genuine, it would have been worth more than the entire ranch. His new boots squeaked groaningly on the porch floor.

The collie, wondering at such change in his friend's costume and bearing, halted in his scarce-begun journey toward the approaching car and stared, with head on one side.

"Sure!" growled Fenno. "Sure! Keep a-lookin' at me, Trevy. I'm sure wuth it. If 'twasn't that he's leavin' here for good, in a day or two, I'd 'a' saw him in blue blazes before I'd 'a' rigged me up like this, on a hot week-day; jes' 'cause he took a idee to ask her over to eat supper with us, to-night. I feel like I was to a fun'ral, Trevy."

As he spoke, Joel was strolling down the dusty walk, toward the gateway, to give such sour welcome as he might to his partner's sweetheart. The collie abandoned his own intent to gambol ahead; and paced sedately along at Joel's side.

The average high-class collie has reduced snobbishness to an art. Witness the courtesy wherewith many of them hasten to greet a well-dressed stranger, as contrasted with their fierce rebuff of a tramp.

Perhaps it was Fenno's unwonted splendor of raiment which made Treve elect to continue the gateward walk in his company, rather than dash on ahead. Yet of late, he had more than once chosen Joel's companionship rather than Mack's. As they walked, Joel continued to mutter under his breath.

"She said she 'wanted to meet her darling Royce's dear old partner,'" he sniffed. "Well, Trevy, the pleasure's all her'n. (Not that I'm a-grudgin' her the treat of seein' me.) Nothing'd do but she must come over to supper with us, Trevy. And if Sing Lee don't cook no better'n he's been cookin' lately, she's sure due to remember this supper for quite a spell. She— Whatcher smellin' at, Trevy?" he broke off.

The dog had slowed in his walk, and was moving stiff-legged. His nostrils were sniffing the still air with queer intensity. The car was drawing to a stop, in front of the gate, twenty feet away;—quite near enough for the hated lily-of-the-valley perfume to reach the collie's acute senses.

But it was not perfume he was smelling. It was something far more familiar and far more detested; something still too faint to reach Fenno's grosser powers of scent.

The noisy little car stopped. Mack, on its far side, got out and hurried around the runabout, to help Reine Houston to the ground. He did not even pause in his loverly haste long enough to turn off the noisy engine; an engine whose coughing reverberations drowned all lesser sounds.

Reine did not wait for her lover to reach her side and assist her in the wholly simple task of opening the car door and stepping to earth. Coming toward the gateway, from the direction of the house, were Joel and the dog. Anxious to make a good impression on Fenno, the girl jumped down before Mack could come around from the far side of the car. Her plump hands outstretched in friendly greeting to Joel, she ran forward to meet him.

There was a patch of roadside tumbleweed between the car and the gate. The girl prepared to clear this in her stride. But she did not do so.

This because Treve suddenly abandoned his stiff-legged suspicious advance and made one lightning bound at her.

The dog did not growl, nor did he show his teeth. But he sprang with the incredible speed of a charging wolf. Clearing the patch of tumbleweed by fully twenty inches, he sent his

body crashing with all its force against the
white-clad girl.

He did not bite. His lowered head and much
of his furry body smote her amidships. Back
she shot, under that swift impact, banging hard
against the side of the car and using up what
little breath she still had in a loud screech.

Royce Mack rounded the side of the car just
in time to see the dog hurl himself at the all-
precious Reine.

With a yell of fury at such vile sacrilege to
his angel, he sprang at Treve and kicked him.

The kick struck the dog in the short ribs with
an agonizing force that doubled Treve and sent
him rolling over and over in the dust. Furiously, Mack followed him up, his boot drawn
back for a second and heavier kick. The girl
did not cease from screaming as she gathered
herself up, bruised and hysterical with fright.

As his foot swung back for the kick, Royce
chanced to see Joel Fenno from the corner of his
eye. The old man was also in violent action.
At sight of his partner's activities, Mack checked
himself with one foot still in air.

Fenno, regardless of his own rheumatic
limbs, was doing a vehement dance in the center
of the low tumbleweed patch. Beneath his
stamping feet writhed and twisted a fat four-
foot rattlesnake.

The nasty odor of crushed cucumbers—certain sign of the pit viper—was strong enough in the air now, for even these blundering humans to get the scent which Treve had caught twenty feet away.

"I ain't got my gun on me!" wheezed Joel, to his partner, as a final drive of his heel smashed the rattlesnake's evil, arrow-shaped head. "But if you kick that dog ag'in, I swear t' Gawd I'll go in an' git it, an' blow your mangy face off! I seen the hull thing. This gal of your'n was jes' a-goin' to plant her foot in the tumbleweed, when I seen this rattler h'ist up his dirty head an' bend it back to strike her ankle. Trevy seen it, too. An' he pushed her out'n death's way, when there wa'n't neither one of us humans near enough nor quick enough to. An' you kicked him fer savin' her! Lord! Kicked—kicked—*Trevy!*"

He had left the slain snake and was hustling across to the dog.

Treve had gotten gaspingly to his feet. No whimper had been wrung from him by the anguishing pain of the kick in his tender short-ribs. No snarl nor other sign of wrath had shown resentment at this brutality—a brutality for which any human stranger would have been attacked by him right murderously.

Instead, the great dog stood stock-still in the

road, his glorious coat dust-smeared, his mighty body a-tremble. His soft eyes were fixed on the man who had kicked him—the man who had been his god—the man whose sweetheart the collie had risked his own life to save.

This was the man to whom he had given loyal and worshipful service since long before he could remember. And now his god had turned on him;—had not punished him, for punishment implies earlier fault; but had half-killed him for no fault at all.

The deepset dark eyes were terrible in their heartbreak. Royce Mack, blinking stupidly, felt their look sear into him. Slowly he stared from the stricken dog to the dead snake. Then his eyes fell upon Reine Houston.

At sight of the snake, and at comprehension of what Treve had averted from her by that wild leap, Reine collapsed, blubbering and quaking, on the running-board of the car.

Drawn by supreme impulse, Royce turned his back on the collie and hurried over to her. Treve was forgotten.

With babbled love words Mack sought to re-assure and comfort the girl and to learn if she were badly hurt. In this tender employment he was interrupted by Joel Fenno's rasping voice. The old man had been examining Treve, with the tender touch of a nurse, and crooning softly to the hurt collie. Now he turned grimly on his partner.

"Best boost your young lady into the car," he snarled, "an' trundle her back to Ova. She ain't li'ble to have much ap'tite left, after what's happened. Besides, Sing Lee's salaraytus biscuits ain't no good example for a new-mown bride to take to heart for future use. More'n that, she's met me. That's what she come here for, wa'n't it? She's met me. Likewise, she's saw me dance. She's met Treve ag'n, too. Met him reel sudden an' personal. That's why she's still alive. S'pose you traipse back to Ova with her; an' leave me an' Trevy to ourselves. We kind of need to be left thataway. If you don't mind. So long!"

His wizened hand on the dog's ruff, he strode back to the house, shutting the door loudly behind Treve and himself.

It was late when Royce Mack got back from Ova, that evening. Joel was sitting up for him. Royce said nothing to his partner, but went at once to Treve, who had come slowly forward to meet him.

His hands roamed remorsefully over the dog, and he seemed trying to say something. Treve was looking up into Royce's face with that same strickenly reproachful expression that the man had not been able to get out of his memory all evening.

"If you're huntin' for broken ribs or for rupture," commented Joel as he watched his partner's exploring hands, "there ain't any. Small thanks to you; an' by a mir'cle of heaven. Treve's all right. Except you've smashed suthin' in the heart an' the soul of him that you can't unsmash. That's all you done."

The old man's toneless voice irked Mack.

"Can you blame me?" he challenged. "What else could I do? I saw him spring at her and knock her down. I thought he was killing her. It seemed the only way to—"

"To prove you're a born fool?" supplemented Joel. "You didn't need to prove it to me. Nor, when she's knowed you a while longer, you won't need to prove it to her, neither. Why would he be killin' her? Hey? We've had him all these years; an' he never yet did a thing that wa'n't wiser'n the wisest thing *you* ever did. Nor yet he never did anything that was rotten. You might 'a' knowed he had some reason for actin' so. Anyhow, there's lots better ways for a man to show he's a dog's inferior, than by kickin' him."

"Let it go at that!" muttered Royce, sullenly;

harder hit than he cared to show, by the look in his collie chum's dark eyes. "I'll make it up to him, somehow. I—"

"Make it up to him?" mocked Fenno. "How? By tellin' him you've forgave him, maybe? Or by gettin' him a nice gold watch an' wearin' it for him till he's old enough to take care of it? 'Make it up to him!' *Lord!*"

Royce turned wrathfully on his expressionless partner.

"I don't see what business it is of yours!" he snapped. "You've always hated the dog. You've always called him worthless and said you wished we could be rid of him. Well, you'll be rid of him, all right. In less than a week he and I will be out of here for good."

"Where do you get that stuff about 'him and you?' *You'll* be gone. But Treve's as much mine as he's yours."

Royce glanced at his scowling partner in genuine surprise.

"You don't mean to say you're going to be cantankerous about *that,* too?" he exclaimed. "Why, Joel, you hate the very sight of the dog! You've hated him from the beginning. You've never had a decent word for him. I don't believe you ever spoke to him in his life, except to give him some order or else to swear at him. And now you talk about his being as much yours as mine. Well, let's come to a showdown. What do you want for your share in him?"

Joel made no immediate answer. He was peering through the dim candle-light at Treve. The old man's thin lips moved rhythmically, as though he were chewing the mysterious cud of senility. His chin quivered. Otherwise his leathery face was blank. It gave no sign of the turmoil behind it.

But Treve understood. With all a collie's strange trick of reading human emotion behind a wordless and expressionless mask, he knew his friend was acutely unhappy. The dog got to his feet and came over to Fenno, pressing his furry bulk against the rancher's lean legs and thrusting a sympathetic muzzle into the tough palm. He whined softly, his gaze fixed on Joel's.

From long habit, in the presence of others, Fenno made as though to repulse the dog's friendliness. Then, with a little intake of breath, he bent over the collie and caught the classic head almost roughly between his hands.

"Treve!" he mumbled, thickly. "Trevy, you and me know all about that, don't we? We're —we're good pals, me and you, Trevy. The best pals there ever was."

Royce Mack looked on, dumbfounded. There

was caress in Fenno's thin voice and in his rough
grasp of the dog. Treve, too, was behaving as
though he were well accustomed to such signs of
affection from the man.

"I—I thought—" began Mack, "I thought—"

"No, ye didn't!" crossly denied Fenno, the
barriers down. "You never 'thought,' in all
your born days. If you'd knowed what it meant
to think, you'd 'a' knowed a white man couldn't
go hatin' Trevy, like I made out I hated him.
Nobody could. And likewise you'd 'a' remembered how he kept me alive that day down by
Ova, when I was throwed and crippled up and
couldn't stir to help myself; an' how he brang
water to me; an' how he flagged you and brang
you to me, besides. An' now you go jawin'
about takin' him away; an' askin' what do I
want for my share of him. Well, I want just a
even billion dollars for my share of Trevy. I
ain't sellin'. I'm buyin'. Now whatcher want
for *your* share of him? Speak up! If I got it,
I'll pay."

Royce pondered a moment. He could not
fathom this phase of the old man. Then a solution came to him.

"Remember the day we got him?" asked Mack.
"Remember how we made dice marks on a lump
of sugar, out to the foreman shack, to see which
owned him? He ate the sugar, and we compro-

mised by owning him between us. Suppose we
throw dice again to see who owns him? Loser
to give up all claim to him. How about it?"

"Nope," refused Joel, stubbornly. "Lemme
buy him off'n you, Mack. I'll pay—"

"I'm not selling him," as stubbornly insisted
Royce, enamored of his own sporting idea. "I'm
giving you your chance. Take it or leave it.
You ought to be glad I don't suggest we let him
go to whichever of us he chooses."

Joel winced. Then, despondently, he clumped
across the room to the shelf where lay the par-
cheesi game. Choosing a cylinder cup and a pair
of dice, he came back to the table. On the way
he paused to pat furtively the collie's silken ears.

"Best two out of three?" suggested Royce.

"Nope," said Fenno. "One throw. When a
tooth's got to come out, a single yank is best.
You throw first."

Royce took the dice-cup and shook it with
relish. Nothing could beat him. He knew that.
In his present streak of luck, when a glorious
bride and a legacy were falling to his lot, a bout
of chance with his Jonah-like old partner could
not fail to bring him success—and Treve.

Expertly he chucked the dice out on the table,
in the flickering candle-flare. Over and over the
white cubes tumbled and hopped and rolled;
coming to a halt, at last, barely an inch from

the table edge and almost side by side. Both men leaned forward to read the pips on the exposed top surfaces of the dice.

A six and a five! Eleven! Unbeatable except by a next-to-impossible Twelve.

Joel's face set itself like wrinkled granite. He made no other outward sign of distress. Treve, at sound of the noisily rattling dice, had gotten interestedly to his feet, and stood with his head on a level with the deal table, watching.

Royce swept up the dice and tossed them into the cup; passing it across to Fenno. With hand as steady as a boy's, the old man accepted the cup and sulkily he threw the two dice upon the board.

The jar of a heavy tread on the porch made both men turn their heads. Visitors at such an hour were unheard-of. Toni, the chief herdsman, stamped in to report the straying of a bunch of sheep that had nosed a hole in the rotting wattles of the home fold. Instinctively the partners glanced back to the dice.

There lay the little cubes, just under the candle's nearest rays.

Two sixes! Twelve!

There had been fewer than nine chances in a hundred that Joel could have made such a throw. Yet, his proverbial hoodoo was broken. Luck, for once, seemed to have gravitated his way.

Fenno made no comment, but bent over to pat Treve with an odd new air of personal possession, while Mack listened scowlingly to Toni's tale of the lost sheep.

"Suppose you and *your* dog chase out with Toni and round 'em up?" said Royce, at last, turning maliciously to his partner. "They're not mine any longer, you know. Any more than Treve is. For once I'll have the fun of going to bed and letting the rest of the outfit do the hustling. Good-night."

At dusk, three days later, the one livery car from Santa Carlotta stopped at the ranch gate to carry Royce Mack and his belongings to the distant railroad, whence the night train was to bear him eastward to his bride.

Herders piled the car with luggage; then stood at the gate to say good-by to their former boss. Joel loitered in the doorway; Treve beside him. Fenno was frowning and fidgeting.

Royce came up to him with outstretched hand. For a moment the old man ignored the hand. Once more his jaws were at work with senility's cud. Suddenly he burst forth:

"Trevy's your'n! Take him along East with you!"

There was a world of stifled heartache and stark misery in the grouchy old voice.

"What the blue blazes!" sputtered Royce in amaze. "D'you mean to say you don't want him, after all the fuss you made? He—"

"Yep!" snarled old Fenno. "I want him more'n I want my right leg. An' I reckon I'll be twice as lonesome without him as I'd be without the two of my legs. But I—I don't want him the way I won him. I thought I did. But I don't. It—it sticks in my throat. He's a square dog, Trevy is. He ain't goin' to be won by no crooked trick. So I— Oh, take him along an' shut up!"

Royce continued to stare in bewilderment. His owlish aspect angered Joel.

"We shook dice for him," expounded Fenno, sourly. "You throwed a six an' a five. I throwed a six an' a one. You looked back to see who was buttin' into the room that time of night. I flicked the one-spot over, an' made it a six. Take him along. I—I— Trevy, son," he ended, a frog in his throat as he laid a shaky hand on the collie's head, "you see for yourself, I couldn't keep you, that way; you bein' so clean an' decent; an' me cheatin' to get you. I—"

To his astonishment, Royce Mack broke into a shout of laughter.

"When I put Reine on the Pullman to go East," said Royce, "I told her about our throwing dice for Treve. I was still sore over losing him. D'you know what she said? Said she was tickled to death that I'd lost. Said she can't bear dogs, and that she'd never be able to endure having Treve around after the savage way he upset her. She said she'd always be afraid of him, and that she'd have insisted, anyway, on my leaving him behind. That settles it. . . . Good-by, Treve, old friend. Good-by, Joel. Luck to the pair of you!"

Late into the warm evening, Joel Fenno sat silent on the porch. At his feet, in drowsy contentment, lay Treve. The old man's face was aglow with wordless happiness. Every now and then he would stoop to stroke the sleeping dog. Then he would listen delightedly to the responsive lazy thump of Treve's tail on the boards.

Life was worth while, after all. It was great to have a chum that was all one's own, and to sit thus with him at the close of day. No more bickerings, no more jawing, no more need to pretend he didn't like this wonderful collie of his. It was *fine* to be alive!

"Trevy," he exhorted, solemnly, as he knocked out his final pipe and prepared to go indoors, "don't you ever let me ketch you throwin' dice crooked. But if ever you do, don't go blabbin' about it. Not one time in a trillion-an'-seven, c'd you expec' to find a girl who'd square it all for you, like that pudgy Reine person done for

me. An', Trevy, lemme say ag'in, for the sev'-
ralth time, right here,—of all the dogs that ever
happened—you're—you're that dog. Now le's
quit jabberin' an' go to sleep!"

CHAPTER XII: AFTERWORD

I HAVE drawn upon one of our Sunnybank collies for the name and the aspect and certain traits of this book's hero. The real Treve was my chum, and one of the strangest and most beautiful collies I have known.

Dog aristocrats have two names; one whereby they are registered in the American Kennel Club's immortal studbook and one by which they are known at home. The first of these is called the "pedigree name." The second is the "kennel name." Few dogs know or answer to their own high-sounding pedigree names. In speaking to them their kennel names alone are used.

For example, my grand old Bruce's pedigree name was Sunnybank Goldsmith;—a term that meant nothing to him. My Champion Sunnybank Sigurdson (greatest of Treve's sons), responds only to the name of "Squire." Sunnybank Lochinvar is "Roy."

Treve's pedigree name was "Sunnybank Sigurd." And in time he won his right to the hard-sought and harder-earned prefix of "CHAMPION";—the supreme crown of dogdom.

We named him Sigurd—the Mistress and I—

in honor of the collie of Katharine Lee Bates; a dog made famous the world over by his owner's exquisite book, *"Sigurd, Our Golden Collie."*

But here difficulties set in.

It is all very well to shout "Sigurd!" to a collie when he is the only dog in sight. But when there is a rackety and swirling and excited throng of them, the call of "Sigurd!" has an unlucky sibilant resemblance to the exhortation, "Sic 'im!" And misunderstandings—not to say strife—are prone to follow. So we sought a one-syllable kennel name for our golden collie pup. My English superintendent, Robert Friend, suggested "Treve."

The pup took to it at once.

He was red-gold-and-snow of coat; a big slender youngster, with the true "look of eagles" in his deepset dark eyes. In those eyes, too, burned an eternal imp of mischief.

I have bred or otherwise acquired hundreds of collies in my time. No two of them were alike. That is the joy of collies. But most of them had certain well-defined collie characteristics in common with their blood-brethren. Treve had practically none. He was not like other collies or like a dog of any breed.

Gloriously beautiful, madly alive in every inch of him, he combined the widest and most irreconcilable range of traits.

For him there were but three people on earth;
—the Mistress, myself and Robert Friend. To
us he gave complete allegiance, if in queer form.
The rest of mankind, with one exception—a girl
—did not exist, so far as he was concerned; unless the rest of mankind undertook to speak to
him or to pat him. Then, instantly, such familiarity was rewarded by a murderous growl and
a most terrifying bite.

The bite was delivered with a frightful show
of ferocity. And it had not the force to crush
the wing of a fly.

Strangers, assailed thus, were startled. Some
were frankly scared. They would stare down in
amaze at the bitten surface, marveling that there
was neither blood nor teeth-mark nor pain. For
the attack always had an appearance of man-
eating fury.

Treve would allow the Mistress to pat him—
in moderation. But if I touched him, in friendliness, he would toss his beautiful head and dart
out of reach, barking angrily back at me. It was
the same when Robert tried to pet him.

Once or twice a day he would come up to me,
laying his head across my arm or knee; growling
with the utmost vehemence and gnawing at my
sleeve for a minute at a time. I gather that this
was a form of affection. He did it to nobody
else.

Also, when I went to town for the day, he would mope around for awhile; then would take my cap from the hall table and carry it into my study. All day long he would lie there, one paw on the cap, and growl fierce menace to all who ventured near. On my return home at night, he gave me scarcely a glance and drew disgustedly away as usual when I held out my hand to pat him.

In the evenings, on the porch or in front of the living room fire, he would stroll unconcernedly about until he made sure I was not noticing. Then he would curl himself on the floor in front of me, pressing his furry body close to my ankles; and would lie there for hours.

The Mistress alone he forbore to bite. He loved her. But she was a grievous disappointment to him. From the first, she saw through his vehement show of ferocity and took it at its true value. Try as he would, he could not frighten her. Try as he would, he could not mask his adoration for her.

Again and again he would lie down for a nap at her feet; only to waken presently with a thundrous growl and a snarl, and with a lunge of bared teeth at her caressing hand. The hand would continue to caress; and his show of fury was met with a laugh and with the comment:

"You've had a good sleep, and now you've waked up in a nice homicidal rage."

Failing to alarm her, the dog would look sheepishly at the laughing face and then cuddle down again at her feet to be petted.

There was another side to his play of indifference and of wrath. True, he would toss his head and back away, barking, when Robert or myself tried to pat him. But at the quietly spoken word, "Treve!", he would come straight up to us and, if need be, stand statue-like for an hour at a time, while he was groomed or otherwise handled.

In brief, he was the naughtiest and at the same time the most unfailingly obedient dog I have owned. No matter how far away he might be, the single voicing of his name would bring him to me in a swirling rush.

In the show-ring he was a problem. At times he showed as proudly and as spectacularly as any attitude-striking tragedian. Again, if he did not chance to like his surroundings or if the ring-side crowd displeased him, he prepared to loaf in slovenly fashion through his paces on the block and in the parade. At such times the showing of Treve became as much an art as is the guiding of a temperamental race-horse to victory. It called for tact; even for trickery.

In the first place, during these fits of ill-humor,

he would start around the ring, in the preliminary parade, with his tail arched high over his back; although he knew, as well as did I, that a collie's tail should be carried low, in the ring.

I commanded: "Tail down!" Down would come the tail. But at the same time would come a savage growl and a sensational snap at my wrist. The spectators pointed out to one another the incurably fierce collie. Fellow-exhibitors in the ring would edge away. The judge—if he were an outsider—would eye Treve with strong apprehension.

It was the same when I whispered, "Foot out!" as he deliberately turned one white front toe inward in coming to a halt on the judging block. A similar snarl and feather-light snap followed the command.

The worst part of the ordeal came when the judge began to "go over" him with expert hands, to test the levelness of his mouth, the spring of his ribs, his general soundness and the texture of his coat. An exhibitor is not supposed to speak to a judge in the ring except to answer a question. But if the judge were inspecting Treve for the first time, I used to mumble conciliatingly, the while:

"He's only in play, Judge. The dog's perfectly gentle."

This, as Treve resented the stranger's handling, by growl-fringed bites at the nearest part of the judicial anatomy.

A savage dog does not make a hit with the average judge. There is scant joyance in being chewed, in the pursuit of one's judging-duties. Yet, as a rule, judges took my word as to Treve's gentleness; especially after one sample of his biteless biting. Said Vinton Breese, the famed "all-rounder" dog-judge, after an Interstate show:

"I feel slighted. Sigurd forgot to bite me to-day. It's the first time."

The Mistress made up a little song, in which Treve's name occurred oftener than almost all its other words. Treve was inordinately proud of this song. He would stand, growling softly, with his head on one side, for an indefinite time, listening to her sing it. He used to lure her into chanting this super-personal ditty by trotting to the piano and then running back to her.

Nature intended him for a staunch, clever, implicitly obedient, gentle collie, without a single bad trait, and possessed of rare sweetness. He tried his best to make himself thoroughly mean and savage and treacherous. He met with pitifully poor success in his chosen rôle. The sweetness and the obedient gentleness stuck forth, past all his best efforts to mask them in ferocity.

Once, when he bit with overmuch unction at a guest who tried to pat him, I spoke sharply to him and emphasized my rebuke by a light slap on the shoulder. The dog was heart-broken. Crouching at my feet, his head on my boot, he sobbed exactly like a frightened child. He spent hours trying pitifully to make friends with me again.

It was so when his snarl and his nip at the legs of one of the other dogs led to warlike retaliation. At once Treve would rush to me for protection and for comfort. From the safe haven of my knees he would hurl threats at his assailant and defy him to carry the quarrel further. There was no fight in him. At the same time there was no taint of cowardice. He bore pain or discomfort or real danger unflinchingly.

One of his chief joys was to ransack the garage and stables for sponges and rags which were stored there for cleaning the cars. These he would carry, one by one, to the long grass or to the lake, and deposit them there. When the men hid these choice playthings out of his way he would stand on his hindlegs and explore the shelves and low beam-corners in search of them; never resting till he found one or more to bear off.

He would lug away porch cushions and carelessly-deserted hats and wraps, and deposit them in all sorts of impossible places; never by any chance bringing them back.

From puppyhood, he did not once eat a whole meal of his own accord. Always he must be fed by hand. Even then he would not touch any food but cooked meat.

Normally, the solution to this would have been to let him go hungry until he was ready to eat. But a valuable show-and-stud collie cannot be allowed to become a skeleton and lifeless for lack of food, any more than a winning race-horse can be permitted to starve away his strength and speed.

Treve's daily pound-and-a-half of broiled chuck steak was cut in small pieces and set before him on a plate. Then began the eternal task of making him eat it. Did we turn our backs on him for a single minute—the food had vanished when next we looked.

But it had not vanished down Treve's dainty throat. Casual search revealed every missing morsel of meat shoved neatly out of sight under the edges of the plate or else hidden in the grass or under nearby boards or handfuls of straw.

This daily meal was a game. Treve enjoyed it immensely. Not being blessed with patience, I abhorred it. So Robert Friend took the duty of feeding him. At sound of Robert's distant knife, whetted to cut up the meat, Treve would come flying to the hammock where I sat writing. At a bound he was in my lap, all fours and all fur—the entire sixty pounds of him—and with his head thrust under one of the hammock cushions.

Thence, at Robert's call, and at my own exhortation, he would come forth with mincing reluctance and approach the tempting dish of broiled steak. Looking coldly upon the food, he would lie down. To all of Robert's allurements to eat, the dog turned a deaf ear. Once in a blue moon, he consented to swallow the steak, piece by piece, if Robert would feed it to him by hand. Oftener it was necessary to call on Wolf to act as stimulant to appetite.

"Then I'll give it to Wolf," Robert would threaten. *"Wolf!"*

Treve got to his feet with head lowered and teeth bared. Robert called Wolf, who came lazily to play his part in the daily game for a guerdon of one piece of the meat.

Six feet away from the dish, Wolf paused. But his work was done. Growling, barking, roaring, Treve attacked the dish; snatching up and bolting one morsel of meat at a time. Between every two bites he bellowed threats and insults at the placidly watching Wolf,—Wolf who could thrash his weight in tigers and who, after Lad and Bruce died, was the acknowledged king of all the Place's dogs.

In this way, mouthful by mouthful and with an accompaniment of raging noise that could be heard across the lake, Treve disposed of his dinner.

Yes, it was a silly thing to humor him in the game. But there was no other method of making him eat the food on which depended his continued show-form and his dynamite vitality. When it came to giving him his two raw eggs a day, there was nothing to that but forcible feeding. In solid cash prizes and in fees, Treve paid back, by many hundred per cent., the high cost of his food.

When he was little more than a puppy, he fell dangerously ill with some kind of heart trouble. Dr. Hopper said he must have medicine every half hour, day and night, until he should be better. I sat up with him for two nights.

I got little enough work done, between times, on those two nights. The suffering dog lay on a rug beside my study desk. But he was uneasy and wanted to be talked to. He was in too much pain to go to sleep. In a corner of my study was a tin biscuit box, which I kept filled with animal crackers, as occasional titbits for the collies. Every now and then, during our two-night vigil, I took an animal cracker from the box and fed it to Treve.

By the second night he was having a beautiful time. I was not.

The study seemed to him a most delightful place. Forthwith he adopted it as his lair. By the third morning he was out of danger and indeed was practically well again. But he had acquired the study-habit; a habit which lasted throughout his short life.

From that time on, it was Treve's study; not mine. The tin cracker box became his treasure chest; a thing to be guarded as jealously as ever was the Nibelungen Hoard or the Koh-i-noor.

If he chanced to be lying in any other room, and a dog unconsciously walked between him and the study, Treve bounded up from the soundest sleep and rushed growlingly to the study door, whence he snarled defiance at the possible intruder. If he were in the study and another dog ventured near, Treve's teeth were bared and Treve's forefeet were planted firmly atop the tin box; as he ordered away the potential despoiler of his hoard.

No human, save only the Mistress and myself, might enter the study unchallenged. Grudgingly, Treve conceded her right and mine to be there. But a rush at the ankles of any one else discouraged ingress. I remember my daughter stopped in there one day to speak to me; on her way for a swim. As the bathing-dressed figure appeared on the threshold, Treve made a snarling rush for it. Alternately and vehemently he bit both bare ankles.

"I wish he wouldn't do that," complained my daughter, annoyed. "He *tickles* so, when he bites!"

No expert trainer has worked more skillfully and tirelessly over a Derby winner than did Robert Friend over that dog's shimmering red-gold coat. For an hour or more every day, he groomed Treve, until the burnished fur stood out like a Circassian beauty's coiffure and glowed like molten gold. The dog stood moveless throughout the long and tedious process; except when he obeyed the order to turn to one side or the other or to lift his head or to put up his paws for a brushing of the silken sleeve-ruffles.

It was Robert, too, who hit on the scheme which gave Treve his last show-victory; when the collie already had won fourteen of the needful fifteen points which should make him a Champion of Record.

Perhaps you think it is easy to pilot even the best of dogs through the gruelling ordeals that go to make up those fifteen points. Well, it is not.

Many breeders take their dogs on the various show-circuits, keeping them on the bench for three days at a time; and then, week after week, shipping them in stuffy crates from town to town, from show to show. In this way, the championship points sometimes pile up with reasonable speed;—and sometimes never at all. (Sometimes, too, the luckless dog is found dead in his crate, on arriving at the show-hall. Oftener he catches distemper and dies in more painful and leisurely fashion.)

I am too foolishly mush-hearted to inflict such torture on any of our Sunnybank collies. I never take my dogs to a show that cannot be reached by comfortable motor ride within two or three hours at most; nor to any show whence they cannot return home at the end of a single day. Thus, championship points mount up more slowly at Sunnybank than at some other kennels. But thus, too, our dogs, for the most part, stay alive and in splendid health. I sleep the sounder at night, for knowing my collie chums are not in misery in some distemper-tainted dogshow-building.

In like manner, it is a fixed rule with us never to ship a Sunnybank puppy anywhere by express to a purchaser. People must come here in person and take home the pups they buy from me. Buyers have motored to Sunnybank for pups from Maine and Ohio and even from California.

These scruples of mine have earned me the good-natured guying of more sensible collie breeders.

Well, Treve had picked up fourteen of the fifteen points needed to complete his championship. The last worthwhile show of the spring season—within motor distance—was at Noble, Pa., on June 10, 1922. Incidentally, June 10, 1922, was Treve's third birthday. His wonderful coat was at the climax of its shining fullness. By autumn he would be "out of coat"; and an out-of-coat collie stands small chance of winning.

So Robert and I drove over to Noble with him.

The day was stewingly hot; the drive was long. Show-goers crowded around the splendid dog before the judging began. Bit by bit, Treve's nerves began to fray. We kept him off his bench and in the shade, and we did what we could to steer admirers away from him. But it was no use. By the time the collie division was called into the tented ring, Treve was profoundly unhappy and cranky.

He slouched in, with no more "form" to him than a plow horse. With the rest of his class ("Open, sable-and-white"), he went through the parade. Judge Cooper called the contestants one by one up to the block; Treve last of all.

My best efforts could not rouse the dog from his sullen apathy.

It was then that Robert Friend played his trump card. Standing just outside the ring, among the jam of spectators, he called excitedly:

"*Wolf! I'll give it to Wolf!*"

I don't know what the other spectators thought of this outburst. But I know the effect it had on Treve.

In a flash the great dog was alert and tense; his tulip ears up, his whole body at attention, the look of eagles in his eyes as he scanned the ringside for a glimpse of his friend, Wolf.

Judge Cooper took one long look at him. Then, without so much as laying a hand on the magnificently-showing Treve, he awarded him the blue ribbon in his class.

I had sense enough to take the dog into one corner and to keep him there, quieting and steadying him until the Winners' Class was called. As I led him into the ring, then, to compete with the other classes' blue ribboners, Robert called once more to the absent Wolf. Again the trick served. The collie moved and stood as if galvanized into sparkling life.

Cooper handed me the Winners' rosette; the rosette whose acquisition made Treve a Champion of Record!

It was only about a year ago. In that little

handful of time, the judge who made him a champion—the new-made champion himself—the dog whose name roused him from his apathy in the ring—all three are dead. I don't think a white sportsman like Cooper would mind my linking his name with two such supreme collies, in this word of necrology. Cooper—Treve—*Wolf!*

(There's lots of room in this old earth of ours for the digging of graves, isn't there?)

Home we came with our champion—Champion Sunnybank Sigurd—who displayed so little championship dignity that, an hour after our return to the Place, he lifted my brand new Panama hat daintily from the hall-table, carried it forth from the house with a loving tenderness; laid it to rest in a patch of lakeside mud; and then rolled on it.

I was too elated over our triumph to scold him for the costly sacrilege. I am glad now that I didn't. For a scolding or a single harsh word ever reduced him to utter heartbreak.

And so for a while, at the Place, our golden champion continued to revel in the gay zest of life.

He was the livest dog I have known. Wolf alone was his chum among all the Sunnybank collies. Wolf alone, with his mighty heart and vast wisdom and his elfin sense of fun and his love for frolic. Wolf and Treve used to play a complicated game whose chief move consisted of a sweeping breakneck gallop for perhaps a half-mile, to the accompaniment of a fanfare of barking. Across the green lawns they would flash, like red-gold meteors; and at a pace none of their fleet-footed brethren could maintain.

One morning they started as usual on this whirlwind dash. But at the end of the first few yards, Treve swayed in his flying stride, faltered to a stop and came slowly back to me. He thrust his muzzle into my cupped hand—for the first time in his undemonstrative life—then stood wearily beside me.

A strange transformation had come over him. The best way I can describe it is to say that the glowing inward fire which always had seemed to shine through him—even to the flaming bright mass of coat—was gone. He was all at once old and sedate and massive; a dog of elderly dignity —a dignity oddly majestic. The mischief imp had fled from his eyes; the sheen and sunlight had vanished from his coat. He had ceased to be Treve.

I sent in a rush for the nearest good vet. The doctor examined the invalid with all the skilled attention due a dog whose cash value runs into four figures. Then he gave verdict.

It was the heart;—the heart that had been

flighty in puppyhood days, but which two competent vets had since pronounced as sound as the traditional bell.

For a day longer the collie lived;—at least a gravely gentle and majestic collie lived in the marvelous body that had been Treve's. He did not suffer—or so the doctor told us—and he was content to stay very close to me; his paw or his head on my foot.

At last, stretching himself drowsily to sleep, he died.

It seemed impossible that such a swirl of glad life and mischief and beauty could have been wiped out in twenty-four little hours.

Not for our virtues nor for our general worthiness are we remembered wistfully by those who stay on. Not for our sterling qualities are we cruelly missed when missing is futile. Worthiness, in its death, does not leave behind it the grinding heartache that comes at memory of some lovably naughty or mischievous or delightfully perverse trait.

Treve's entertaining badnesses had woven themselves into the very life of the Place. Their passing left a keen hurt. The more so because, under them, lay bedrock of staunch loyalty and gentleness.

I have not the skill to paint our eccentrically

lovable chum's word picture, except in this clumsily written sketch. If I were to attempt to make a whole book of him, the result would be a daub.

But I have tried at least to make his *name* remembered by a few readers; by giving it to the hero of this collection of stories. Perhaps some one, reading, may like the name, even if not the stories; and may call his or her next collie, "Treve"; in memory of a gallant dog that was dear to Sunnybank.

We buried him in the woods, near the house, here. A granite bowlder serves as his headstone.

Alongside that bowlder, a few days ago, we buried the Mistress's hero collie, Wolf; close to his old-time playmate, Treve.

Perhaps you may care to hear a word or two of Wolf's plucky death. Some of you have read his adventures in my other dog stories. More of you read of his passing. For nearly every newspaper in America printed a long account of it.

It is an account worth reading and rereading; as is every tale of clean courage. I am going to quote part of the finely-written story that appeared in the *New York Times* of June 28, 1923; a story far beyond power of mine to improve on or to equal:

"Wolf, son of Lad, is dead. The shaggy collie, with the eyes that understood and the friendly tail, made famous in the stories of Albert Payson Terhune, died like a thoroughbred. So when Wolf joined his father, in the canine Beyond, last Sunday night, there was no hanging of heads.

"Wolf died a hero. But yesterday the level lawns of Sunnybank, the Terhune place at Pompton Lakes, N. J., seemed empty and the big house was curiously quiet. True, other collies were there; but so, too, was the big bowlder out in the woods with just 'Wolf' graven across it.

"Ten years ago, when thousands of readers were following Lad's career as told by his owner, Mr. Terhune, an interesting event took place at Sunnybank. Of all the puppies that had or have come to Sunnybank, that group of newcomers was the most mischievous. Admittedly, Lad was properly proud, but readers will remember his occasional misgivings about one of the pups. The cause of parental concern was Wolf. He was a good puppy, you know, but a trifle boisterous; maybe—yes, he was, the littlest bit inclined to wildness.

"In 1918 Lad passed on; and the whole country mourned his departure. Wolf succeeded his famous father in the stories of Mr. Terhune. The son had long since abandoned his harum-scarum ways and had developed into a model member of the Terhune dog circle. Wolf was the property and the pet of Mrs. Terhune.

"He became the cleverest of all the collies. One could talk to Wolf and get understanding and no back talk. One could depend on Wolf and get full loyalty. One could like Wolf and say so; and the soft cool nose would come poking around and the tail would begin to wag till it seemed as if Wolf would wag himself off his feet.

"Wolf constituted himself warden of the Sunnybank lawns and custodian of the driveways. When motoring parties came in and endangered the lives of the puppies playing about the driveways, Wolf, at the first sound of the motor, would dash importantly down into the drive and would herd or chase every puppy out of harm's way.

"Each evening it was the habit of Wolf to saunter off on a long 'walk.' Three evenings ago he rambled away and—

"Down in the darkness at the railroad station some folk were waiting to see the Stroudsburg express flash by. It was a few minutes late. A nondescript dog, with a hunted, homeless droop to his tail, trotted onto the tracks.

"Far down the line there came the warning screech of the express. The canine tramp didn't pay any attention to it, but sat down to scratch at a flea.

"The headlight of the express shot a beam glistening along the rails. Wolf saw the dog and the danger. With a bark and a snap, the son of Lad thrust the stranger off the track and drove him to safety.

"The express was whistling, for a crossing, far past the station, when they picked up what was Wolf and started for the Terhune home."

All dogs die too soon. Many humans don't die soon enough. A dog is only a dog. And a dog is too gorgeously normal and wholesome to be made ridiculous in death by his owner's sloppy sentimentality.

The stories of one's dogs, like the recital of one's dreams, are of no special interest to others. Perhaps I have talked overlong about these two collie chums of ours. Belatedly, I ask your forgiveness if I have bored you.

ALBERT PAYSON TERHUNE.

"Sunnybank,"
Pompton Lakes,
New Jersey.